THE SECRET DUCHESS

What Reviewers Say About
Jane Walsh's Work

The Inconvenient Heiress

"Reading a Jane Walsh novel is a dream with every page. It's a reminder that we have always been here, that we have always been finding community and finding love, that we have always risked it all and been rewarded for our bravery, that queer love is about the quiet moments as well as the loud ones, that we deserve to wear flowy gowns and make our art and find our future, that we deserve to have our love and care returned to us in spades, that we deserve and deserve and deserve."—*The Lesbrary*

"I enjoyed every moment of this. Those forbidden feelings and moments Arabella and Caroline shared were magical, but when everything changed for Caroline and she had to contemplate marriage my heart broke for them both. I was completely invested in them being together and so being on that emotional rollercoaster with them, especially Arabella I could only hope they might get their chance. …[Jane] has a real talent for delivering exciting regency romances that are rich, loving, and deeply sentimental."—*LESBIreviewed*

Her Duchess to Desire

"One of Walsh's strongest points is her ability to build a strong, positive queer community in a time period that is known to have sometimes been hostile to them. …I love an Ice Queen heroine who melts in the hands of the right person, and Anne is a great personification of that." —*Courtney Reads Romance*

"What a fantastic story. Not like anything I have read before so it was exciting and new and captured my imagination right from the start.

Everything is so regal, from the characters, to the lifestyle, to the exquisite designs that Letitia draws up and produces. I just closed my eyes and could picture it all perfectly. It was the element of forbidden romance between Anne and Letitia that had me hooked because it was delicious, came with risks, and none of us knew what the consequences would be."—*LESBIreviewed*

Her Countess to Cherish

"This book was a nice surprise to me in its portrayal of gender fluidity, along with a delightful romance between two sympathetic characters. If you love queer historical romance, you should absolutely check this out."—*Courtney Reads Romance*

Her Lady to Love

"If you are looking for a sweet, cozy romance with grounded leads, this is for you. The author's dedication to the little cultural details do help flesh out the setting so much more. I also loved how buttery smooth everything tied together. Nothing seemed to be out of place, and the romance had some stakes. …Highly recommended."—Colleen Corgel, Librarian, Queens Public Library

"Walsh debuts with a charming if flawed Regency romance. …Though Honora's shift from shy curiosity to boldly stated interest feels a bit abrupt, her relationship with Jacquie is sweet, sensual, and believable. Subplots about a group of bluestockings and a society of LGBTQ Londoners add depth…"—*Publishers Weekly*

"What a delightful queer Regency era romance. …*Her Lady to Love* was a beautiful addition to the romance genre, and a much appreciated queer involvement. I'll definitely be looking into more of Walsh's works!"—Dylan Miller, Librarian (Baltimore County Public Library)

"…it's the perfect novel to read over the holidays if you love gorgeous writing, beautiful settings, and literal bodice ripping! I had such a brilliant time with this book. Walsh's novel has such an excellent sense of the time period she's writing in and her specificity and interest in the historical aspects of her plot really allow the characters to shine. The inclusion of details, specifically related to women's behaviour or dress, made for a vivid and exciting setting. This novel reminded me a lot of something like Vanity Fair (1847) (but with lesbians!) because of its gorgeous setting and intriguing plot."—*The Lesbrary*

Visit us at www.boldstrokesbooks.com

By the Author

Her Lady to Love

Her Countess to Cherish

Her Duchess to Desire

THE SPINSTERS OF INVERLEY:

The Inconvenient Heiress

The Accidental Bride

The Secret Duchess

THE SECRET DUCHESS

by

Jane Walsh

2024

THE SECRET DUCHESS

ISBN 13: 978-1-63679-519-5

THIS TRADE PAPERBACK ORIGINAL IS PUBLISHED BY
BOLD STROKES BOOKS, INC.
P.O. BOX 249
VALLEY FALLS, NY 12185

FIRST EDITION: JANUARY 2024

CREDITS
EDITOR: CINDY CRESAP
PRODUCTION DESIGN: SUSAN RAMUNDO
COVER DESIGN BY TAMMY SEIDICK

Dedication

For Mag, who makes my ordinary life feel
extraordinary every day that we are together

CHAPTER ONE

Shropshire, 1814

Joan, the Duchess of Stanmere, widow of two weeks to a man she couldn't bring herself to think of as dearly departed, had always liked being a duchess. She danced at Almack's most Wednesdays and found it delightful. She took tea with the Queen whenever she was beckoned. She attended church at St. George's and plays at the Theatre-Royal and never wore the same gown twice to a ball.

But when the mourning wreath was fixed to the front door of Astley Park, Joan had a change of heart. Beneath the glamorous surface, the dukedom had turned out to be nothing more than a nest of vipers. She had simply never looked down long enough to notice.

The day that the duke's will was read was bright and beautiful, with birds chirping and nary a cloud in the sky. It was a stark contrast to the library, teeming with black-clad ducal relations and dark rumors. Joan sat by herself near the doorway, unable to think through the roar of voices. She had yet to touch the cup of tea that steamed beside her on the checkerboard table.

None of the conversation was directed at her.

And yet, all of it was *about* her.

Stanmere's two brothers, clad in superfine wool and gleaming Hessians, were laughing by the window. Jackals, the pair of them. Lord Peter, the younger, was slim and elegant and smirking. He kept brushing his hand over his pocket where Joan knew he kept his cigars. Lord Paul, the elder, was slouched against the windowsill sipping his second brandy despite the early hour.

Stanmere's sister, Lady Mary, was fanning herself on the settee. Her eyes were bright above the painted silk fan and her hair towered with feathers. She leaned forward so far that she almost toppled from her perch in her efforts not to miss even one word from the lawyers.

The late duke's two daughters were eying the refreshments that had been laid out on the side tables, uninterested in the proceedings as their papa's will contained not a single mention of a ball, a rout, or a handsome gentleman.

And Stanmere's only son, the new duke and the head of the family, was flanked by the family's lawyers as he gazed at the documents spread across the oak desk.

His only *legitimate* son, that was.

"I don't understand," Joan said.

Her voice sounded hoarse to her own ears, as if she had shrieked her outrage. Maybe the tea would help after all. She grasped the teacup, heard it rattle against the saucer, and then set it down and clasped her shaking hands in her lap.

"It is simple." The Marquess of Chetleigh gestured at the head of the firm that had been employed by the duchy for decades, a gentleman who squinted at Joan as if she were nothing more than a clause that needed removal. "However, Mr. Walton can go through it again for you."

"I understood the words well enough, Chetleigh."

"Stanmere," he corrected her gently with a slight cough. "I know it may take time to accustom yourself not to use my lesser title now, but I do implore you to try."

Before today, Joan hadn't thought herself capable of hating anyone. But as she stared into Chetleigh's pale blue eyes, devoid of even a hint of kindness, a mess of anger and hatred bubbled in her chest. He was her stepson, a mere two years younger than her five and twenty. His perfectly trimmed sideburns touched the crisp height of his collar, his lips held the faintest impression of a sneer. He was the perfect appearance of a perfect gentleman, and Joan's fury knew no bounds.

It startled her.

She wasn't accustomed to emotions of *any* sort of intensity. What need did she have for anger? Doors opened for her if she glanced at them, events were planned on her behalf if she thought of them, and shopkeepers fawned over her the instant she stepped a toe past the threshold.

"If everything is clear, then there is nothing to discuss," he said, leaning back in his armchair.

"It does not make any sense that my husband would leave a fortune to his illegitimate children, and yet leave his widow with nothing." Joan's hands started to shake again, and she clasped them firmer together.

"*Nothing* is not quite true, Your Grace." Mr. Walton raised a finger, his brow creasing as he glanced at the will. "It is unfortunate that everything is tied up in entail, or you would have been entitled to one third of the income from the land as is right and proper for a widow. But Stanmere did bequeath you two hundred pounds per annum to use at your discretion."

"And I say, we do deserve something!" cried Alexander, one of the sons of whose existence Joan had learned about a half hour prior. The eldest of them at nineteen years old, he was the spit of his father, down to his sandy hair and pointed chin.

"Indeed we do," his younger brother, James, piped up. "Does ducal blood mean *nothing* to anyone?"

There were five of them crowded together on the Chesterfield, sprawled together like puppies with knobby knees and elbows. All of them unmistakably cast from the Astley lineage.

Family secrets, large as life and thrust into the sunlight.

Joan's cheeks were hot, which was strange because the rest of her felt made of ice. "And yet I have not been left enough funds to pay for one year's worth of candles at Hanover Square."

Lady Mary fanned herself. "Then it is a good thing that you shall no longer be living there."

Joan sucked in a breath. "It was a figure of speech. Obviously I shall depart soon to the dower house."

Chetleigh's lips twitched into a true sneer now. "Actually, no. You won't."

Any moment now, she would wake up from this nightmare and laugh at these absurdities. Maybe Stanmere was still alive and she would learn to appreciate the devil she knew. If she half-closed her eyes, she could almost see him there, tall and broad-shouldered, joining his brothers in laughter. She shuddered and blinked away the illusion.

"My mother still resides in the dower house, and my father specified in his will that she shall remain there," Chetleigh said. "Perhaps if you were a more attentive listener, you would not have so many questions."

Stanmere's daughters tittered.

Joan stared at them. Had they always been so disrespectful?

"I won't be ousted by that gel with the atrocious hair," Stanmere's mother boomed. "I'm staying right where I've been since my Richard departed this earth, and I'll move for no one."

Joan tucked one of her curls behind her ear, as if she could hide the mass of bright red hair that her mother-in-law had decried as dreadfully unfashionable since the day they had met.

"Oh, Her Grace won't be inconvenienced in the least, would you?" Lady Mary smiled at her. "Mother is *so* comfortable where she is. It would be a great disservice to remove her from her rightful place when she has been there for so many decades. Think of the hardship for our frail mother!"

Stanmere's mother was a woman of excellent health at seventy-five years of age, who could ride better than any in the county and was always the first to shout tallyho at a fox hunt. She might well outlive them all.

"Then I shall live on the income from the rents on the land I brought as my dowry." She glared at Mr. Walton.

"Sadly, your land has not generated profit in some time. It operates at a loss."

"How can that be?" Joan stared at him. "I was an heiress upon my marriage."

"Circumstances change," he said with a shake of his head. "I remember drawing up the papers with Stanmere and your father. You had a pretty enough amount tied up in investments, all of which have failed over the years. And you have a nice parcel of land, but there have been years of drought and hardship. Someday it may yet generate money again."

Her father had explained her marriage settlement as best he could, but she had not been much interested at twenty to learn the details of something that might affect her so far in the future.

It turned out that the lesson once delayed was learned much more harshly now.

"If that is true, then Stanmere would have left a larger sum to me. He wouldn't have done this. Not to *me*."

This was beyond the pale for any husband, let alone one of the wealthiest dukes of the realm.

Chetleigh sighed. "You are assigning blame where there is none to be had. Your bereavement has gotten the best of you. As great a man as my father was, not even he could know when the bell would toll for him. These circumstances are beyond the control of man."

She really ought to have that tea now. She needed every reinforcement she could get in the onslaught of such shocks. Joan picked up the cup and drank deep, but it didn't do her any good. It would have felt rather better to have thrown the teacup at Chetleigh's head.

Shocked at her own thoughts, she shrank back in her chair.

"But you raise a valid point. My father must have had good reason for doing what he did." Chetleigh tapped his finger on his chin. "He never made mistakes. You should know that better than anyone."

Stanmere's daughter bit into a biscuit and licked the cream from her crimson lips. "Is there no indiscretion on your side that you can think of, which may have led my father to make these decisions?"

Joan staggered as if she had been slapped. "I cannot believe you have the poor manners to imply that I have been adulterous." She glanced at the brood of ill-begotten sons, grinning like fools as if they were attending a farce on a London stage. "I am not the one who strayed from my marital bed."

"It *is* the primary reason when a widow is left with nothing." Mr. Walton cleared his throat. "In light of such events, two hundred pounds was generous of His Grace. Many women live in great comfort on a good deal less."

"Are any of those women duchesses?" Joan asked. "I would be hard-pressed to believe even a genteel lady raised with nothing could be satisfied by such an income."

Lord Peter fished out a cigar and lit it. "You are getting high in the instep. You were a duchess for a scant five years."

"I am still a duchess, and the daughter of an earl. Until this moment, I thought I was also a member of this family."

"You ought to have thought of that before you were unfaithful!" Lord Paul shook his head. "Disgraceful."

Joan found it hard to breathe as she gazed around the room without finding a single sympathetic face. Panic clawed its way up her throat as she watched them nod at each other and smirk at her. They were united by blood. It appeared that relations by marriage were of little concern.

"She clearly did it," one of the daughters said to the other.

"Of course she did. Brazen as anything. Why, the evidence is in the inheritance. Or in the disinheritance, I should say."

They giggled.

"Our father must have known what you were about." Chetleigh shrugged. "It is against God to challenge his decision. We will abide by his ruling."

"There are no such sins in my past," Joan said, striving for dignity. "I shall excuse myself if all I am met with are insults."

Joan fled up the grand staircase and down the long hallway to her bedchamber, her heart racing. Her wedding was a blur in her memory, grand and elaborate and exhausting as it had been. But she remembered how her father had mopped his brow and her mother had beamed, and she had gazed up at Stanmere's stern face and thought—this is the end of all trouble, and the start of all happiness.

More fool she.

❖

"Must we endure the tonic? I much prefer the seaweed treatments. Or sea bathing."

Maeve Balfour knew her voice was plaintive, but the situation was dire. The seaside resort of Inverley was lovely. Why ruin it with tonics that tasted like sulphur mixed with brimstone? Mama had lectured her into enough glasses of it over the past two summers for her to know to avoid it at all costs.

"I credit it with my improved good health." Mama downed it in one gulp. "You would be wise to drink up so you may avoid my many indispositions when you reach my age."

Mama was in her late forties, with a few lines on her face and a handful of silver streaks in her black hair to attest to her age, but she had complained of everything from megrims to stomach pains to swollen ligaments to stressed nerves since they had left Ireland three years ago on a tour of England's resort towns.

Maeve poked her nose in the glass. It smelled worse than it tasted, but she finished it. "Do let us have a seaweed treatment. I must insist." "I suppose we have time."

They followed Miss Alice down a stone hallway to a small chamber with a window overlooking the sea, where a cauldron of water bubbled on a small fire and released steam into the room. Miss Alice was their usual attendant, a portly woman with cheerful manners who could always be relied upon for good conversation and excellent treatments.

It was a relief to lie back in a comfortable chair while Miss Alice chatted with her and massaged crushed seaweed paste onto her cheeks and forehead before draping long strips of seaweed to cover her face and neck. Maeve sighed and tipped her head to rest against the padded back of the chair. It was much better to sit than to stand, and a gentle incline was even better. One's figure showed to every advantage in a recline, after all. It didn't matter that there was no one here to admire it. She always liked to look her best, for herself if for no one else. This was much nicer than the tonic, and it was ever so comfortable to listen to the waves crash upon the shore and to think of nothing at all.

"I shall never understand why you enjoy this so much," Mama said after Miss Alice left them. "My seaweed is always too cold. It tingles the face in a most disagreeable manner."

"I have never found anything so refreshing," Maeve replied without opening her eyes. "I am told it has marvelous benefits for the skin. It's a necessity that we have greatly overlooked in our time here. You always say we cannot put a price on health."

"With a visit to the doctor costing what it does these days, I think one can. I suppose our money is better spent here at a fraction of the price."

"You always say you feel better after one of our spa days."

"I must admit you are wise to think of such things as radiant skin now," Mama said. "You still have youth on your side, but you are getting no younger. Such things matter when one is out to catch a husband."

Maeve was grateful that the seaweed on her face obscured her frown. "Is husband hunting to be the sole use for any improvement to my health? Whyever can it not be for my benefit, instead of a future lord and master?"

"Because it is most unnatural to declare yourself destined for spinsterhood, and from such a young age! I remember you being but a girl of fourteen when first you mentioned it."

Maeve remembered it well. She had been in a fever over a girl who lived in the next parish and had realized then and there that there could be no room for men in her life when feelings such as these existed for the fairer sex.

What use did she have for the cold hands of a mealy-mouthed suitor when her heart fluttered at the merest glimpse of a fine-faced lady in Spitalfields silks or French lace?

"My spinsterhood has allowed me to be your traveling companion. How dismal you would have found the journey without me!"

"You shall be released from your duty as your mother's companion in a month's time."

Maeve bolted up. Seaweed slimed off her cheeks and plopped to her lap in a sodden mess. "I do beg your pardon?"

"The banns have been cried for a week now." Mama stared straight ahead.

"What banns?" Her heart pounded. "Whose banns?"

There was but one church within the confines of the town, and of course it was the Church of England. As Catholics, neither Maeve nor her mother had ever attended the Sunday service. Or so Maeve had thought.

Mama peeled the seaweed away and wiped her face. "Did you never wonder what all of this travel was for?" Her voice was muffled through the towel, but Maeve could hear her exasperation as clear as if she had shouted.

"For your health. For our pleasure. Because Scotland's dramatic hills should not be missed if one can help it, and Bath is a lovely place to spend one's winters, and Inverley in summer is the most charming place I have ever encountered in all my life."

"I thought I raised you better than this." Mama clicked her tongue. "You are clever enough, little as you like to exert yourself. Did you not notice how I have been in pursuit of the Count of Aducci since your stepfather died last year? Why, we even followed him to London when he left Bath in the autumn. I cannot believe how it escaped your notice. But you have always been in pursuit of your own pleasures."

Water from the seaweed on Maeve's lap seeped into her skirts. To avoid looking her mother in the eye, she scooped up the sodden mess and dumped it onto the table. "The count is distasteful," she said. He was the type of man who leered at the actresses when they had attended the theatre together.

"He is rich."

"And that excuses his behavior?"

"You know that it does."

"We shall live with him in Italy?" That wasn't such a bad prospect. The ruins of Rome would be a marvel to see, and the country had plenty of art and wine to recommend it. She could find plenty of ways to avoid the count.

"My dear, it is no longer we."

It felt as if a fresh piece of seaweed had slipped down the back of her dress. Maeve stared at her, but now it was her mother who did not meet her eye. "Whyever not?"

Mama's face softened. "I tried to tell him that you should come with us. I tried, my dear. But he won't listen. He says you are a grown woman and need to care for yourself. And he's right. You are eight and twenty, and clever enough. You shall be fine."

"I very well shan't be." She tried to think of a life without her mother's presence, and failed.

"Of course you shall. There is plenty of summer left. You will find a man to marry."

"I don't wish for a husband!"

"A sensible sentiment, as they are a nuisance. But they are a necessary nuisance. We could not have spent such a merry time these past three years without a husband to fund it, and all I needed to do was send a letter each quarter inquiring after his health. Being a wife need not be such an onerous task. You shall see."

"I won't do it."

"You will have six months of money for room and board, and then you will see how difficult it is for a single woman of no fortune." Mama's jaw was set. "But if it takes more than three, I would be surprised indeed. I am leaving you in choice pastures, Maeve. There are plenty of eligible men here on holiday. You have the looks, you have the charm. All you need is the will. Now let us be off for home, dear."

Maeve's hands were shaking as she tossed the towel aside and picked up her reticule.

What would become of her if she was left alone with no protection?

Why, what if this was the last seaweed treatment she ever received, and she had squandered it?

It didn't bear thinking about.

CHAPTER TWO

L ondon was a welcome respite after the duke's burial in Shropshire, where Joan had been the recipient of pitying looks and sly laughter until she could bear it no more. With the family still at Astley Park, the Hanover Square townhouse was empty save for a small village of footmen and housemaids and other sundry staff, none of whom would dare gossip about her.

At least, Joan didn't think they would. But her life had been topsy-turvy since Stanmere's death, and it would be a wonder if she could be surprised by anything anymore.

She stood in the center of her bedchamber and tried to find happiness in the fact that the adjoining door would never again reveal her husband, but all she felt was dread.

Perhaps it was because she still carried him with her.

Chetleigh had thrust a small linen bag at her the day after the will had been read, and she withdrew it now from her pocket and took the memorial jewelry out. The brooch was crafted of ivory, with fine silver filagree encasing a lock of Stanmere's sandy hair. It was a showy piece, almost as large as her palm. It was sure to look gaudy on her if she were ever to wear it.

She didn't know why he would have bequeathed it to her when he had arranged his will so cruelly. Joan had always thought he was horrid, and he hadn't seemed to think much of her at all even while he had been among the living, but the will was beyond all comprehension.

The inscription on the back of the brooch—*memento mori*—seemed to mock her.

As if he sensed her heartache, her foxhound Maurice padded in from the sitting room and nudged Joan's hand. She rubbed his chest just where he liked it and pressed a kiss to his white and tan head, grateful for his presence. Stanmere had meted out his version of justice casually, and it was so commonplace to him that he never thought twice about his violence afterward. He had treated Maurice so viciously during a hunt last summer that he would never walk the same again, but he didn't seem to recall it though he had mocked her for insisting on keeping a now-useless hunter in the stables.

Shuddering, Joan went to put the brooch in her jewelry box but— how odd. It was missing. It had always sat on her dresser, a small box of etched glass and silver. Anything extravagant had been kept in the safe, but she had a handful of favorite jewels in the box, along with some sentimental pieces from her late mother.

"Have you sent my jewelry for cleaning?" Joan asked.

Her first lady's maid, Tilda, sat in the chair by the window, squinting down at a pile of pins in her lap. "No, Your Grace. Were instructions given before we left for Astley Park?"

"Not that I recall."

"The housekeeper must have arranged for it during your absence. After all, you cannot wear any of it now, so it is as good a time as any to clean them. I have been blacking your pins all afternoon so that no hint of shine will show in your hair, or on your fine mourning clothes." She sighed. "I have done this far too often for the Astleys in my years."

Tilda had been the lady's maid for each of Stanmere's four wives, and Joan had inherited her service when Tilda refused to leave it for the little cottage she had long been promised for her retirement. She insisted on staying to train the next generation to serve the duchy.

Sarah, Tilda's granddaughter, entered the room with her arms piled high with clothes. She was a tall, slender girl of nineteen, anxious to do well since Tilda had obtained the position for her last year as Joan's second lady's maid. Though Joan was only five years older, nineteen seemed a lifetime away.

Sarah bobbed a curtsy, then bit her lip as she looked down at the dress at the top of the pile. "Apologies if the sight distresses you, Your Grace. I intended to have all this put away before you came home from the lawyers, but I was later returning from the dressmaker's than I anticipated."

Joan noticed with a start that it was her funeral dress in Sarah's arms. In fact, all the dresses that lay in wait for Sarah to hang were black. Most of her mourning wardrobe had been ordered the instant she left London, to be made up while she was away in Shropshire.

Why should she mourn the man who had destroyed her life now that his was gone?

These thoughts felt treasonous. The duke had been her husband. A good wife would mourn him regardless of what he had done.

What did it say about her that she could not find it in herself to grieve?

What if the Astleys had been right, and there was something wrong with her? Not adultery, she had never even considered such a thing—but was there some flaw writ large in her character that she was blind to see within herself?

She clutched the brooch, the silver biting into her palm. "You are right, Sarah. I have no wish to see that dress again. You may keep it."

It was devoid of the jewels and beadwork that decorated the frocks she tended to gift to her maids, as those would have been unthinkable to wear in deepest mourning. But the yards of fine bombazine crepe were worth a good deal of money, enough for Sarah and Tilda to resell at a high cost. They would have better use of it than she would.

Although perhaps soon that would no longer be the case. For although she had been all morning with the lawyers that her father had always used, they had proved to be of little help. If all the ducal land was entailed, and if her own dowry provided no income, then they explained it was an unfortunate truth that she had nothing more to her name. When she insisted on investigating, they recommended a Bow Street Runner.

It had felt most unusual to talk business with anyone. These matters had always been handled by the men in her family. But her father had died years ago, and so had her uncles. She had no brothers, and her husband's family was clearly not inclined to help her.

She was on her own.

Tilda snatched the funeral dress from Sarah and folded it, her arthritic fingers still nimble at certain tasks. "This is kind of you, Your Grace. We are grateful."

There was a knock on the door, and Lady Mary swooped in. "Your Grace! I am glad to see you here. We did not nearly have enough time to talk at my dear brother's funeral. Oh, terrible times these are."

She dabbed at her eyes with the weepers attached to her sleeves, the white cotton a stark relief to the black crepe of her dress.

"I did not realize you had also returned to London," Joan said, rumpling Maurice's ears one last time before she stood. She hadn't forgotten Lady Mary's laughter at the will reading. But perhaps her throat had been dry that day. If she was here to visit, she must be willing to make amends.

"What on earth is that beast doing in your bedchamber?"

"I am happy for him to have the run of the house. Maurice is my faithful companion." She struggled to say something that conveyed the truth of the matter but did not praise the dead, for she was wretched at lying. "These are indeed terrible times. It is good to have friendship to rely on."

Lady Mary gazed at the pile of black dresses. "I have yet to receive my mourning clothes, but I see now the dressmaker must have been busy with yours first. London's finest always has a wait list, I suppose, even for a duke's family."

Perhaps she wasn't here to make amends after all. Joan felt her eyes well up and prayed that no tears would fall. She and Lady Mary had shopped together, dined together, and visited the opera countless times together. Joan had considered her a sister in truth.

Had she always been so jealous?

"I am sure your new wardrobe will be ready soon." Joan hesitated. "My jewelry seems to be gone. Has your staff also taken this as a convenient time to send your jewels for cleaning?"

"Of course not. No one dares to touch my jewels without my express permission. But I am shocked, Your Grace. Shocked! For all your love of fine fashion, you mustn't be tempted by temporal things *now*." She laughed and snapped her fan open. "Why, imagine being concerned about sapphires when my dear brother is dead? I cannot believe it of you."

Joan was flustered. "Of course I don't intend to wear any of it. But it is disconcerting to discover things missing."

"I am surprised your household is so lax." Lady Mary pursed her lips and glanced at Joan. "Perhaps not so surprised. You aren't a woman of much experience, after all, and now you have no husband to guide you. Poor lamb. Anyway, I stopped by to say my farewells."

"Farewells?"

"Well, you aren't staying here, are you?" Her brows were raised so high that they near touched her hairline. "I thought you came to oversee the packing."

"I have no plans to leave London."

"But you must leave Hanover Square. Stanmere's wife will need to move in." Lady Mary clasped a hand to her mouth. "Oh, Your Grace. You cannot mean to stay! You cannot be so naive as that!"

She struggled to retain her composure. "Chetleigh is not yet married. Nor even betrothed."

"*Stanmere*, my dear. And he may not yet be betrothed, but he will be as soon as it is proper. He has the future of the dukedom to think about, and the Stanmeres never fail with regards to their responsibility. No, you cannot stay. It would be a shocking imposition to start a marriage with one's mother-in-law in residence."

"But where am I to go? Stanmere thought of everything and everyone in his will. Except for me." She couldn't help the bitterness that seeped into her voice.

"You are upset about the children, aren't you?" Lady Mary sighed and shook her head. "What a business that was."

"Children? The eldest is almost twenty. All of London will know of it, if they don't already." The idea made her feel faint. Five sons, all come out of the woodwork.

It didn't seem real.

"Don't be silly. Of course he had to provide for them. They are his sons, of his own body. He had a duty to them."

He had a duty to me. But she didn't say anything.

Lady Mary pursed her lips again, and after grasping her and kissing her cheek, left in as much a hurry as she had arrived.

Joan's hands were shaking, and she stroked Maurice for comfort. There was to be no sympathy from anyone, then. How could Lady Mary be so unconcerned about Stanmere's brood of sons? The scandal would be enormous. The one mourning custom that comforted her was that no one would gossip to her face until she could wear colors again, months from now.

But the next week proved her wrong. She received dozens of callers who came to express their sympathies but arrived with malice in their eyes and a thirst for news. People she had thought were her friends. People she had danced with and laughed with and been in perfect charity with.

Now, no more.

Joan sat in horror after visitor after visitor left her parlor, pressing her for news of who the lucky men had been that had caught her eye during her marriage.

For it wasn't Stanmere's children that interested anyone. It was her own alleged harlotry.

Her name was ruined.

"You could always go to Inverley," Tilda suggested one night as she brushed Joan's hair. Maurice whined from his perch on her bed, waiting for his grooming as well. She urged him onto a length of toweling before picking up a coarse cloth and rubbing it over his back and chest as he wagged his tail and pawed at her knee for attention.

"Where on earth is Inverley?"

"It's by the seaside," Sarah said. "My cousin went last summer and said it's all the crack."

Joan was perplexed. "And why would I go?" She couldn't imagine enjoying anywhere that a maid's cousin thought was fashionable. It was as likely as anything to be a dismal spot of sand next to a straggly patch of grass.

"Because you own a house there," Tilda said.

"I do?"

"Do you not remember purchasing it the year that your father gifted you with five thousand pounds to spend at your discretion?"

She did remember. Five thousand pounds were hard to forget. It had been an extravagant gift one summer, apropos of no occasion that she could think of. Her father had pressed her to tell no one of it. An odd request, but she had never questioned Papa.

A romantic whim had encouraged her to purchase a house that she had never seen. As a duchess, all it ever took was a passing thought and an open pocketbook for any of her fancies to be satisfied. She had wanted a charming little house that she could visit on holidays with her children if she were to have any. She didn't think she had been more descriptive than that when giving her instructions to the land agent.

The task was done without much fuss and before she knew it, she had a deed in her name.

Which she had then promptly forgotten about, given that children never did appear.

Joan drew in a breath. She couldn't recall it being listed in the will. And why should it be? It was *her* house.

For the first time since the funeral, she felt a glimmer of hope.

"By all means, let us go to Inverley."

❖

On the morning of her mother's wedding, Maeve packed her worldly belongings into four trunks and two carpet bags. A hired man tossed them into his wagon as if they were of no importance at all and drove them down the road to where she would stay for the rest of the summer with her friends, Caroline Reeve and Arabella Seton.

It shouldn't have felt so strange to look over the rented lodging one last time. After all, she and Mama had stayed in numerous places during their travels, none of which felt like a home. This was a collection of cramped rooms stuffed with other people's furniture and paintings and taste.

It held no sentimental value.

And yet, her chest felt tight as she latched the front door for the final time and slipped the key under it.

The church was full by the time Maeve arrived, and the ceremony almost over before she could focus on it. Even the wedding breakfast passed by at triple speed in a blur of jumbled details. The count's proud smile at her mother, his new bride. The honeyed wedding cake, gleaming from the center of the table. Her mother's rebuke at her tardiness, which ended up being the last real piece of conversation between them.

Mama and the Count of Aducci left with half the cake still on the table, and Maeve only had time for a kiss to her cheek before Mama was waving farewell with her white linen handkerchief from the barouche landau. Her new stepfather littered the ground with a spray of coins as the horses whinnied, and children screeched with glee to pocket a farthing or a ha'penny, with one lucky boy the recipient of a silver crown.

"Are you ready?" Arabella clasped her hand in Maeve's own and gave it a squeeze. She was a short plump woman with round spectacles and a heart made for sympathy and love. She was one of her dearest friends, though she was altogether far sweeter than Maeve could ever imagine being.

Arabella's lover, Caroline, nodded. "It's time, Maeve. Come on home with us."

Caroline was tall and slender and had already turned to walk toward the cottage that she and Arabella shared together by the seashore.

"Today shouldn't have felt so strange," Maeve said as they walked, forcing herself to laugh although her heart was as bruised as if the wheels of the barouche landeau had trampled it. "People do marry. Weddings happen all the time."

"You are welcome to stay with us as long as you like," Arabella told her. "Until it no longer feels odd."

Would it ever feel that way? Maeve wasn't sure.

"When are you sailing to Ireland?" Caroline asked as they entered the whitewashed cottage. Maeve had visited for tea many times, but she saw it with new eyes as she tried to consider it her temporary home. It was simple, without much in the way of furnishings, but there were Arabella's paintings on the wall, and a quilt that Caroline's sisters had clumsily stitched when they had been girls, and a rope basket that Arabella's brother had given her. Her chest tightened once more. There was a sense of family in this house.

Maeve's trunks were stacked by the door, and she realized with a start that she would need to unpack them herself. Although she wasn't used to anything more than a maid-of-all-work about the house, now she didn't even have that. It was exhausting to think of doing for oneself.

"I have no plans to return to Ireland."

"I thought you had family there?"

"Yes, my last letter found my grandfather in good health. But I did not much care for Ireland while I lived there, and I doubt it has changed much in the interim."

"Oh." Arabella's brow creased. "I suppose I haven't heard you talk much of your home."

Maeve smiled at her. "Well, Inverley is my home now, is it not? We shall make very merry together here and never a cross word shall be spoken between us."

That night, Caroline built a fire on the beach, ringed with stones smoothed from the ocean. Maeve was charmed by the dusky summer sky, the stars that started to peek out from the heavens, and the ever-present sound of the water lapping at the shore. Woodsmoke filled her lungs and sand filled her shoes.

Her heart ached from the loss of her mother's companionship. The beach was a far cry from the elegant eating establishments of London, or the dainty teashops in town. Caroline had brought a quilt with them, and Maeve pulled a corner of it over her shoulders. It smelled of salt and lavender, and it warmed more than her body.

Arabella spread out a blanket for them to sit on, then unwrapped a loaf of bread and a wheel of cheddar. "We often like an impromptu supper of toasted cheese in the summer," she told Maeve. "Messy, but satisfying."

"There are few things better than a good cheese," Caroline said, cutting slices into a neat pile.

Arabella poured wine. "To the future," she proclaimed, raising her glass and grinning at Maeve.

Maeve touched her glass to Arabella's. "May there be no wedding and no husband in mine. Only the friendship of such lovely companions."

Caroline laughed and drank her wine. "To friendship. Meeting you and Grace last year changed my life, you know. I don't know if I would have had the courage to talk to Arabella about our feelings for each other if we had not all met."

"I am so happy that you did," Arabella said, her heart shining in her eyes.

Arabella, Caroline, Maeve, and their friend Grace had all revealed their sapphic inclinations the year before when Maeve and Grace had first come to Inverley. Now Caroline and Arabella were in love with each other, and Grace had found love with a prickly botanist who was the daughter of the wealthiest man in Inverley.

Maeve poked a slice of bread on her thin metal tine, balanced a bit of cheese on top, and stuck it in the sand close to the fire. "I am more grateful than I can express that you have offered your home to me. All of Inverley must be filled to the brim with visitors now that the weather has turned so hot this summer. I cannot imagine it would have been easy for me to find somewhere to stay."

"That's what friends are for," Caroline said.

Maeve burnt the roof of her mouth with the bubbling hot cheese and spilled wine on her dress as she tried to balance her glass and her plate, but it was the tiny seed of jealousy that itched under her skin like a burr to see her friends so in love.

Where was her love story?

How had all of her best friends found love, and her own mother had married for a third time, and Maeve had nothing of her own? She longed for kisses, and sweet nothings, and to lean against another woman's shoulder as naturally as Arabella was leaning against Caroline.

She took another sip of wine. If friendship was all her future held, she would learn to be content with it.

No matter how much she wished for more.

CHAPTER THREE

Before a week had passed, Maeve was quite ready to give up the simple life if only an alternative would present itself to her. She cut uneven slices of vegetables for dinner with Caroline, struggled to hang laundry on the line with Arabella, and her earthly reward each night was to retire to a lumpy pallet in the drafty second bedroom that Arabella used as a studio for her watercolors. It was stacked high with papers and frames, was permeated with the odor of paint, and inhabited by Arabella's two cats who insisted on showing their delight at her presence by sleeping on her knees.

Maeve was grateful. Truly, she was.

But her back ached and her legs cramped, and her feet begged for tender mercies. She was more exhausted than she had ever been. Why, yesterday she had carried a leg of mutton for a quarter hour through town after a visit to the butcher, and her arms reminded her of the indignity each time she raised her teacup to her lips.

"Do either of you wish to visit the spa with me before you start your other errands?" Maeve asked her friends at breakfast. "I would move heaven and earth for a seaweed treatment."

"I don't have the coin for extravagances these days," Caroline said with a shrug. "We are saving our money for the boarding house for girls that we wish to open, though I am still hoping to secure funding from a wealthy sponsor someday. We shall be hard-pressed to get anywhere without more money than we are bringing in."

"My portrait work does well enough to keep body and soul together with a tidy sum leftover to contribute, but it's never enough."

"I suppose I cannot afford a seaweed treatment either." Maeve slid down in her chair and tipped her head up, gazing at the ceiling. "Perhaps I shall never have anything fine again in my whole life."

Why must the price be so dear on all the things she liked best? She had thought nothing of it when she had never had to open her purse strings to pay for any of it. She and Mama had often visited the spa in the morning and enjoyed a cup of chocolate at the teashop in the afternoon, and there had always been enough coin left over for a length of fabric at the draper's should anything catch her fancy on the way home.

Mama might have left her with six months of room and board, but it was not enough to maintain the pleasures of her previous lifestyle. And given that she had no intention of marrying and securing pin money after those six months passed, she needed to stretch her funds as far as she could in order to survive.

She wished for the seaweed treatment more than ever.

But it wasn't so much the loss of luxury that worried her. It was the stark reality that this would be but the start of privation. The meanest soiree in Inverley still had a pack of cards and a thimble of wine and a sliver of cake to offer its guests. But even that cost something to attend, and soon she would be able to afford less and less than ever before. Who knew what would become of her then?

"If you're looking for money, you will have to earn it," Caroline said. "You could always become a companion, like Grace was before she found love."

"Grace is sweet and amiable. I am nothing like that."

"Then you will need to take employment."

That had even less appeal. "I'm afraid I'm not good for much. And I have not the faintest idea of how to go about such a thing." Her stomach tightened. Her mother always said that a spinster was next to useless, putting little stock on a woman's value beyond that of a wife or a mother. "I know how to dance and I play a neat hand of whist, but I have no real experience at anything."

"You have plenty of experience," Arabella said stoutly. "You have traveled. You are wonderful with people."

"That doesn't count much as a talent."

"You shall have to learn to change if you are to survive," Caroline said, and though it was delivered gently enough, each word felt like a barb that twisted in her heart. "Otherwise it's the parson's mousetrap for you."

"That dress you're wearing must have been expensive," Arabella said, looking at the lace that adorned her bodice.

"Oh yes, do let us speak of fashion instead of finance!" Maeve warmed to the subject. "This is one of my favorite day dresses, you know. The lace was from another dress that I had made up in Ireland, but when it grew shoddy, I removed the trim and attached it to this one instead." She gazed down at the ivory muslin. "How I wish I could afford another dress of its ilk!"

"I meant that you could sell it."

"*Sell it?*" Maeve shuddered at the thought, sending the pintucked cotton rippling against her skin. "To whom? And then what would *I* wear?"

"We have a secondhand clothing emporium in town."

"I didn't know that."

"It isn't close to the shops where visitors frequent."

"Oh."

That stung, but she recognized the truth in it. She was no longer a fashionable visitor, spending her time at leisure. There were to be no more trips to fine shops, no more evenings at the assembly rooms. And yet surely her personal standards were not so expensive that she could no longer afford them? She lifted her chin. "I cannot be expected to sell the clothes from my very back and parade around Inverley in the nude. Do be sensible."

"You can sell *some* of them," Arabella said. "You need the money."

"Think of it as helping the townsfolk become more fashionable by granting them access to your castoffs," Caroline said, rolling her eyes.

Maeve pursed her lips. "You are saying it would be more of a charitable act, then."

"I was funning, but if it would help you—then yes, please do think of it in such terms."

"I would prefer to consider myself generous instead of desperate." She stared down at the Irish lace. She supposed she could always remove it once more if she had to sell the dress itself. And yet was she really considering such a thing?

"There's nothing wrong with making money by buying or selling," Arabella said. "My brother works in the rope trade and provides well enough for his family. The laborers who work for him are good honest men. There is no shame in needing money. We all need it. My portrait work is *work*, and I am not embarrassed by it."

To be in the position of earning one's keep! Maeve disliked the notion. It wasn't for people like her. But then who was it for? People like Arabella? Like Grace? Women she considered to be her dearest friends?

It was shameful to have thought herself above it all. She hadn't realized until she moved in with Arabella and Caroline how simply they lived. And oh, how happy they were together.

"But my clothes mean so much to me." Maeve struggled to find the right words. "My satins make me feel glorious and confident. Silk is like my second skin. Each stitch feels part of me. And each dress is attached to memories that I will no longer be able to make, attending soirees and libraries and horse races and the like. Even if I could scrape together the subscription fees for such events in the future, what good would it do me if I gave away the wardrobe that would allow me entry? I cannot attend such things in sackcloth." Her heart felt heavy. "It may seem silly, but my clothing has always helped define me."

"A bonnet defines nobody, no matter how fine the trim," Caroline said. "You make too much of it."

Caroline would never understand. She saw clothing as a necessity. But Maeve's identity was wound up in her silks and linens, and if she was stripped of her social standing, then her identity was all she had, as threadbare as it might become.

Despite it all, she knew they were right. She needed a way to make money.

And surely the sale of one garment wouldn't be *too* disastrous to her way of life.

❖

Standing on the shoreline at the edge of England, Joan felt she could have gone her whole life without having experienced the alleged pleasures of the seaside. It proved troublesome to walk on the sand in her laced-up ankle boots. The sound of the waves was thunderous. Watching the ocean swell and heave made her stomach dip and her eyes cross.

The sun's heat was trapped against her skin by the miles of black bombazine that made up her walking dress, and her head ached under her black bonnet. The waves were gray-blue, murky and mysterious, with foam-tipped wavelets creeping up the shore like tendrils of some beast yearning to grab her and pull her under.

It was eerie. Endless.

Terrifying.

Joan shuddered and turned her back to it. Maurice, delighted to have the run of the countryside, gamboled about in front of her as she made her way up the path to the gardens around the house.

But the house was another problem.

For Fairview Manor was nothing like the charming cottage she had in her mind's eye when she had purchased it sight unseen. Boasting but seven bedchambers, it was modest when compared to any of the ducal holdings. Yet instead of ivy-covered stone and mullioned windows and charming wood trim, the architect had thrown up walls of dark red brick with pitch-black iron trellises marching along the premises. Turrets with yawning windows stuck out like an eyesore at each corner of the house, menacing any onlookers. Spires upon spires dizzied the eyes, ringing round a widow's walk that stretched the length of the roof and overlooked the sea.

She could almost imagine a ghostly figure up there, dressed in black and staring out into the endless depths of the sea.

Instead of Joan's pastoral fantasy, it was her nightmare.

She walked along the hedgerow that divided her property from the road so she could look at Fairview Manor again from the front. It was as imposing from this angle as it had been from the back.

"Afternoon, ma'am," a man called out from behind, startling her.

He had a round face and white hair and puffed at a pipe, putting Joan in mind of one of the cottagers from Astley Park. He tipped his hat as he walked past the house on the road to Inverley. He paused for a moment, as if he wished to speak further, but the sight of her mourning attire seemed to change his mind.

"Good day," she said to him before fleeing up the path to the house. She had been in town for three days and had seen no one. She had hoped it would stay that way.

"Is there any chance that the locals here know who has the deed of this house?" she asked the butler.

"I've never heard anyone rumormonger about it. Mrs. Evenson and I have lived here all our lives, Your Grace. Even we did not know that it was a duchess who purchased the house. The land agent we had met with had been most vague about the whole affair. Upon your instruction, we haven't breathed a word of it to the staff."

Joan went to her bedchamber and rang for Sarah, but Tilda bustled through the door instead.

"You should be taking your rest," Joan told her. "I was calling for Sarah to help me out of my dress."

"I'm not ready yet for pasture, Your Grace. I can do as well for you as my granddaughter." But her fingers were slow to unbutton the dress, and she scowled as she rang the bell herself for Sarah's help.

"You've earned your retirement," Joan said. "You can have all the time you like to do whatever you like. I do wish you would consider it."

Tilda sat in the armchair and frowned out the window as Sarah made quick work of undressing Joan and helping her into a black muslin frock with an overdress of imperial gauze.

Joan plucked at the sheer black fabric, thin as breath. Tiny pleats made for a distinctive tonal stripe on the bodice where the gauze doubled over itself. There was a velvet ribbon around her waist and another at the hem of her skirt.

It was beautiful.

But it was dreadful knowing that it had been created to proclaim a grief that she did not feel, as decorative and ornamented as the widow's walk on the roof, but wholly without substance.

Sarah's brows knit together as she stared at the vicinity of Joan's shoes.

"I am not displeased," Joan said to reassure her. "I simply wish I was wearing colors already."

But Sarah shook her head and glanced at Tilda.

"Out with it, girl. A lady's maid doesn't fidget like a schoolgirl! If you have something to say to your mistress, say it. Her Grace would not think ill of you. I gained the trust of all of the duchesses by speaking my mind and giving sound counsel."

Joan nodded. Tilda had been invaluable to her since her wedding day.

"The mail came today," Sarah blurted out.

Tilda sighed. "That is a fact less than worthy of sharing, my dear. But don't worry. With time, you shall understand what is important and what is not, and what your mistress needs from you."

Sarah's face turned crimson. "The housemaids are all agog at today's scandal sheets."

"Scullery maid gossip is even less befitting a duchess's ear!" Tilda cried. "Oh, Your Grace, I do apologize. I have yet to finish my Sarah's training. This is no time for retirement."

She shook like a leaf, but she stood her ground. "Her Grace needs to see it."

Joan doubted it but took pity on her. "Do be so kind as to fetch the papers, Sarah."

And when Sarah returned, Joan was glad she had listened.

The newspaper wasn't crisply ironed, as befitted the correspondence she was accustomed to receiving in Hanover Square. But while the shabby state of the paper might raise her brow, it was its contents that had her reeling.

CHAPTER FOUR

THE MISSING DUCHESS, the scandal sheet headline stated in big bold letters.

"What is the meaning of this?" Joan whispered. Tilda peered at it over her shoulder.

The article was written in a flowery hand, decrying the sad state of affairs that a mighty Duke had not only fallen prey to his scheming harlot of a duchess, but now that the noble figure was dead, her illegitimate children danced on his grave.

"They make it sound as if I murdered him. And they aren't even my children." Joan sank into a chair, her knees weak. "The eldest is but five years younger than myself."

"The papers don't care as much about proof as they do about profit," Tilda said.

Joan snatched up the gossip rag again. "What do they mean that I am *missing*?"

The second half of the article detailed the mysterious disappearance of the duchess in the dead of night with all the ermine her coach could carry, leaving behind a devastated family who would do all in their power to forgive her if she was returned to their bosom.

There was a caricature underneath the article, showing her with a mincing air and a face full of cosmetics, her long hair in wild disarray. She touched her curls with both hands, reassuring herself that her ringlets were as neat as ever. "I look nothing like this. I don't even wear lip rouge."

"It is a poor likeness, Your Grace," Sarah agreed.

"But they do describe you, red hair and blue eyes and the way your nose tilts up a little," Tilda said.

"I didn't want anyone to know that I am here, but I didn't mean to raise a hue and cry about my whereabouts." Joan frowned down at the paper.

"Did you truly not tell anyone where we were going?" Sarah asked, her eyes huge.

"No one asked," she said, trying to remember if she had spoken to anyone after Lady Mary had visited her. "They didn't seem to care where I was going when I left Shropshire, so I thought nothing of it when I left London."

She hadn't wanted anyone in Inverley to know that the Duchess of Stanmere was here, because she didn't think she could bear any more snide gossip about her alleged infidelity. But she had never imagined that the scandal sheets would catch wind of anything, or that they would take things so far as to proclaim her the mother of the illegitimate sons.

She also hadn't deliberately intended to hide her whereabouts from the Astleys. But if no one knew of Fairview Manor because it wasn't part of the dukedom's holdings, how would anyone know she was here when they didn't know where *here* was?

Joan felt something that she couldn't quite name. "The duchy took everything from me." She took a deep breath. *Satisfaction.* That was what this long-forgotten feeling was. "Well, they can't have this, can they?"

Sarah gaped at her. "Your Grace! You don't mean to stay missing, do you?"

Joan took another breath. The sea air was said to be healing, after all. Maybe that was what was fueling this strange mood. "I certainly do. This is sensationalist gossip. No matter what the papers print, the Astleys do not care enough about me to wish for my return. Send the scullery maids back to London, and hire local women to replace them. I don't want anyone from London in this household who could have any inkling of who I am." She frowned. "There was a man outside when I came inside. What if he recognized me from the description in the papers?"

"A disguise, my lady!" Tilda's eyes brightened. "That's what you need. Nothing easier. That will throw 'em off the scent."

"I don't wish to do anything drastic." She ran a hand through her hair. Unbound, it curled well past her shoulders. Stanmere had liked it long.

"In my day, girls used to dye their hair with walnut leaves," Tilda said. "We could do such a thing to yours to darken it a shade or two."

"Would it not stain my face?"

"We shall be careful. Besides, if you don't, you will run the risk of someone in town finding you out, and you will be besieged by nosy visitors. No one shall be the wiser that a duchess is amongst the pigeons, Your Grace. You won't be caught."

Being caught made it sound like she was doing something wrong. But a sin of omission was not so grave, was it? Missing duchess indeed. What a wild tale the papers spun, when they had nothing else to print!

Joan tugged at one of her curls, looking at it. Her hair was dark auburn, the red showing more when she was out of doors in the bright sunlight than when she was inside. "If I wear a bandeau to cover most of it when I am indoors, and keep my hair tucked up beneath my bonnet when I am out, then I won't have to dye it."

"However will we get all that hair beneath a bonnet?" Sarah's nose crinkled in confusion. "You have ever so much of it, Your Grace."

There was one option besides the walnut dye. "Tilda, how handy are you with a pair of scissors?"

❖

Maeve clutched her canvas bag to her chest as she stared at the secondhand clothing emporium. Caroline had marched her to its doors and nipped off down the alley to the grocer's, leaving Maeve alone to conduct her business. She supposed she must resign herself to doing things on her own now, much as the idea made her want to turn around and bury her head under the blanket in the back chamber of the cottage.

Sea salt had rusted the door hinges and eaten away at the painted letters proclaiming it to be the premier location for used goods. The building looked well-used itself. The stone steps had grooves worn into them and the brickwork needed repairs near the roof.

It was a far cry from the sparkling chandeliers and fresh plaster that adorned the buildings on the other side of town where the visitors laughed and danced and ate at the assembly rooms and fine hotels and shops.

Whatever was she waiting for, frozen here on the steps? A miracle? A handsome knight to sweep her away and solve her problems, like the count had done for her mother? Then again, that had been no miracle. Her mother had set herself to the task and done the work to accomplish what she had wanted.

Maeve needed to find the same resolve within herself.

Besides, she wanted no knight. They were more trouble than they were worth.

She shoved the door open and blinked in the dim light. Stacks of clothes and hats and boots and belts greeted her, some in neat bundles on the shelves against the wall, and some in haphazard piles. A musty aroma enveloped her, and she sneezed.

"I've plenty of handkerchiefs if you're looking to buy one. Finest cotton England has to offer! Some with good quality lace, too!" A man sat behind a desk piled high with fabrics. Dust motes danced in the sunlight, but his collar was crisp and white and his coat had nary a crease in it. He sprang to his feet when she came closer. "Oh! Well now, I suppose you have plenty of your own, a fine and fancy lass such as yourself?"

"In fact, I am looking to part with my plenty, instead of increasing the contents of my linen chest."

"A lady not from our shores. You're from beyond the Irish sea, are you?"

She and Mama had met with plenty of censure in their travels through England. Her stepfather's coin had paved the way for most people to be polite to them, but there were a few who looked at any Irishwoman with distrust.

For a moment, her resolve crumbled and she wished Caroline had entered the establishment with her.

"Yes, near Dublin. But I have spent years in England."

"Very good, miss." His eyes roved over her garments in a way that Maeve would have found insulting had they been at a social engagement, but when he lingered on the extravagance of her silk-lined poke bonnet and the braided trim of her skirts instead of on her bosom, she felt her shoulders relax.

Now this was something she was comfortable with.

Her dress, after all, had not been cheap. After her conversation with Caroline about fashion, it was a relief to be in the presence of someone who appreciated sartorial detail.

"If you like the cut of my gown, sir, then I think you will be best pleased with the contents of my bag."

Maeve heaved her bag onto his desk, and he swept aside piles of papers and fabric scraps to make room for her to pull a dress from its depths.

She hadn't been able to part with her cream satin or her robin's egg blue muslin or her green velvet or her beribboned pink silk, though they might have garnered more money. This gown was simple, but fine enough. It had a striped blue and white sarsnet skirt with a white bodice and short puffed sleeves, and being her least favorite, it was in excellent condition. She tugged a blue spencer from the bag as well, and a petticoat that had a matching striped flounce at the hem. "It's all meant to go together."

"We pay by the piece, not the outfit." He stripped off his gloves with a murmured apology to her female sensibilities at seeing his bare skin and touched the clothing. "The spencer is in good shape."

"It's *all* in good shape. A lady will want an outfit that is meant to be worn as a whole, and not scraped from the piecemeal assortment from your shelves." She looked around, then realized that she may have given offense. "I do beg your pardon."

"Do you think we entertain many ladies here?" He gestured around him. "Come now. I know the people who shop here, and they don't want such things. We don't charge much and we can't pay much."

Maeve took in a deep breath and another lungful of dust, which resulted in another sneeze. "Then perhaps this is your opportunity to market your wares to a new clientele."

A quarter hour passed as fast as any had in an assembly room. He introduced himself as Mr. Culpepper and offered her a cup of tea as they talked, and Maeve found herself enjoying herself as they haggled.

Maeve shook her head. "Obviously the dress is worth more than the paltry sum you are offering! Look at the amount of Valenciennes lace."

He rolled his eyes up to the ceiling. "They all want to talk about trim when it's the *fabric* that makes up most of the worth."

She jabbed a finger at the lace flounce. "Because this is good quality trim! I'm starting to think you can't tell worsted wool from cloth of gold if you think this lace isn't fine enough for you."

She was so engrossed that she didn't notice at first that the door had opened and they were no longer alone. But Maeve's breath halted when she looked up and saw the woman who entered.

CHAPTER FIVE

The woman who walked into the emporium was shorter than Maeve and swathed in so much black crepe that the stiff fabric rustled as she walked toward them, and her face was obscured by a heavy veil. Not a hint of shine gleamed from her shoe buckles or hatpin. Maeve caught the scent of her perfume as she came up to the desk, the aroma delicate and floral, like violets. She breathed deep. It was a welcome change from the must of the shop.

"I am looking for clothing, sir," she said to Mr. Culpepper. "I'm told you have the best wares." Her voice enthralled Maeve. It was light and airy, the words beautifully articulated.

He bowed. "Thank you, madam. I do like to think I have a selection that would please the most discerning of customers. You may take your time to peruse, if you wish."

She drew herself up, which gave her a scant quarter inch more in height. "I can scarcely see what's in front of me through my veil. Please do select something appropriate."

"We don't have much in the way of mourning."

"Anything but black, sir."

"I am happy to hear that you are past the worst of times. My condolences on your loss, but time does heal all wounds. Now, we do have a good selection of lavenders and grays."

"No half-mourning, either."

This gave Mr. Culpepper some pause. "Ah. Of course."

"I don't wish to spend more time than necessary, sir."

The widow moved her head, and Maeve imagined she was taking in the same sights she herself had. By the way she shook her head, she must have come to the same conclusions as Maeve. This was no place for a woman in such finery to shop. However had she come to be here?

Then she looked down at the garments that sprawled out of Maeve's bag. "Have these just come in? They seem finer than the other things here."

The maid darted between them and took the bag, spilling its contents over the counter.

"I have not even finished showing Mr. Culpepper," Maeve said.

"Were they yours, then?" Her eyes roved over Maeve for an instant, and she felt hot all over. "These seem satisfactory to me." She let the striped walking dress fall from her gloved hand.

"They are more than satisfactory," she snapped. "I purchased them in London."

"Not from a well-known modiste," the widow said, gazing down at them. Her tone was thoughtful instead of critical, but Maeve bristled.

"Oh? And do you know all of the fashionable modistes in town?"

"I spread my custom widely enough, yes." Then she paused. "That is, my husband did." She seemed flustered. "Well. I can see that the stitching is not fine enough to be from the best of shops."

"I beg your pardon, but why are you even in a secondhand shop? If you are so well acquainted with the best of the London dressmakers, perhaps you ought to have something custom made."

Mr. Culpepper coughed. "Miss Balfour, let us not get carried away here. I would be more than happy to purchase your clothes and sell them to Mrs.......?"

She dismissed his query for her name with a wave of her hand. "This dress isn't the first stare of fashion—"

"The *lace* is *Valenciennes*," Maeve interrupted, throwing up her hands. "Does no one recognize true quality anymore?"

"Despite the lace," the widow said, nodding to her in acknowledgment, "nothing is remarkable here."

"I received dozens of compliments when I wore this on the promenade the other week," Maeve said coldly.

"The local promenade? Yes, I suppose it would pass muster here in Inverley."

The notion of selling her clothes to be immediately donned by someone else felt invasive. Intimate. It hadn't occurred to her that she would ever meet the person who bought them, nor that they wouldn't even appreciate them.

"I will take everything," the widow said, gesturing to the counter and nodding at her maid, who bundled the clothing up.

Mr. Culpepper blinked at her.

"Everything," the widow repeated.

"Eighteen guineas and five shillings," he said, and Maeve sucked in a breath. Why, that was far too much, was it not?

But the maid plucked the coins from her reticule and then she and the widow left in a flurry of crepe, Maeve's canvas bag clutched between them.

"Eighteen guineas?" Maeve stared at Mr. Culpepper.

"I thought she could well afford it."

She stuck out her hand. "And what of my share?"

He pushed half the money across the desk. "Mind you, if you have anything else to bring me, I won't have the luxury of paying so much. I've never had such an easy hour's work as this, and it's unlikely that a woman like her would return."

Nine guineas would go a long way toward her living expenses. Perhaps she could get used to selling things after all. Especially when the clientele had proved so intriguing.

❖

Joan tried to walk as fast as she could as she and Sarah returned to Fairview Manor. "This was a terrible idea," she muttered as she averted her gaze from onlookers.

"No one can identify you through the veil," Sarah said from half a pace behind her.

"Maybe not, but will they wonder who I am, given that I am in mourning deep enough to befit a prince?"

Joan hadn't given it a second thought when she had left the manor. The veil shielded her face and protected her identity from anyone who might have studied that dratted drawing from the gossip rag. But it wasn't common to wear such a heavy veil, and the quality of her clothes might raise more questions than it answered. It felt as if everyone was staring at her as she hurried through town. She hadn't given much thought to how people who were not accustomed to rubbing shoulders with royalty dressed, but she saw in an instant when she walked among them that her dress was worth far more than any she saw.

Why, she had bought a bag of clothing for the paltry sum of eighteen guineas! *Those* were the sort of people she was amongst. Would they not raise a brow at her attire, the same as she raised hers at theirs?

Joan had never worried so much in her life as she had since the will was read. Deep thoughts were for other people, her mother had reassured her when she was a girl. People like her were intended for much more important things. Like dukes. She was pretty, and that was supposed to be enough.

Joan was fast discovering that *pretty* didn't matter a whit in her new circumstances.

"People may wonder, Your Grace, but they will never guess at the truth."

Joan winced at the use of her title. "Let us be silent for now." The last thing she needed was for anyone to hear the truth from their own lips. No disguise in the world would save her then.

Fairview Manor was not far from town. It had been built beyond a small hill, but it was not so hidden that townsfolk had no reason to pass by it. After all, there were more houses located past her own, though not as grand, and charming vistas abounded all about Inverley. There was no guarantee that she would not be seen by either townsfolk or visitors, unless she truly never stepped foot out-of-doors.

New clothes would help hide her from scrutiny, and she had to admit that she was eager for an excuse to discard her blacks.

She hoped it had been worth the risk of venturing outside today.

Tilda was delighted to see her new attire once they were back in the house. If nothing else, Joan was heartened by the fact that her maids were so taken with the subterfuge. Seeing them happy was a balm to her heart.

"We shall launder everything tomorrow, Your Grace," Tilda promised. "No dust from the shop shall linger on them, you may put your mind at ease on that."

Joan picked up the striped sarsnet dress. It was well made, though nothing compared to the tiny even stitches of Madame Bastien or Madame Desmarais. She had been no less than honest. She had patronized the best dressmakers that London had to offer. *All* of them. But the dress was nicer than she had admitted.

She had been out of sorts in the clothing emporium, fretting that she would be recognized and wishing to be done with the errand as soon as possible. She had never been in a shop that sold things that weren't new, unless of course they were so old that they were antiques. She had not intended to be rude to the shopkeeper or to the woman who had been selling her wares.

But she had been.

Joan wasn't sure if she had ever behaved so curtly. It wasn't becoming of a duchess.

"You were lucky to find these pieces, Your Grace. We could have been an hour or more in that shop and not come out with anything half as nice as these. Are you sure you do not wish me to give your measurements to the dressmaker in town?"

"Perhaps that would have drawn less attention. But they would not have anything ready today, and I have no desire to wear black a day longer than I need to."

It was a shocking thing to throw off mourning a husband within the month of his burial, and scandalous to wear colors without first observing the period of half-mourning.

But Stanmere didn't deserve to be mourned.

Besides, no one knew her here.

The dress held the faint aroma of rose petals, and Joan thought of the woman who had sold it. She had the type of face that was beautiful at first glance and became more alluring the longer one looked. She had a mass of pitch-black curls cascading from beneath her straw bonnet, and a long neck with a graceful arch. Her lips were full, and she had a smattering of freckles across her high cheekbones and nose. It was most charming.

Not that it mattered what the woman looked like. Joan's reason for studying her was so that she could guess whether or not she could fit into her clothing. Her beauty was but a footnote. Joan was shorter by a few inches, and a trifle less full in the bust, but she thought it would be a close enough match.

Joan wanted to protest when Sarah scooped the clothing back into the bag and bustled out of the room to add them to the other garments to be laundered that week. But they were simply clothes. Nothing more.

She caught sight of her hair in the mirror. Tilda had cut it to her shoulders, which made it easier to pile on top of her head to hide it beneath a bonnet if she were outside, and a bandeau if she were inside. Most of her hair would be out of sight, which was never how she had worn it previously, for she was proud of her hair. She hoped the change to her hair and clothing would be enough to prevent discovery from the prying eyes of neighbors as she focused on getting what she deserved from the duchy. It would rub salt in the wound if the people of Inverley knew that she was the so-called scandalous duchess.

Luke, her trusted footman and Tilda's great-nephew, had agreed to act as messenger back and forth to London with any sensitive messages, as Joan had no desire to set foot in the capital unless it was of dire necessity.

He was there now to oversee hiring a Bow Street Runner to investigate her dowry. It sounded unbelievable to her that an heiress worth twenty thousand could be worth precisely nothing five short years later. And to have been left with a mere two hundred a year when she had been a true and faithful wife!

If she had been adulterous, why had it been left to assumption and not part of the legal document to remove her from the will entirely? Two hundred was insulting, but it could have been even less had he truly believed it of her. And what had become of the lands to the north? They could not have been added to the entail, for they had not been listed among the other properties in the will.

It was all very mysterious.

Joan drafted a letter to Mr. Boyd asking if the firm could help collect her personal jewelry and her wardrobe and send it to her direction in Inverley. She didn't mind her own lawyers knowing where she was, but underlined in the letter that she wished for discretion. Her jewels must be cleaned by now, and she would welcome her own clothing to replace the few secondhand pieces she had bought today on impulse.

Perhaps if the lawyers were more involved, the Astley family's betrayal would feel less personal.

Though she wasn't sure if anything could heal the gaping wound in her heart where trust had once held it together.

CHAPTER SIX

Maeve dug the tips of her shoes into the sand. She sat on a stool beside Arabella, who was painting a tiny watercolor for a visitor as a keepsake. If Maeve had such a talent, it would be so helpful in her current situation. And yet thinking of all the hours Arabella spent sketching and painting and purchasing frames for her work made Maeve's head spin. Selling her clothes had been a quick enough venture. Maeve couldn't conceive of the labor it would take to learn an art and perfect it.

She had received a letter yesterday from Mama, vague and breezy, scrawled in haste between dinner with the count and an evening engagement at a London theatre before they departed for Italy next week. That was what Maeve missed most about her old life—always having something to do and somewhere to go.

The beach was a good enough replacement for a soiree in that regard. There were plenty of people strolling today, with interesting countenances and fashions to study. The scent of the sea breeze was lovely, tinged with the aroma of hot nuts and meat pasties that the vendors were offering.

A man was strolling along the shore, a basket in each hand as he called out that he had pies for sale, fresh pies, baked up that morning and ideal for anyone and everyone to enjoy on a beautiful afternoon.

"I could do with a pie," Maeve said, eying him.

Seeing her looking, the man loped up the beach toward them. "Fancy a toss, lass?" he asked, winking at her.

Maeve gasped and glared at him, but Arabella smiled. "We would love a toss, sir."

"Right you are then, I can set you up fine. Two pretty ladies deserve a good show." He set down his baskets and rolled his sleeves up his arms, and then postured a bit, flexing his arms before flipping over the cloth and revealing mounds of golden crusted pies. "Now, you know the rules, don't you?"

"I most assuredly do not." Maeve gave him a pointed look. "I wish for nothing more than pie."

"Then pie you shall have! Or you shall have not. The fates decree it, you see. For the price of one mere shilling, you buy a toss. I throw the pie up in the air—"

"No," Arabella cried, laughing. "Sir, it is not the pie you toss!"

"Ah, you have done this before! I would have never guessed it of such a fair maiden. You are right, we toss no pies here. Flaky and delicious they are, and liable to get pastry in your pretty hair were I to use my might and toss a pie. No, we toss shillings, according to the custom of the land. You throw your coin in the air, I shout out heads or tails, and if you win, you get a fine pie worth thrice as much as the throw."

"And if you win?"

"I keep your shilling." He grinned. "It's a popular pastime on both sides, I will have you know."

"It seems rather more certain that I would instead enjoy a paper cone of peanuts from that man over there if I must part with a shilling for no certain reward from you."

"But the good are always rewarded," he said with a wink. "Now, do you wish for pie or shall I find another pair of hungry ladies?"

"We shall take you up on the toss," Arabella said.

"Toss a coin each, then. High in the air, make it count."

Arabella took a shilling for them each from what she had earned that afternoon, and they both threw their coins up.

"Tails!" the man boomed.

The coins flashed in the sun and fell to the sand. They peered at the results. One was tails, one was heads. He scooped up both shillings. "One pie to split between the two of you today, and two shillings for me, if you please."

"Do you have cherry?" Arabella asked.

"We have everything you might desire." He took a pastry from his basket but handed it to Maeve. "I believe Doubting Thomas was the winner, though." He winked at her before bundling up his wares. Shouting of his victory, he resumed his stroll along the shore, attracting others to his game.

"It's rigged, you know," Arabella said as she took a bite. "He fancied you and made sure you won the pie. Not that I am complaining, because this is delicious."

Maeve glared down at the pastry. "What makes you say that?"

"Because I never win. I never had many suitors here, and I don't think anyone considered me a good prospect. I always ended up paying a shilling with no pie."

"Then I don't want it. The nerve of that man." She squinted down the beach at him, too far away to scold but plenty near enough to scowl at.

"I'll finish it then."

"I won't even charge you for my share, though I don't have the faintest idea how else I shall be in a position to make more money. I suppose I shall have to part with another dress before long."

Arabella bit her lip. "Indeed you may need to."

"Oh?"

"Caroline's youngest brothers were meant to spend the year with their eldest brother, Jacob, and their sister, Sally, in Somerset. But there has been an outbreak of scarlet fever in their area, and all of them are on their way home to Inverley for the rest of the summer to avoid it. We received the letter this morning."

"Scarlet fever! How dreadful. I am glad to hear that they have not caught it."

"We are soon to have a cramped cottage. It's three brothers and one sister who are coming, though the sister might stay with their other sister in Inverley."

"There will be no room for me," Maeve said quietly. "I understand. Family comes first, and they are escaping a dire situation."

"You are welcome to stay! We would never abandon you. But it will be tight quarters."

She should have realized that this could happen. Without the bond of her own family, the promise of marriage, or an agreement of employment, it was unsteady living for a spinster with little means.

Was this to be her future? To rely on the kindness of friends when they had their own obligations and responsibilities?

She had been living with Arabella and Caroline for a month. It was wonderful staying with her friends, but she had felt guilty at taking up space in their cottage when they refused any offer of money from her. Though she tried her best to do her fair share, Maeve had to admit that she was slow and unpracticed at cleaning and cooking.

Even without the scarlet fever outbreak, she supposed she would not have been able to rely on them forever.

The idea of moving was daunting. She knew from previous experience with Mama that there were *never* any rooms to rent in Inverley in the height of summer. Every spare room was pressed into service for boarders between June and October, and the hotels were at full capacity. To find even the meanest accommodations for a new groomsman in a stable would be next to impossible now that it was July and the town was brimming with people.

But the other solution was marriage, and she was determined never to follow that path.

"The widow." Maeve's thoughts were tumbling round and round as she tried to think. "Your neighbor told you that she lives in that big manor house by the cove, right?"

"The woman who bought your clothes? Yes. The house was deserted for years until she came this summer. No one has properly seen her aside from you, and our neighbor who chanced to catch a glimpse of her as he walked past her property some weeks ago. I am sure he described the same woman. There are always a handful of widows visiting town in grays, but never in such unrelieved black. Her loss must be recent."

"I doubt she brought a house party with her. It wouldn't be at all the thing during mourning. We have walked the hills near her manor. How many bedchambers do you reckon it holds?"

"At least five, I would say. Maybe more. I have painted it many times. Visitors take a particular interest in Fairview Manor as it looks so dramatic on the bluff."

"Perhaps she would welcome a lodger."

It was the only place in Inverley that might have empty bedchambers in it. Maeve warmed to the idea. A manor house would have nice soft beds in it, and she could stop imposing on the generosity of her friends.

"You said her clothing was very fine," Arabella pointed out. "She must be wealthy."

"Mine is also fine and yet that does not convey the reality of my situation, does it? She may have lost her wealth a dozen times over in her widowhood. We don't know."

"You cannot mean to disrupt her mourning, Maeve!"

"She may well not even be mourning. Remember, she did buy my clothes."

"You don't know *why* she bought them! Maybe they weren't for her."

"If they were not for her, then her maid would have taken care of the errand and spared her the trouble."

"I don't know if your plan will work."

"Oh, it shall," Maeve said brightly.

After all, it would have to.

❖

Everson came to Joan's sitting room as she was writing another letter to her lawyers. "Your Grace, you have a caller."

She stared at him. "We have talked about such an occurrence a dozen times. Please do tell them that I am not at home."

"I did, Your Grace. However, the lady insists on speaking with you. She is claiming some prior acquaintance."

Her heart sped up. Would Lady Mary have traveled all the way to Inverley? Or was it one of Stanmere's daughters? They couldn't have found her. Not yet. Unless Luke had been followed from London, but he had not even returned yet.

If it wasn't family, she might pass as someone else. Her curls were pinned up and Sarah had wrapped a wide bandeau around her head and tied a bow near one ear, which was a style she had never worn in the past. She wasn't in her widow's weeds and her dress was simpler than usual. She had to admit to being in a great deal of comfort during her country sojourn. Why, her closest friends in London would not recognize her, as accustomed as they were to the glamor of her usual attire.

But still, Joan quailed at the thought of confronting the visitor.

"Where is she?"

"She is waiting in the Blue Parlor."

"I will tiptoe after you and peek in the door to determine if I know them or not. Then you may tell them that I am indisposed and shall not see anyone."

As well-trained as he was, Everson's brows raised. "Your Grace, this is most unusual."

"Lead the way, Everson." Joan slipped off her shoes so that she would make no noise. "I shall follow."

It was unusual for a lady of the manor to glide down the hallway in her stockings. A month ago, she would have laughed at such an absurdity. But now she felt as if her life depended on such subterfuge. Once they neared the parlor, Joan waited for the butler to move into the doorway, and then she peeked through the crack between the open door and the doorjamb.

Only to be met with a wide green eye staring back at her.

CHAPTER SEVEN

Joan gasped and stepped back from the crack in the parlor door, then realized there was now no choice but to enter the room and greet her visitor as if she had meant to do so all along.

She straightened her back and walked into the room, her shoulders back and chin up. Joan cleared her throat. "Thank you, Everson, that will be all."

He bowed and left, and Joan found herself staring into the eyes of the raven-haired beauty from the secondhand clothing emporium. "You!" she exclaimed, then clapped a hand to her mouth upon realizing how ill-mannered she sounded.

The woman's lips quirked. "I am most gratified by the enthusiasm of your greeting. We were not properly introduced the other day. I am Miss Maeve Balfour."

"I am Joan—" but she caught herself, about to say the Duchess of Stanmere. Here she was at the first test of her disguise and she was ready to spill everything at the barest invitation. Even as a girl she had never been good at falsehoods. "The captain's widow," she finished. Everson had told her that the house had belonged to a sea captain, who had built it some twenty years previously and sold it upon his death.

"It is a pleasure to meet you, Mrs.......?"

"Oh! Yes." She tried to recall what the butler had told her the captain's name was, and finally recited "Mrs. Firth" as if she were a schoolgirl at her lessons. This would never do. She never behaved so awkwardly. Tea would help—tea *always* helped—so she pulled the bell for Sarah. "Do sit down, Miss Balfour."

Her masses of coal black curls and the glitter in her green eyes were enough to launch fashionable trends in the ladies' magazines. She was hardly elegant, but she had such presence that Joan thought she would do whatever she bid, without a thought. Miss Balfour was languid, almost limpid. She sat in the chair as if she were boneless, which would have been a disgrace if they were in public and was still rather improper in company together, but she leaned against the plush chair as if nothing could compel her to ever arise from its depths again. Her breathing was so light that her bosom hardly moved, and if Joan didn't say another word, she wondered if Miss Balfour would drift to sleep given another quarter hour.

This was a woman whose every inch cried out to be pampered. Like a princess in a Banbury tale. And yet, from Joan's memory of their exchange in the emporium, she possessed a tongue sharper than any brambles that would ever hold her hostage in a villain's tower.

That tongue touched Miss Balfour's lips, and Joan sucked in a breath.

"I suppose you are wondering what I am doing calling on you."

"I confess to being surprised that you know where I live."

She shrugged. "There are few secrets in a small town."

"What kind of secrets?" Joan asked sharply.

"The one I'm currently interested in involves a woman and her sartorial habits. I am happy to welcome anyone to the neighborhood who shares my taste in clothes."

Could it be that her reason for visiting was so straightforward? There was no guile on Miss Balfour's face, no hint of recognition that she was talking to a duchess. Joan felt the tension leave her body. She had not wanted any social calls, and although this was a most unusual one, she could tell that there was no danger here.

"Thank you for calling on me."

"It is good to see houses such as yours well-occupied, instead of remaining empty summer after summer." Miss Balfour tapped a gloved finger on the arm of her chair. "I beg your pardon for coming to the point so directly, but I was wondering if perhaps we could do one another a favor."

Disappointment crashed through her. As a duchess, she had fielded regular requests for favors. It was upsetting to place Miss Balfour in the category of people she recognized after all, if only in her manners. "Oh?"

"This is dreadfully forward, and I do apologize, but I was wondering if you had any rooms to let?"

"Rooms?" Joan blinked. This was not what she had expected. "Oh. No, I am afraid I do not. You cannot stay here."

God above would have to help her if this creature were to slumber every night in her own home. She had no idea where such a vehement response came from, but she felt the certainty of it in her bones.

Miss Balfour's eyes wandered over the mahogany grandfather clock, the marble statuary visible in the garden through the window, and the gold patina on the picture frames. An open doorway led into a music room on one side, and a breakfast parlor on the other.

"I don't suppose that it is for lack of space," she said, her voice thoughtful.

Joan took a deep breath. "I am not looking to house any lodgers."

"I could make do with a garden shed," she said. "I am not particular, as long as I have space for a mattress and could beg a bowl of gruel from your cook in the mornings."

Her face remained placid, though Joan caught sight of a wicked glint in her eyes before she lowered her lashes to hide them. A bowl of gruel indeed. What cheek.

Those cheeks, alabaster and high, freckled and pale, would get Joan in trouble if she had to stare at them each day. But whatever did these feelings mean? She didn't recognize them.

"I am sure you will have better luck in town."

"Summer is in full flush, Mrs. Firth. There are no rooms in town. And yet you have this big, empty house all to yourself. Widowhood must be lonely. Surely you could use someone else to rattle along with?"

"Many people keep manor houses, regardless of the size of the family."

"There are not so many such estates here in Inverley. There are two near town, in fact. Martin House, which is already full of wealthy guests and beyond the range that I could pay even if they had space to let....... And yours. All twenty-three rooms of it, seven of them bedchambers, if the bricklayer in town can be believed."

It had nothing to do with money. What she couldn't afford was a woman like Miss Balfour nosing her way around her secrets.

"After all, you have taken the very clothes from my back." Miss Balfour's eyes were large and sorrowful.

Joan wondered if she were some sort of actress with how smoothly she spoke.

She looked down at her dress. She hadn't even realized that she was wearing Miss Balfour's striped blue sarsnet frock in front of her. On what occasions had she worn it? Had it pinched her in the same place as Joan where it laced up in the back?

The intimacy of wearing another woman's clothes—*this* woman's clothes—made her feel warm.

"I apologize for raising a question of some indelicacy. But might you be experiencing some financial strain? Perhaps your coffers might welcome the funds from a boarder. After all, you were shopping for secondhand clothing."

"That meant nothing," she said as dignified as she could.

Miss Balfour's eyes trailed lower. "Perhaps not. I do beg your pardon for mentioning it, but you do not even have shoes on your feet."

Her *feet*! Embarrassment flooded her. She had forgotten that she had left her shoes in her sitting room, intending on peeking into the parlor and fleeing without being seen.

Joan stood, her heart pounding. "I am afraid that is all the time I have today for social calls, Miss Balfour."

Miss Balfour rose, her lithe body unfolding like a flower seeking the sun. Joan half expected her to stretch like a cat getting up from its perch where it had dozed for most of the day. "Thank you for your time, Mrs. Firth. I do appreciate it. I expect I shall see you about Inverley."

She would not, but Joan held her tongue as Miss Balfour departed. She would have to make sure of it.

For it appeared that Inverley was as full of trouble as London.

❖

By the end of the week, Maeve's nerves were stretched as thin as the fabric of her best evening gown. Her nights were the least comfortable that she could remember, the thin pallet becoming harder and less welcoming with each hour of each night. Her days were not much better, filled as they were with the worry that any day now,

Caroline's siblings would arrive and she would be in dire straits with no housing.

The longer she stayed in the cottage, the more difficult it was to see how happy Caroline and Arabella were. The thought ashamed her. She was delighted for Arabella and Caroline and wished nothing more than their shared joy and love for one another. But each longing look between them, each casual kiss or squeeze of their hands sent a pang straight to her heart. The jealousy was as bitter as sea tonic, as much as she told herself not to partake.

Maeve had spent her days calling on the hotels and boarding houses and knocking on the doors of the cottages that lined the shore next to Arabella's, hoping that someone would have a room available, but there was no such luck.

She sold two more dresses to Mr. Culpepper at the secondhand clothing emporium. She watched Arabella work on the beach as she painted visitors and locals, and she talked to Caroline in the evenings as she made plans for the boarding house that she hoped to establish next summer.

Maeve had started to think more about her own future, but she didn't have any answers.

She didn't have dreams and goals like Arabella and Caroline did. She wasn't sure if she wanted anything in particular at all except to return to the life that she had left. And yet that was as impossible as finding a room.

"It is unfortunate that the widow didn't have any space at Fairview Manor," said Arabella as Maeve fretted to her over a cup of tea. "Perhaps life as a lady's companion would suit you after all. You could still live in some comfort, and you would not have to worry about arranging your own lodgings."

Maeve frowned. "Mrs. Firth's behavior was the oddest thing I have ever seen. Not wearing shoes to greet a guest! I don't understand it at all."

"Eccentricities aside, it appears that she is more than well off enough not to need boarders."

"It doesn't explain why she needed to cast her custom at the secondhand shop."

It had given her a start to see Mrs. Firth in her own clothing. It was like some sort of strange mirror, showing Maeve the life that she could have had if she had been wealthy herself. They were of similar build, though Maeve was taller. But more than that, it felt decidedly familiar to see a stranger wearing the dress that Maeve had purchased in Bath to attend the pump room and the circulating library. Maeve wondered if Mrs. Firth had as many compliments in it that she herself had garnered, for she had to admit that without the widow's veil, she was a lovely woman.

"What kind of woman is the widow?" Arabella asked.

"She's gorgeous." Maeve sighed. Mrs. Firth's hair had been swept away from her face and Maeve had not seen much of it beneath her bandeau, but the style had served to put all attention on her face. And oh, what a face. She had a pert uptilted nose, straight brows that accentuated her large dark blue eyes, and a high forehead. She was elegant, and refined…and most odd. "She wasn't very interested in talking. In fact, she seemed almost confused that anyone had come to call on her. Perhaps her neighbors have not wished to disturb her, but why wear colors again if not to signal to everybody that her mourning was over?"

"That house always had an air of mystery," Arabella said. "It's why my paintings of it always sell so well. I suppose it's suitable that the woman herself is as mysterious as her abode." She looked dreamy, as if thinking of a dozen fanciful scenarios.

"I shall have to continue to knock on doors. At some point, some of the visitors will start to leave Inverley, and I can rent a room somewhere."

But although she found herself in that fortuitous situation the next day with a baker who had rooms available, she found herself turned away. "Irish aren't trustworthy," she was told. "And we heard about your mother marrying and leaving you behind. You can't be a good sort and I doubt you've much coin. I'll keep my room for an Englishman, thank you."

Maeve felt as if she'd been slapped. "I'm an honest person, and I have enough for one month right here." She dug into her reticule and held up a fistful of coins. "I can pay up-front."

"I'm looking for a man, or a married lady. A single woman looking as you do might cause some ruckus with the lads wanting to hang about all day and all night. Can't have that. We're a decent establishment. My other boarders would be outraged at the inconvenience."

"That won't happen."

The baker looked at her, his eyes skimming the length of her body. "Won't it?"

She fled back to the cottage, outraged.

She hadn't considered the possibility that people would want better prospects to rent their rooms. She hadn't expected to be turned away if she had money on hand.

Mrs. Firth truly was her only hope.

She hadn't been approachable, but she did have plenty of space. And if there was anyone that Maeve could persuade to take a chance on her, she thought her odds were best with the shoeless widow.

She just needed to convince her that it would be best for both of them.

Maeve grabbed her bonnet and strode out the door.

Chapter Eight

Joan insisted that Tilda take the day off her duties and sit with her in the morning.

"You were always more than a maid," Joan said. "You have been my friend and I insist that you enjoy your retirement."

Tilda grumbled but sat down in the parlor, a cup of tea steaming beside her and a pile of fabrics to be cut up and sewn into piecework on her lap.

They were soon interrupted by news that Tilda's great-nephew had finally returned from London. When the butler brought Luke to them, Joan was surprised to see another man in tow.

"Your Grace, may I introduce Mr. Northam to you? He is the Bow Street Runner who has agreed to help with the investigation." Luke's face was serious. "I know it is a liberty, but I thought it best if he accounted to you himself. The situation is more dire than I suspected."

Joan fought to steady her breathing. "I am pleased to meet you, Mr. Northam."

He bowed. "I am happy to be of service, Your Grace." He was young, a tow-headed lad with round cheeks and bright brown eyes. "Most exciting thing to happen to me in my career."

"I want as much news as you can share," Joan said.

"First off, I must admit that I have not uncovered any details regarding your dowry. I will continue to look into the matter for you and I promise I will give you news as soon as I have found anything out."

She was disappointed, but not surprised.

"Now, the jewels. As you instructed, your lawyer had written to the ducal household for your jewelry and clothing, but that turned into a sad state of affairs." He sat back in his chair, shaking his head.

"What do you mean?"

"They deny that you have any jewels or clothes."

Joan stared. "I am a duchess, and I assure you I was attired as such." She looked down at her striped dress. If Luke and Mr. Northam hadn't brought her clothes with them from London, then she would need more dresses from the emporium to supplement her wardrobe. She couldn't continue to wear the same frock day after day. "I am usually accustomed to finery."

"The housekeeper insists that you requested your wardrobe to be sold, on account of going into mourning and the items being rendered sadly unfashionable by the time you could wear color again."

"But my furs and my coats—my nightclothes—all of my gloves and reticules and dance slippers—why, my wardrobe was so vast that it would be wasteful in the extreme to have rid myself of all of it." She shook her head. "I gave no such orders!"

"And the jewels?" Tilda asked.

"The duke himself rebuked your lawyers when asked about the jewelry. He said to remind you that everything you wore was an heirloom and belonged to the duchy, so of course you would have no claim to it."

Joan pressed her hand to her lips to prevent a strangled cry from erupting. Her jewelry had never been sent for cleaning after all.

It had been stolen.

"I had plenty of personal jewelry," she said after regaining what little composure that she could. "Gifts for birthdays and to wear at certain balls and events. Those were no heirlooms. A widow is entitled to her personal effects. I know little of the law, but I know that this cannot be disputed."

"The duke begs to differ. He says that you have received all that you are owed."

"That is a blatant falsehood." Joan's mind raced, and she grabbed a pencil and a sheet of paper from her secretary desk and started writing. "These are the jewelers where I spread my custom. They must have some record of the pieces that they sold to Stanmere over the years, proving that they are not part of the ducal legacy. I had diamonds. Emeralds.

Sapphires. They were worth a small fortune." She swallowed, for this part hurt the most. "And I had less costly items, passed down to me from my own mother. Are those not to be accounted for?"

Luke stood and handed her something wrapped in fabric. Joan thumbed the scrap open and felt sick when she saw the ivory memorial brooch with the lock of Stanmere's hair.

"This is all they gave to us," Luke said.

She ran her thumb over the engraved inscription. *Memento mori.* Oh, but how she wished she could forget ever having met the duke.

Mr. Northam took the paper with the jewelers' names from her desk. "We will explore all avenues, Your Grace. But you're up against a formidable foe. I don't know what you did to make them angry." He held up his hands as Joan started to splutter. "Now, it isn't my business what they print in the scandal sheets! I know better than to take them at face value. But I think you will be on the losing side of this one."

"I can't afford to lose." Joan sat back down. "All I have is this house, and I dislike it immensely." A shiver went up her spine. "You weren't followed from London, were you?"

He barked out a laugh. "No one can follow me when I've a mind to move stealthy like."

"You did a fine job," Tilda told Luke and Mr. Northam. "Now go beg a cup of lemonade from Cook, the pair of you. You've well earned it."

Joan's thoughts were a muddle after they left.

She had worked hard on being a good debutante. She had attended each ball she was invited to, patronized the highest-born ladies at court, and did what her parents said at every turn. She had worked even harder at being a good duchess. She had visited tenants who were ill or in the family way, invited the servants to Christmas parties at the estate, and had been gracious to their peers and neighbors.

None of it mattered now.

Joan was in a far worse position than she had realized.

"Why would Chetleigh be so ruthless to deny me my belongings?" she asked Tilda. "I am not asking for more than what is owed to me."

"Because they are a ruthless family. They are raised that way from the cradle, and greed is all any of them know, Your Grace." Tilda sighed. "There is no excusing it. But you cannot expect them to be kind. That is a fool's errand."

Luke had left the newest gossip rags for her, and Joan read the latest on the missing duchess. "They are still claiming that they do not know where I am but that the Astleys want my safe return. Look, they have even posted a reward. They will not give me a single farthing, but they would pay a stranger a handsome three thousand pounds."

"It's best if no one finds you, Your Grace," Tilda said. "I don't think they want to prepare a fatted calf for your return."

An icy shiver went up her back.

The disguise was all well and good, but this was all a good deal more serious than she had bargained for.

She could not afford for anyone to guess that the Duchess of Stanmere was here. Not when there was enough money on the line for someone to do something rash in bringing her to London for the reward. Not when she didn't know what she would face if she returned.

"I am going to take a boarder," she said slowly, thinking it through.

"A boarder?"

"No duchess would stoop to do such a thing. So if *I* were to do such a thing, no one would ever suspect me of being other than what I claim to be. They will think me on straightened circumstances." She took a deep breath. "And with any luck, the boarder will act as a liaison to the people of Inverley. If I can convince her that I am a sea captain's widow, then all of Inverley will believe it too."

She had a specific person in mind.

If Miss Balfour was so industrious as to have uncovered her address from their brief meeting in the secondhand clothing emporium, then it must mean that she had a network of gossipmongers who she talked with. She could count on Miss Balfour to talk with the townsfolk, to spread rumors that Joan was a simple widow.

All she needed was to locate Miss Balfour. She thought about asking Mr. Northam. He should be able to uncover her whereabouts with what little information she had about her.

But in the end, it wasn't necessary.

For a quarter hour later, Everson told her that she had another visitor, and she only knew one other person in Inverley.

Relief rolled through her like the sea tide. Now all she had to do was act as if her life depended on the stage.

She took a deep breath and entered the parlor stage right.

❖

Maeve felt breathless when Mrs. Firth walked into the parlor. This time she had braced herself for the shock of seeing her wearing Maeve's dress, though it was paired with an enormous paisley shawl that she didn't recognize. Maeve could tell from the way that it hung and the lustre of its yarn that it had not been cheap.

Very curious.

Her will faltered. Perhaps Mrs. Firth didn't need money after all.

And yet she was smiling, and it was no mere tilt of the lip in amusement. "Miss Balfour, it is so good of you to call on me again."

Maeve tried to collect her thoughts. Surprise at the warmth of her greeting had her rooted in place, unable even to nod let alone curtsy. Mrs. Firth was beautiful, but nothing short of a goddess when she smiled. Maeve felt the pull of attraction almost against her will.

"You are the woman I most wanted to see today, Miss Balfour."

"How intriguing. It is always a pleasure to know that one is wanted."

Mrs. Firth poured her a cup of tea, and Maeve took it with gratitude. Fairview Manor offered the finest brew she had enjoyed in weeks. She debated with herself how to broach the subject at hand, given that it had been so unwelcome before. "I have given more thought to our conversation," Maeve said finally.

"I am most gratified to hear it, for I have as well."

"What have been your conclusions?"

"The idea has merit."

Maeve sipped her tea. She couldn't understand what had happened to change Mrs. Firth's mind, but she would accept it without question. "I was hoping you would reconsider. I am still interested in renting a room."

"I have stipulations."

"Oh?"

Mrs. Firth's brow furrowed and she pushed an errant curl up on top of her head. Maeve could see more of her hair today, and what little she saw was a lovely rich warm brown. "You would stay in the back bedchamber on the second floor, and have access to the kitchen, but the rest of the house is off limits."

"You will hardly know I am in the house." Maeve glanced out the window. "Would I have leave to walk the grounds?"

"Oh. Of course."

"Then I shall be content. I love the seaside."

Mrs. Firth shook her head. "Better you than I. I despise the ocean."

Curious that she had chosen to live here, but Maeve remembered that her late husband had been a captain. Maybe the sea had taken him. Her heart ached for her.

"Are there other rules? I am sure I will be able to follow them. I am not the rebellious sort."

"There are to be no visitors."

"Not even to my chamber?"

"Not even there."

Mrs. Firth was indeed eccentric if she disliked visitors so much that she would forbid anyone from entering for any reason. "That should not be a problem." Maeve could always walk to Caroline and Arabella's cottage instead of inviting them to walk the grounds with her. The conversation reminded her of haggling with Mr. Culpepper when they were both ready to accept the next offer, and she relaxed. It would be a yes. It had to be a yes. "Are there any other requirements?"

"No gossip rags are to cross the premises. Ever."

"I do love them, but alas they are too dear for me to purchase. You shall have no worries there. Would you prefer to review all of my reading material before I dare to step past the threshold?" Maeve smiled. "I promise there is nothing scandalous."

Mrs. Firth fumbled. "That won't be necessary." She cleared her throat. "Would five guineas be fair?"

"Per week?"

"Per month."

Maeve paused. Mrs. Firth could charge far more at the peak of the summer months. Was her motivation not financial after all? But whatever it was, it didn't matter. "More than fair. I am happy to agree to your terms."

Mrs. Firth extended her hand, and Maeve shook it.

A foxhound bounded into the room and gave a short woof in greeting, his tail wagging.

"I didn't realize you already had a boarder," Maeve said as he sat on the floor and dropped his head onto the cushion beside her, his eyes imploring her to pay attention to him. Charmed, she rubbed his ears and heard him sigh. He was a beautiful dog with an elegant face and a strong chest, the patches on his fur the color of cream and coffee, though his leg seemed to give him some trouble.

Mrs. Firth frowned "I do hope you like dogs, for Maurice is permitted the run of this house. It is not negotiable."

It was one more part of the mystery of the fog-enshrouded manor house that wouldn't have been out of place in a gothic romance. "I am delighted to share the house with such a fine dog."

An odd feeling stole over her. These were uncharted waters.

She hadn't roomed in a family household in years, more accustomed to hearing her neighbors through the thin walls of lodging houses, and having the safety of plenty of other people around at all hours of the day. Fairview Manor was remote, its facade was intimidating, and there were only to be two inhabitants. Herself and Mrs. Firth.

And the servants, she reminded herself. They would not be completely alone. It would be safe enough. After all, she didn't have to view the room that she was being offered to know there would be no lumpy pallet in it. It was a good opportunity.

"It's not haunted," Mrs. Firth added in a rush. "I understand that it looks like it might be. But it isn't."

She patted Maurice. "I think we shall all get along just fine. Ghosts or no."

CHAPTER NINE

When Maeve moved into Fairview Manor the next morning, she was delighted when the butler showed her to a guest room in the southern turret. In fact, she was delighted by the fact that there *was* a butler, dressed as fine as any she might have seen in Bath or London. The housekeeper who ushered her through the front door had refined manners, and the aroma of buttery pastry wafting through the house proved that there was an excellent cook on the premises. This was rich living, and worth the guineas that would trickle out of her accounts each month that she stayed here.

She could almost pretend that she was a guest instead of a boarder, as if her standing hadn't sunk so low as to be beneath anyone's notice.

Her bedchamber was the sole room that she was granted leave to inhabit, but it was a grand one. Located as it was in the turret, the walls were rounded in a most charming manner, and the windows overlooked the sea. Less charming were the oxblood drapes and the heavy wood trim on the walls. Oppressive, and not to Maeve's taste, but rented lodgings never were.

Maeve suppressed a shiver. Mrs. Firth was right that the manor was assumed by most to be quite haunted, but she couldn't give it credence. After all, it had hardly even been *lived* in. She had talked to Arabella and Caroline's neighbors to find out all anyone knew of the situation and learned that Captain Firth had arranged the house to be built, but his residence of choice had been a London address. Maeve believed in spirits as much as the next person, but it would be an odd choice for a ghost to haunt a place that his corporeal self had rarely stepped foot in.

Ghosts or not, it was a relief that the issue of her lodgings had been resolved.

Now she needed to find employment, or soon enough she would be without any clothes to wear.

But with no skills, no talents, and (she could admit it to herself if to no one else) little enough inclination for exerting herself for more than a dance or two of an evening, that task was proving difficult.

Another difficulty was her attraction to the mysterious widow of the manor.

Maeve flopped back onto the bed, staring up at the ceiling.

Mrs. Firth had seemed more anxious than pleased to invite her to live here. Maeve understood that she was paying for the four walls around her and little else, but given Mrs. Firth's behavior when they had met, it was strange that she was allowed to stay here in any capacity.

She wouldn't question it, though her curiosity gnawed at her. She had needed to move out of Arabella and Caroline's cottage, and not only had she moved out, but she had moved up. This was a far grander establishment than any other she had rented, in Inverley or elsewhere. She and Mama had often dined with the family on the rare occasion that they rented quarters in a genteel establishment, but Mrs. Firth was clearly a cut above. Maeve wondered at the circumstances of her birth. She spoke so well with such articulation that she was sure Mrs. Firth came from a situation better than the one she had married into.

It wouldn't do to speculate. She was best off if she didn't encounter Mrs. Firth more than necessary. Especially since each time she saw her, Maeve's eyes strayed where they ought not.

Thoughts like these would get her into trouble if she wasn't careful. She couldn't afford to be thrown out of the manor for any kind of indecency.

Not that she considered herself or her desires to be indecent. But though she may be attracted to Mrs. Firth, she didn't *know* her, and flirtation was not worth the risk of discovery if she did not share her inclinations.

The best part of living with her mother, and then with Caroline and Arabella, was that she always had someone to talk to at the end of the day. There was always someone available to gossip with over a cup of tea, or to join her on an errand. The thought of spending all of her time by herself was depressing. She had never lived alone and had never desired to.

As guests were forbidden, the sole reprieve from her loneliness would be to talk with Mrs. Firth herself, but she did not seem to welcome conversation.

Maeve hadn't paid for her lodgings yet, and she yearned to see more of the house that she had been forbidden to wander. Surely one meeting between them couldn't hurt, could it? Her spirits were immeasurably cheered as she eased herself off the bed and went through the contents of her reticule.

One meeting. That was all she would allow herself.

No matter how much her curiosity burned inside her.

❖

Joan was shocked when Miss Balfour entered the Blue Parlor as bold as brass on her first day in the manor. She had thought it clear that Miss Balfour was *not* to be in the family rooms under any circumstance. Joan hated that her tongue felt tied in a knot worse than her bonnet strings on a windy day. People didn't behave out of the norm around a duchess, and so she had no experience reprimanding anyone. It felt terribly ill-bred to point out that Miss Balfour was reneging their deal a mere day after having struck it.

What kind of woman was she to do such a thing?

It would be a good deal easier if only she didn't wish to find out the answer.

Miss Balfour sauntered up to her and dropped a fistful of guineas into her palm. "One month upfront."

Joan blinked. "Oh. Thank you."

"I thought I should seek you out straightaway to pay my dues. Everson told me that you were here. So here I came."

Joan wasn't in the habit of carrying coins, being rather more used to a maid or a footman handling the petty finances when she shopped. She didn't have a reticule on her person, and her linen day dress had no pockets. The weight of the guineas felt strange in her palm.

Maybe because they were still warm from Miss Balfour's hands.

Joan clattered the coins onto the nearby desk and Miss Balfour cocked her head. Too late, she realized that the sum was meant to be significant, and she was pretending to be a widow of straightened means. Money was not to be strewn aside where the servants might pilfer it. For the benefit of her boarder's opinion of her, she rang for Sarah and made a show of instructing her to put the money away. She didn't think she would win any accolades on the stage, but hopefully it was enough to dupe Miss Balfour.

"I trust that you have found everything to be satisfactory?" Joan asked her, deciding not to answer the impertinence of her appearance in the parlor with her own impoliteness. After all, there was no time like the present to lay the foundations of her story. The sooner she started speaking of her alleged past, the sooner Miss Balfour could gossip to all and sundry that the widow of Fairview Manor was dull as dishwater—and certainly no duchess. "My husband was ever so fond of the view from the South Tower. He loved to gaze out to the sea that he spent his lifetime sailing."

"I hadn't realized Captain Firth had ever lived here. I was told that it didn't seem as if *anyone* had really lived here before now."

"Oh?" Had she put a foot wrong already? Joan tensed. At least it was proof that Miss Balfour truly would take any opportunity to gossip about her, if she had already uncovered information that she herself didn't have.

Miss Balfour shrugged. "The manor has a remote air, so I suppose people presumed it to be uninhabited. Except for the staff, of course. You and your husband must have been impressively discreet to have visited without the inhabitants of Inverley catching wind of it."

Joan's confidence plummeted. She had assumed that people would believe any falsehood she uttered. As a duchess, the mere *thought* of something seemed to summon it from thin air, whether it was a desire for fine champagne, a pair of matched bays for the carriage, or an invitation to dine with royalty. Someone was always listening, whether the words were spoken aloud or not. Someone always made it happen.

It didn't seem to be the case here.

"The yellow linen." Miss Balfour pointed at Joan's dress. "A fine choice. I have always loved mameluke sleeves. I find they are dashing, are they not? I wore it to a Venetian breakfast last spring."

"It is a lovely color."

"You must have returned to the emporium since our chance meeting. I sold it three days ago." Her smile was mischievous.

Actually, Sarah had gone in her stead, with explicit instructions to purchase anything that Miss Balfour may have given up. The fact remained that Miss Balfour's castoffs were the nicest clothes available to her without risking a trip to the dressmaker's where her face and form would be carefully studied.

The intimacy of wearing her clothing still gave her pause. And yet there was something friendly in it. The clothes were so gently worn that they were almost new, and there was something about donning them that helped her feel confident. She wondered if any of their previous owner's personality had somehow been imprinted on the cloth, for the woman standing before her didn't seem like she would have been cowed in the least by Stanmere.

God. *Stanmere.*

The thought of the brooch upstairs flashed through her mind.

"I shall leave you to your ruminations, Miss Balfour. The door to the gardens is down the hall through the conservatory, if you wish to take your daily constitutional."

"Shall we walk together? It is a fine time of day for a stroll." Miss Balfour's green eyes were filled with light and sparkle, her mouth curved into a lush smile, and Joan's imagination fevered up once more.

"I have no time," she said shortly, and was nevertheless disappointed to see the smile fade from those cherry blossom lips. "I shall see you anon."

CHAPTER TEN

The next morning, Maeve arrived at the general store, located at the busiest intersection in the center of Inverley. She wore her next-next-best day dress for the occasion, which had now become her best. The dress that Mrs. Firth had worn yesterday previously held that title, the yellow linen twill walking frock given to Mr. Culpepper in exchange for four guineas (and eight extra shillings when Maeve had refused to hear any slander against the darling ivory bows at its neckline and hem).

Mr. Culpepper was proving to be an indispensable friend. He had been the one to suggest Maeve seek out employment at the general store, as the owner was a dear friend of his and he had put in a good word for her. Today was her first day as a shop attendant.

It wasn't something she had ever expected for herself. She was a patroness of such establishments. Selling her belongings had been difficult enough, but *working* was another thing entirely. This was the true beginning of her descent from good society. After today, acquaintances from her former evenings at the assembly rooms would no longer even acknowledge her, and it would be a surprise if anyone invited her even to the smallest event that Inverley had to offer. It was not that she was no longer a visitor, but that she was casting off her gentility to soil her hands and fraternize with a different sort of people altogether.

She adjusted her favorite straw bonnet with its arrangement of ribbons and faux fruit, glad enough that she had been able to keep her best of *something* for herself, and sailed inside.

"Good morning, Mr. Jackson," she greeted the owner.

"Good morning, Miss Balfour. Happy to have you here with us today." He glanced at the clock in the corner. "We open at ten sharp, you know, and it's best to arrive a little early to help open up."

It had taken longer to walk from Fairview Manor than she had thought. "I can do that, sir."

"Good, good."

After listening to a lecture on the running of the store and keeping the till and counting the inventory, Maeve was put behind the big wooden desk where the money and ledgers were kept and was told to keep the customers happy and to give them what they wanted.

That was when Maeve realized that working in a shop was akin to the very best part of a party. A good soiree had dancing and a light supper, all of which was enjoyable, but her favorite part of such an evening was talking with friends and exchanging the best on dits about the latest goings-on.

At the general shop, *everyone* wanted to gossip.

They were people she had never met before, and who wished nothing more than to talk about themselves and their predicaments. Mrs. Frances wanted a new jelly mold, on account of her daughter-in-law making off with hers and refusing to return it, and so she wanted to show her up with a fancier dessert at her next dinner. Maeve happily looked through molds with her, but in the end recommended an elegant lemon tart instead. "Much more refined than a jelly," she promised Mrs. Frances, who left the shop empty handed but filled with good cheer.

Then Mr. Talcott needed a new leather harness for his horse because his son had come home drunk. Maeve understood it to be a common trouble, given the level of his exasperation. He had somehow lost the harness when he had put the horse to stable in his condition. "Ought to be him in here paying for a new one," he said with a shake of his head, "but I reckon he's best off where he is sleeping it off."

Maeve frowned. "He should learn to take his responsibility! He should search every inch of the stable until he finds the harness instead of wasting your time and money to purchase new. I do hope he finds it, sir."

A bevy of young ladies came in, giggling over the merits of the brawny sailors compared to the red-coated militiamen stationed outside of town, and Maeve passed a comfortable half hour with them as they fawned over handkerchiefs and lace and beads before they left without even purchasing half a length of ribbon.

Mr. Jackson touched Maeve's elbow. "Now, mind that we have to encourage people to make purchases," he said. "Not while the hours away with chatter. How about you go handle the inventory? We received bolts of cloth from London this afternoon, and they need counting and sorting."

Maeve brightened. She did love fabrics.

But the storeroom was dark and dull with no one to talk to. Maeve lost track of time while she was stroking the velvets and patting the corduroy and sorting the leather hides.

Mr. Jackson's face fell when he checked in on her. "How have you sorted these?" He poked one of the piles.

Maeve smiled up at him. "By color, of course. Don't they look lovely?"

"It's more practical to sort by purpose, isn't it?" He scratched at his beard. "People will come in looking for cloth by type, for whatever they want to make of it. They're not going to look by color."

She recognized the truth of it immediately. It was what she would be looking for herself as a customer. Her face burned. "Of course. I will re-sort them."

"It's a bit late, I'll finish up." He hesitated. "But I'm not so sure I need the help after all, Miss Balfour. Mr. Culpepper was right that you're a good enough lass, but you're altogether a bit too chatty for my store."

Maeve was exhausted when she left the general store. It had been most obliging of Mr. Culpepper to recommend her to Mr. Jackson, but her heart was heavy. She was left wishing that she had not tried her hand at working after all. What if she could never find permanent employment? Her shillings would drift away from her like grains of sand being pulled back into the ocean. And then how would she live?

The thought haunted her more than anything she had seen thus far at Fairview Manor.

Oh, what a predicament Mama had left her in.

It was a struggle not to think of her with bitterness, though she also missed her terribly. It was still so odd to think that she wouldn't be at home waiting to pour her a cup of tea when Maeve returned.

Mama hadn't always been wise, nor had she always been thoughtful. But she had been quick with an observation or a pithy comment and had been wonderful company through their travels.

Mr. Jackson may have thought her too chatty, but it had been a balm to her soul to finally talk to people again. It was lonely whiling away the hours in her new bedchamber by herself.

Wouldn't Mama have been surprised to see Maeve working at the general store where they had passed so many hours shopping together? She had always called Maeve a layabout, and she knew it to be no less than the truth. Today had been a test of her mettle, standing for far longer than she typically did in a day. Her shoes pinched her feet, which felt swollen twice their size. She frowned down at the beribboned shoes. They hadn't been a practical choice, but she didn't own much that wasn't ornamental.

It was most distressing to wonder if perhaps the truth was that *she* was merely ornamental too.

❖

For all that Miss Balfour had kept out of Joan's sight during the past week, she nevertheless made her presence felt.

She left for her daily turn about the garden each afternoon at half past two, when Joan always caught sight of her from her bedchamber window.

She left a prettily embroidered handkerchief in the Blue Parlor where she was not supposed to have been at all, and which Joan asked Sarah to return to her posthaste.

And on Thursday afternoon, she slammed the front door so hard that Joan heard it all the way from her sitting room on the second floor.

Miss Balfour's voice was agitated as she spoke with Everson— and loud, for the walls in the manor were thick and sound didn't travel easily.

Joan swallowed. It was none of her business. Miss Balfour was a boarder, and a reluctantly invited one at that. It wouldn't do to further their strange acquaintanceship.

And yet the truth of the matter was that Joan was starting to wish for more than the society of her maids. With her self-imposed solitude, the only available person who could provide her with some distraction was Miss Balfour.

Perhaps Miss Balfour might welcome a distraction from whatever was troubling her today. She had seemed to enjoy talking on the day that she had moved in. It had been Joan's coldness that had ended their conversation before it could properly begin.

That decided the matter for her. Eager to see Miss Balfour in the flesh after days of encountering nothing more than ephemera, Joan put aside her letter.

She found her in the kitchen. Miss Balfour looked up from the cup of tea cradled in her hands, her face cross. Joan realized with a start that although she owned this house, she felt like she was trespassing where she did not belong.

Cook had been patting Miss Balfour's arm but stood when Joan entered. "Ah, Your oh, Mrs. Firth! May I offer you a cup of tea? The pot is still fresh."

Joan had never in her life been offered tea in a kitchen. Not when she had been a girl, and certainly never as a duchess. She looked around, uncertain if she had even set foot in the kitchen since her arrival in Inverley. It was as unfamiliar to her as an alchemist's laboratory. Everything was scrubbed neat and clean, and mysterious herbs hung from the ceiling and perfumed the air in a most pleasing manner.

"I would like a cup of tea," she said, surprising herself. She took a step into the room, then hesitated. A divide still existed between mistress and servant among the middle class that she was pretending to belong to, and yet here was Miss Balfour, a gentlewoman, ensconced in the kitchen as comfortable as you please. Perhaps she should follow her instinct. "And of course you must join us," she said to Cook, in a bluster of counterfeit confidence. Whether or not it was normal for other households, it was going to happen in hers.

Sarah bustled in, her arms full of laundry, and stopped short when she saw Joan.

"You must have a cup of tea with us, Sarah," she said, desperate for a familiar face around the table.

"Oh!" Her mouth was an oval of surprise, and the bundle in her arms teetered. "Yes, I would be most appreciative of tea." She sounded uncertain, and her brow was creased as she deposited the sheets in a basket by the door. She sat down, glancing at Joan while Cook poured fresh cups for everyone.

This was promising. It wasn't *comfortable*, and Joan was sure that both Cook and Sarah would talk about this with some confusion between themselves later, but her priority was to provide comfort for Miss Balfour.

Miss Balfour, however, did not appear comforted. She still had a storm cloud on her face, and she scowled into her teacup.

Joan sipped her tea, unable to recall whether she had put lemon in her cup or honey. Perhaps she had worsened the situation. Should she ask Miss Balfour what was the matter, or had the opportunity passed? It would be gauche to bring up her ill temper in front of Cook and Sarah.

Tilda wandered in and of course she must be served her own dish of tea, which meant that a crowd of chattering women now sat around the big scarred table. Dishes clacked against each other, spoons clinked against the china, and then a plate of biscuits appeared. Without knowing quite how it happened, Joan realized that it was a little party.

She met Miss Balfour's eyes. They were expressive, luminous and large, and held a wry sort of humor. Despite the awkwardness she had felt upon entering the kitchen, she felt her shoulders relax.

"Thank you for joining me," Miss Balfour said, her lilting voice hardly above a whisper. She leaned close and touched Joan's wrist with a gloved finger.

A shock of awareness flooded her at the contact, though it lasted no more than a moment.

Was this how people touched when they were not of the noblesse? How intriguing. She knew well enough that the common folk touched all the time. She had heard vague tales of footmen and maids cavorting in stables and storage closets. But she had never thought much about those in between the ranks of service and the nobility.

She wanted to reach out and touch Miss Balfour too. Her fingers twitched, but she managed to restrain herself.

The conversation continued to swell, and somehow they were enclosed within their own pocket of air and space, even as Luke came in cheekily begging for a cup of his own and Cook was reprimanding him and the roars of laughter crashed around them like the waves.

Joan felt a funny warmth in her chest.

It was pleasure.

She was startled to recognize the truth of it. It had not been duty that had compelled her to find Miss Balfour, nor curiosity. It had been *pleasure*. She wasn't sure how much she wanted to dwell on that. She had always been happy to see her friends, but she knew that this was not in the same category.

She didn't know *how* she knew, given that she had never felt this way, but it was a truth that she felt to her marrow.

With everyone else around them occupied, she could speak freely. "Are you feeling better now?" she asked, her voice as soft and low as she could make it.

Miss Balfour frowned. "How did you know that I was upset?"

"Forgive me, but I heard you enter the manor and you did not sound like yourself."

Miss Balfour swirled the dregs of tea in her cup. "I am in dire need of employment and have yet to find a position. My services, limited as they are, were declined last week at the stationer's shop and the circulating library. Today, after starting in a position at the general store that I thought would suit me, I made a fool of myself trying to fit in and I was let go." She drew in a deep breath. "I am feeling vexed."

Joan nodded. She was feeling much the same these days. She didn't belong in her new life any more than Miss Balfour did. "That sounds most concerning."

Miss Balfour looked away. "Worry not, I can pay my room and board for next month. And I would like you to know that I am not taking advantage of your cook. She offered me tea when I came in. I wasn't looking for more than my share."

Joan felt a hot flush start at the base of her throat. "I didn't think any such thing. You are more than welcome to refresh yourself."

"In the kitchens, of course."

Joan could tell there was the hint of an insult there, some disfavor at being forbidden from the parlor, but she felt helpless to correct Miss Balfour. After all, it was true. That was the stipulation that she had set out, and there was nothing unusual in it. As a boarder, Miss Balfour was not a guest of the manor and therefore was not welcomed to the rest of the house beyond her bedchamber and the kitchen.

And yet Joan wanted more than the lingering scent of her rose petal perfume in the great hall and her forgotten handkerchief in the parlor and the sound of her laughter, lush and low, as it floated from the garden to her bedchamber window.

Joan couldn't name the emotion that she felt, but she knew that she wanted to chase it as long as she could, to hold it close to her chest while they were in the same room together.

There was something warm and vibrant about Miss Balfour. It wasn't wise to enter into a friendship, however. She was easy to talk to, which meant Joan was liable to say too much about her past, or to trip over the lies that she must weave to convincingly play the part of the sea captain's widow. Falsehoods didn't come easily to her at the best of times.

But the look on Miss Balfour's face, pale and drawn, decided it for her.

"Would you care for a turn about the grounds, Miss Balfour?" The words rushed out of her in a tumble, leaving her breathless and lightheaded. Nerves such as these were ridiculous. Taking one's constitutional was an unexceptional part of one's day, after all, whether it was alone or with a friend.

Was Miss Balfour a friend, though?

Joan thought she might like it if she were.

The warmth in her chest blossomed when Miss Balfour smiled up at her. "I would like that very much indeed, Mrs. Firth."

CHAPTER ELEVEN

Maeve felt an absurd pleasure at being asked to walk. Mrs. Firth had been so solicitous at tea. Perhaps her earlier reticence had been due to shyness. Or perhaps her grief had rendered her unwilling to socialize and she was now rusty at the practice, preferring to isolate herself in her house on the hill.

"I hope the fresh air brightens your mood," Mrs. Firth said once the kitchen door swung shut behind them.

"It never fails. Inverley is lovely in August, and you own a fine allotment of it."

"Yes, I suppose so."

The disinterest in her voice surprised Maeve. Mrs. Firth had confessed to not liking the ocean, but she must see the merits of the rest of the property. "It must be a far cry from what you're used to in London."

"London?" Her tone was sharp.

"Why, is that not where you both lived when Captain Firth was at sea?"

"Oh. Yes." She paused. "I also spent time in Shropshire with his family."

"Did he have a large family? I always wished for one."

"Two younger brothers, an insufferable sister, and two daughters from a previous marriage. And several sons. I ought not forget about his sons." There was a tight smile on her face.

"I hope they were a comfort to you when he passed."

"They did not care for him, nor for me. Not when he was alive, and certainly not now." Her mouth snapped shut, as if she hadn't meant to say so much.

How dramatic. Maeve was aching to know more, but Mrs. Firth seemed disinclined to elaborate. She had eyes that Maeve suspected would be lovely if they sparkled, but so far Maeve had only seen a nervous sort of energy behind them.

She pushed away the thought that *she* would like to make them sparkle and could think of a way or two to make that happen. She had always enjoyed the company of other women, regardless of whether she could make a conquest. The thought of such desires might well send Mrs. Firth to the fainting couch. Maeve had implied such things before to women who had reacted with confusion or outrage. She wasn't going to take such a chance with the woman she was renting from.

Still, there was much to admire in Mrs. Firth's trim figure as she marched beside her, the summer breeze catching in her bonnet ribbons.

"I meant to hear more about your day, if you wish to talk about it." Mrs. Firth's tone was warm again, her composure regained.

"It is of no import," Maeve said, more to be polite. She ached to say what she felt, to release it and to move on from it. One of the most difficult parts of solitary living was that there was no friendly ear to listen to her woes, and likewise no one to confide in her. She was accustomed to a life intertwined.

"I do not mean to pry, but are you certain?" Her gentle tone was a balm to the hurt that she felt.

It never took much to encourage Maeve to talk, and she seized the opportunity. "No. I am distraught and do not wish to show my ill humors in front of you."

"It must have been a difficult day."

"It was the worst, if I may be honest with you," Maeve said with a sigh.

Mrs. Firth's lips twitched. "The *worst?*"

Maeve laughed. "Perhaps not, but is that not the way it feels sometimes? I know it won't hurt as much tomorrow or the next day, but I fear I have always dwelt too much in the present."

"What happened?"

"I suppose I wasn't being helpful in the way that they needed." Emotion flooded her again, as fresh as it was in the moment that Mr. Jackson had dismissed her. "The part that hurts is that I felt I was doing well, so it was a shock to find I wasn't."

"That is a most difficult position to be in."

"I failed at something that I must succeed at, but at which I have never had to try in my life. It is an exhausting reality, to labor for one's coin." She shook her head, embarrassed. "I am by no means even a true laborer. I am not breaking my back and ruining my eyes with sewing, or anything of the ilk. Instead, I am wretched at the easiest of tasks set to me."

Lazy, and frivolous. Words she had heard time and again from Mama.

"It sounds like you are trying, and you are learning as you go on. It's admirable."

"Do you reckon the learning is as important as the doing?" Maeve asked. "I'm not so certain my pockets would agree, as learning does not seem to help earn my keep."

Mrs. Firth's face was thoughtful. "We all find ourselves in unpredictable circumstances at some point or another. Perhaps all you need is time to adjust to your new surroundings, and the new expectations that come with them."

"Time is another commodity that I do not have in ample supply. But it is kind of you to take the time to listen."

"Sometimes I think time is my *only* valuable commodity. It is the one thing that I can give and no one can take from me." She looked away as she said it, and her voice was sad.

When they reached the edge of the bluff, Maeve turned out of habit toward the path that led to the private cove.

"Where are you going?" Mrs. Firth's tone surprised her.

"I never miss an opportunity to go to the shore when I am walking."

Her fists balled at her sides and her face was blanched. "I don't care much for the sea."

"Of course. I should have remembered." Maeve reached out and touched her arm. "I am sorry, I did not mean to be inconsiderate." It seemed a cruel fate to live by the shore when one was so afraid of it.

"You have no need to apologize. It is normal to speak of the sea when it is so near." Mrs. Firth's smile was strained.

"I see storm clouds gathering. Do let us return to the house." The dark clouds were plenty far enough away that they could have made a half dozen excursions to the shore before any drop of rain landed, but Maeve wished to end the tension that had sprung up between them and to soothe Mrs. Firth from her fears.

"Yes. The house." She said it with a heavy sigh, the subject seeming to displease her as much as the sea.

They were quiet on the stroll back, Maeve pondering the new questions that she had about her mysterious landlady.

❖

Joan lay in bed that night, blankets tossed asunder, wishing she had purchased a house anywhere else in England. The storm had come on after dinner, the sky turning dark as midnight in the blink of an eye. With the rain lashing the windows and the wind howling down the chimney, the house was more melancholy than usual.

The gauzy curtains hanging from her bedposts fluttered even though the windows were latched closed. Joan was disheartened to find that the draft chilled the air enough to wish for the winter woolen socks that had been sold the minute she left London.

Had she become nothing more than a ghost at Hanover Square, the memory of her fading with each day?

But *someone* missed her. Perhaps not with affection, but someone must be thinking of her. There wouldn't be such headlines about her otherwise.

Although she refused to allow the scandal sheets in the house now, she had been as devout a reader as anyone while in London. She remembered how relentless the journalists could be.

And the Astley family was nothing if not relentless.

She had assumed the papers had caught wind of half a story and had run with it, but she was starting to wonder if the duchy had been feeding the fire to catch her out.

Sometime after the grandfather clock downstairs announced the wretched hour of three in the morning, Maurice jumped onto her bed. With a soft whine, he flopped beside her. It was a comfort to lay beside him and run her hand over his thick fur. He was as restless as she was, trembling and anxious.

She curled up closer to him, his warmth steadying her. *The missing duchess*. What folderol. But she wondered if she had ever understood the family at all. How could she have dined with them one evening, and with no evidence at all, the next day they all believed her to be capable of adultery?

She couldn't shake the thought that something sinister was afoot. Beneath the fine clothes, her late husband had been a brute, though she had avoided the worst of it by seldom sharing the same house. It was unconscionable of him to have written the will as he had—but he had been an unconscionable man.

Chetleigh's behavior, however, was incomprehensible. She had almost no connection to her son-in-law beyond showing up to court together on occasion. Why would he continue this campaign of cruelty against her?

For him to have stolen her personal effects was terrifying. To what end was he working toward? Her jewels and furs were worth a fortune, but it was a mere pittance of the duchy's overall wealth.

At least the disguise seemed to be working. And as long as she put her faith in Miss Balfour's ability to gossip about her with all and sundry, then Joan was as safe as she could be in her secret manor house.

Joan buried her head in the pillow. If only she could focus when she spoke to Miss Balfour. Instead of tales of her heroic husband and their idyllic life, she had instead spilled the truth of her situation under a thin veneer. How would telling any version of the truth benefit her?

And yet it had.

In a curious way, talking to her had unburdened Joan's tension, much like when the storm clouds released rain to then make way for sunny skies and calm waters. Miss Balfour had a certain appealing pertness about her. She had been curious but had not pried when Joan seemed disinclined to speak and had not insisted on going to the shore when Joan was reluctant.

Strolling the grounds together, they could have been any two women, instead of a duchess and a mere miss. How liberating it had felt to be so inconspicuous.

And how liberated Miss Balfour was! Joan had never been around someone so honest. In her social circle, everyone had their share of secrets, and it was wise to keep them close to the chest.

It had inspired her to be more honest herself. But she should have been more careful. What if Miss Balfour could piece together her history and guess at her identity? She seemed clever enough.

It had been foolish in the extreme.

It was strange, knowing that Miss Balfour slept somewhere in the house. With someone else in residence and with the house still so unfamiliar to her, it was as if they both were boarders, and the true mistress of the house was elsewhere.

Her mind went to the widow's walk, and the curtains on her bed drifted again. Had she left Stanmere's ghost in London, only to be met with another here in Inverley?

But that was nonsense. Nothing more than fancies born of little sleep and too much stress.

Maurice, normally a well-behaved dog who waited for Sarah to take him outside each morning, leapt off the bed and whined at the door. All she knew of Sarah's routine was that she awoke before Joan did, and she brought Maurice back upstairs with Joan's tea.

It was far too early for tea, much as she wished for a cup.

He whined again and scratched at her door. Evidently, he did not consider it to be too early at all.

Joan grabbed her silk shawl and pulled it over her shoulders. Maurice padded along beside her as she went down the stairs to the grand entrance. She bit back an oath as she tried to shove the heavy latch aside. This was the reason a footman was always stationed there in the day, but there was no one here at this uneasy time before dawn.

There was a door to the gardens from the music room, and another through the breakfast parlor, and Joan hesitated in the hallway. Maurice seemed to understand that she didn't know where she was going, for he headed to the kitchen. Ah, that made sense, as Sarah must arrange her tea while he bounded about outside.

Joan followed him, and stopped short when she saw Miss Balfour perched on a kitchen stool with a ladle of water. She wore a shabby night wrapper, her hair was bundled up in rags to curl it overnight, and her stockings drooped.

Miss Balfour sipped, and Joan's eyes fixed on the movement of her throat as she swallowed.

She was rooted into place, unwilling to disrupt the tension that lay between them, for it wasn't born of uneasiness.

It was more of an awareness.

A feeling that at this odd hour, anything out of the ordinary might happen.

Anything at all.

What shocked her most was how much she wanted *anything* to happen.

CHAPTER TWELVE

Your dog seems in dire need of the necessary," Miss Balfour said, looking at Maurice.

Joan felt all sense of time and place shudder back into place. This was to be an ordinary sort of encounter after all, despite the oddness of the time and place. She didn't understand what it was that she felt when she was around Miss Balfour, but she must be alone in her strange fancy.

That was as it should be. Miss Balfour was not the kind of woman that a duchess should befriend. What could she have in common with a woman who worked?

And yet Joan wore her clothes. And Miss Balfour made her smile. Amid the recent mysteries of Joan's life, she was refreshingly easy to understand.

"Yes, of course. Maurice is why I came downstairs." She lifted the iron hook and swung the door open, and he bolted outside with enthusiasm. She wrapped her shawl tighter around her shoulders in the cool air. An ominous fog whirled around the grounds, and she hoped he wouldn't stray far from the house.

"I am never in the kitchens at this hour," Miss Balfour said, her voice a touch cool. "I assure you I am not here to pilfer the silverware."

"I had no such thought."

"There are many whose first thought of an Irishwoman would be her untrustworthiness." Her tone was still cool. "Besides, I know I agreed not to treat this house as my own. This is nothing more than a sip of water after a long night."

"I consider you to be more than trustworthy," Joan said, and was surprised to find that she meant it. She knew next to nothing about Miss Balfour. For all Joan knew, she was here to fleece her. But she had already been fleeced out of most of her belongings by far more intimidating people, and she doubted Miss Balfour was here to take what dregs remained.

Joan studied the shadows under her eyes. "Was your sleep as poorly affected by the storm as mine was?" Where were these words coming from? They were too familiar. She would never have dreamt to imply that someone didn't look their best. But she couldn't seem to rein in her tongue.

Miss Balfour propped her elbows on the table, watching Maurice bound across the lawns with wild abandon. "A storm always sounds a good deal more romantic than it is in reality. It was rather loud, was it not?"

"I am grateful there was no thunder to accompany it, though the ocean roared enough to make Maurice and I both shiver."

"Does he share your room? How generous a mistress you are."

Joan bristled. "He is a tender-hearted creature, and I have found myself attached to him."

"Was he a gift? He looks to be a fine example of a foxhound."

"He was my husband's hunting dog." She stopped, for though it was the truth, the story was much uglier than she wanted the fictitious sea captain to be.

"Ah. He must be a comfort to you then."

He was, but not in the way that Miss Balfour meant. The sight of Maurice bore no fond memories of her husband. "He is a wonderful companion."

"*Companionship* is important indeed."

There was something in the tone of Miss Balfour's voice, and Joan was reminded that they were in their nightclothes together. She shivered, and she didn't think it was only from the chill in the air.

❖

Maeve felt unaccountably naked.

She prided herself on her wardrobe, comprised as it was of gorgeous fabrics and elaborate lace and threads of gold and silver and bright embroidery floss. She liked nothing more than catching sight of herself in the glass looking as fine as sixpence.

Her night wrapper was not in the same category as the rest of her clothing.

It had been with her through countless seasons of her life in Ireland. She had wrapped herself in it, cozy as a blanket, through every argument between Mama and Papa. She had brought it with her when they moved from the townhouse in Dublin to the cottage in Killarney, and had packed it in her carpet bag after Mama had married her stepfather and they moved to Cork without him. The night wrapper had seen her through the uncertain voyage to England, and then the happiest times in her life these past few years as she and Mama had wandered through various resort towns.

It held the comfort of memory within its threads.

But Maeve was the first to admit that it was worn thin. The flannel was soft from countless washings, and the pink printed flowers were faded. The elbows were threadbare. The sleeves were short, exposing her wrists, and the left one bore a patch from where she had once sat too close to a candle and the fabric had charred.

She was glad that it was in such poor condition that she could never sell it to Mr. Culpepper, for it was the one piece of clothing that she could never bear to part with.

But that didn't mean that she wasn't embarrassed to be seen in it. Especially by the mistress of the house.

Maeve dipped the ladle in the bucket again and sipped, the water cool on her throat. "Now that the rain has let up, your dog is enjoying himself," she said, more to break the silence that had settled over them.

It should have been an uncomfortable silence. They didn't know each other well enough for this fragile intimacy born of the hour before the dawn, as the night lifted its veil to greet the day. But something about it felt familiar. As worn and warm as her wrapper.

Mrs. Firth leaned against the open doorway and pulled her patterned shawl closer around her shoulders. A light mist had landed on her skin and hair from the fog that lay heavy on the lawns outside. She must be cold, for she wasn't wearing stockings or slippers, her narrow feet bare against the wooden floor. "It's getting difficult to see Maurice," she said.

Maeve set the ladle down. Mrs. Firth's voice had sounded shaky. "He's used to the grounds. I'm sure he's safe enough."

"It isn't safe for anyone in weather like this." There was definite worry in her voice.

The sky was dove gray now, and the fog was white and opaque as it encroached on the grounds. It trailed from the sea to the bluffs and eased its way through the alleys of Inverley more often than the guidebooks admitted to the visitors that thronged the area looking for a healthful air.

"There he is, by the holly bush. Look." Maeve went to stand by Mrs. Firth and pointed out the door to where the dog was rooting beneath the greenery.

In the pale light, Mrs. Firth's skin was luminescent. Her hair was in need of brushing, but unbound it was glorious as it tumbled around her shoulders. Her eyes were watchful and worried, glued to the grounds.

Though Mrs. Firth was not presently in the first stare of elegance, being also in her nightclothes, her garments were in impeccable condition. The fine silk yarns of the shawl and its intricate pattern spoke of its expense, and the fact that she wore it carelessly enough that one edge trailed against the floor reminded Maeve that whatever her financial situation was now, she was a woman accustomed to money. It was more suitable for a ballroom than for a kitchen, and she longed to touch its silky surface.

But if she were honest with herself, what she wanted was an excuse to stroke her hands over Mrs. Firth's arms. For the longer she stood close to her, inhaling the light violet scent that she wore, she wondered if she was drifting into a fog of her own, a swirl of emotions that couldn't be pinned down. She wanted to embrace the magic of this hour.

Anything felt possible.

"He's headed down the path to the cove!" Mrs. Firth exclaimed, moving from the doorjamb so fast that she bumped into Maeve.

Maurice was barking now, and racing beyond the garden.

"It isn't safe." Mrs. Firth took off after him, her night rail flapping behind her like a sail, plunging herself into the thick white wall of nothingness.

Maeve hesitated, then took off after her. Almost immediately, she slipped on slick grass and then wasted precious time stripping off her stockings. She hadn't run without shoes since she had been a child. In fact, she wasn't sure she had run anywhere in any circumstances since girlhood. The grass was cold and wet beneath her feet and she worried about slugs and snails for an instant before losing herself in pursuit of Mrs. Firth.

She didn't want her to be alone if something did happen to her beloved foxhound. She also worried that she might take a tumble, which would be dangerous if she was alone and undiscoverable in the aftermath of the storm.

There was also the matter of Mrs. Firth's fear of the ocean.

Maeve found them easily enough, there being but one well-trodden path down to the shore.

Mrs. Firth stood on the beach at a safe distance from the waves, arms wrapped around herself. Her night rail, heavy with mist, clung to her calves. "Maurice seems to be enjoying himself," she said. "Though I cannot find it within myself to care much for the experience."

"The beach does not show itself to best advantage after a storm," Maeve said.

The cove was protected by the bluffs, a patch of beach private to the property. Maeve liked to walk here, listening to the water and the birds, but all of the afternoons had been sunny thus far.

Today, the sand was strewn with rocks and logs and thick foam that had been churned up from the ocean's depth and spewed out. Maeve stuck a bare toe into the foam. She had never been one to leave the coziness of the indoors when the weather was poor and was surprised to discover that she didn't dislike it.

"I like seeing the beach storm-tossed like this. It's interesting," Maeve said.

"I do not."

"The sea will reclaim its broken treasures in the next tide or two, leaving everything serene again. This is but a temporary wreckage."

Mrs. Firth's face was pinched, and her eyes were shadowed. "It's so elemental," she said. "The sea moves and heaves of its own volition. Look at it, unbroken as far as the eye can see. There is none but God to stop or start the ripples that turn into waves that toss men from their ships and snatch the innocents from the shores."

"I can imagine why it must terrify you," Maeve said, coming up to stand close beside her. "Your husband must have seen many such storms in his life."

"My husband." She paused. "Yes, my husband."

"This must be difficult for you."

"I was his fourth wife. It wasn't a love match."

Maeve blinked. She hadn't expected this. She would have preferred to hear that Mrs. Firth had been devoted to her sea captain and would never dream of finding any other. But finding out that this woman had perhaps never been properly loved...

It was tempting.

It made her want to show her what love could look like.

The idea startled her, for though Maeve had dallied, she had never been in love. It was what she wanted most in life, but she wasn't sure if she would ever have it.

Maurice dropped a stick at their feet, whining until Mrs. Firth picked it up and tossed it for him. He raced after it through the wavelets that lapped up onto the sand.

"You were brave to venture forth in the fog after us. I'm still shaking," Mrs. Firth said, holding out her hand.

"There was fog like this everywhere where I grew up." Maeve was surprised at herself. She never spoke of Ireland.

"Do you miss it?"

"I loved the land and the views. But we left my stepfather there, and I was happier with him behind us. He died in the autumn."

"I am sorry for your loss."

"I am not," Maeve declared. "Not all marriages are happy ones. He decided to take a mistress and live with her openly, so Mama decided to take a stipend and travel with me to England to escape scandal. Meanwhile, I decided to avoid the whole situation altogether and never shackle myself to a man."

It wasn't the sole reason or even the primary one, but it was true enough.

"It must be hard to live as a single woman."

"It is rendered harder still, as I have found no employment." She pulled her flannel wrapper close. "Maybe I'm not meant for work."

"If you wish to find employment, someone will take you. You're very......" Mrs. Firth stopped, red spreading over her cheeks as slowly as the fog rolling in.

"Very what?" She held her breath.

"Very easy to talk to. An asset for a shop assistant, I would think."

"Mr. Jackson thought I was *too* easy to talk to. Maybe Mama was right and a husband is all I can catch, despite my grave disinclination."

Mrs. Firth bit her lip. "I used to think there was no greater purpose than being a wife." She stopped, looked down at the stick in her hand, then tossed it again with more force than Maeve realized she had in her slight frame.

"And now?"

It was the time for truth and secrets, it seemed. For both of them.

"Well, I am on my own now. As for marriage… You are right to avoid it. I would not wish it upon the unwary."

CHAPTER THIRTEEN

Although the mail coach from London arrived in Inverley thrice weekly, letters from Joan's lawyers or from the Bow Street Runner were slow to arrive. Perhaps they had the same opinion of her as her in-laws did. Without a husband, her title was but a shadow of its former self.

Her patience was rewarded with the appearance of Mr. Northam himself instead of a letter. "There is too much to share," he explained as he accepted a cup of tea. "I thought it best to visit you again instead of penning a novel in my letters."

"I am grateful for any light you can shed on the situation," Joan told him.

"We are most eager for news," Tilda added. Joan had insisted that Tilda join her, for no one knew the family secrets better than she did.

"What did you know of your dowry, Your Grace?"

"Only that I had one. I don't recall any of the details of the investments, but the lands I brought to my marriage were in Kent."

Whenever she had been curious, Papa had kissed the top of her head and told her not to worry about men's business. They would take care of everything for her. Looking back on it, she remembered the strain on his face, the sweat on his brow. But it had been a warm spring, and she had not been accustomed to challenging anyone in her life, let alone her father.

Mr. Northam shook his head. "It's ugly business. Might be better for you to go to London and talk with the lawyers directly about it, Your Grace." He shifted in his chair.

Tilda frowned. "God granted you a tongue and Her Grace tasked you with a job. She can hear it from you as well as from any other."

He swallowed, the tips of his ears turning red. "It's a matter of some delicacy."

"Please tell me." Joan clasped her hands in her lap to prevent them from shaking.

"You had a good amount of land for your dowry, and it was profitable at the time of your marriage. But afterward, the duke decided to enclose the lands and evict the tenants, replacing them with farmland for sheep."

"A normal enough practice," Tilda said, "though many suffer from it."

"You are correct, Mrs. Tilda, but the duke was also correct. Enclosing the land brings the property ten times more income compared to the rents from the individual cottagers and tenant farmers."

"Then why am I not seeing a return from this?" Joan asked. "Stanmere's lawyer told me that there has been no profit."

Mr. Northam held up a finger. "Because according to the paperwork, the tenants were evicted but the land remains fallow. There is no record of the purchase of the sheep, or the sale of wool or meat."

Joan was puzzled. "What does that mean?"

"I am told by my source that Stanmere needed money in cash, as all of his wealth was tied up in land. He devised this plan to keep everything off the books, so he could use the money without it being traced."

"Why would it matter if it was traced? Money is money, is it not?"

"To prevent scandal. That's the money he has been using to support his illegitimate sons as they grow older and thus more expensive to keep. They need educations at Oxford and fine clothes now, instead of kites and lemon twists. Now that he has died, that's where their inheritance money comes from." He nodded. "It's a neat little bit of work. He passed on the duchy completely intact to his heir, as per the entail, and had enough from your lands to support his sons, as he felt was only right according to his legacy."

"The Astleys always were proud of lineage," Tilda said. "It's no surprise that he cared deeply about the scandal but still wanted to provide for his sons."

There was an odd look on her face, and Joan wondered what exactly it meant.

"Scandal has already erupted, so it didn't seem to have worked," Joan said.

"But it did work, because they turned it all on you, didn't they? Even though the facts make no sense—anyone who looks at you would know right away that you could not be the mother of a twenty-year-old man—people will believe anything they read in the papers. And if they don't, the wise ones will still keep their mouths shut if the news comes from a powerful duke."

"Are you certain that there are sheep on my land?"

"I went to Kent myself and saw them with my own eyes, Your Grace. A fine herd."

"Then I shall write to my lawyers to open a suit with the Court of Chancery to claim my rightful dowry."

Mr. Northam nodded. "Exactly what I was going to recommend. Not even a duke should prevent a widow from getting her fair share."

When her funds started to come in, she could sell this intimidating house and live somewhere surrounded by nice safe land instead of sea.

Joan paused. "Wait. Why did you say I should talk with my lawyers?"

"When the marriage settlement was signed, there was a clause stating that your dowry lands were not to be enclosed. Your father felt strongly about such things and wished to protect the tenants. Stanmere disagreed and put pressure on him about it. I don't know exactly why, but often in this kind of case there are secrets to protect. Your lawyers drew up that paperwork and your father signed away the clause in the end. He received a bit of money from the Astleys for his trouble, but he knew what it could do to you eventually. He looked out for his own interests, I am sorry to say."

She couldn't breathe. Papa had done this to her? Her dear Papa, who used to throw her up into the air in the wildflower patch on the outskirts of their estate? Her Papa, who told her at every turn that everything would be all right as long as she trusted him?

The Astleys had broken her trust, but Papa had broken her heart.

❖

The best distraction from Joan's problems by far had been conversing with Miss Balfour.

But that too had its complications. Joan regretted that she had forbidden her presence in most of the house, and yet this desire to spend more time with her wasn't wise. The aftermath of the storm had created an intimacy between them that she feared as much as she craved.

Had Miss Balfour done as Joan had expected and spread tales of her beyond the walls of Fairview Manor? With what she had disclosed to her on the beach, Joan was no longer sure that was a good idea.

Oh, this had all been ill thought out. How had she thought herself clever enough to see it through? She couldn't recall ever being praised for intelligence—only for her face and form, and for the splendid spread of her table and the décor of her ballroom. None of which had anything to do with *her*.

Miss Balfour had been so kind to follow her and Maurice to make sure that they were safe that morning on the beach. Joan was accustomed to people doing things for her, but because they expected a favor or payment in return.

Miss Balfour had sprung into action without any hesitation.

She had looked so sweet with her hair bound up in rags, in a flannel wrapper so ancient it should have been made into rags itself long before now. She had been disarming and gentle. Unlike the beautiful creature that Joan spied from afar on her walks, in her silk frocks and beribboned shoes and elaborate bonnets.

To Joan's surprise, she wanted the ease of equals between them. She yearned to talk to her again, to learn more about her.

She wanted her as a friend.

Joan had taken to perching on the ledge of her window in the afternoons, waiting for Miss Balfour to start her daily constitutional in the gardens, for the sole purpose of timing her own presence in the hallway to when Miss Balfour entered again. All so that Joan might have the pleasure of asking her how she found the weather.

She began playing the pianoforte with some vigor in the mornings, so that it might draw out Miss Balfour in the hopes of discovering if she was musical. That proved an ineffective gambit, though she tried to find satisfaction in the improvement of her playing.

In the end, Joan was learning a good deal about piecework from Tilda, as she went in search of her maids for conversation when she was unsuccessful in her endeavors to find Miss Balfour.

Tilda had finally allowed Sarah to take over most of the duties of lady's maid. Joan had insisted that she take up residence in one of the third-floor bedchambers instead of the attics, wishing she had a little cottage on the land that she could gift to her. Tilda had spent so many decades in dedicated service and deserved her leisure now.

Tilda sat back in the wooden rocking chair and added a line of tiny stitches to her patchwork. A wicker basket of chintz and cambric scraps sat on the table beside her. Her quilt, a vibrant mix of oranges and blues and greens, was far from finished.

Joan enjoyed fine needlework, spending hours each week adding flowers and her initials to her handkerchiefs and reticules and sometimes to her shifts. It was peaceful work and helped pass time in the long winters that she had spent at one of their minor estates, as Stanmere preferred to stay at Astley Park and there had been few family members who visited her when her husband was not in residence.

But she had never done any quilting, leaving the practical sewing to the servants. It was interesting to watch Tilda piece together the squares and hexagons into a fine pattern that evolved each passing week, building upon itself with straight edges and clear borders and unbroken lines. There was a method to it that was soothing.

Paper piecing was an old-fashioned method that Tilda told her she preferred to use when quilting. She had to explain it to Joan, who had never done it before. Tilda wrapped a fabric scrap tight around a piece of paper to create a clean shape, and then basted the paper and fabric together to hold that shape as it was sewn to the next square of the quilt. At the end, Tilda told her, the baste stitches and all the paper was removed, and a beautifully sharp pattern emerged.

Joan's task was to cut the paper shapes using the template that Tilda gave her.

"This is a lovely way to spend an afternoon," Joan remarked as she snipped a triangle. There was a breeze from the window, and she tucked the papers beneath a brass candlestick holder so they wouldn't scatter.

"It's lovely for a woman like me," Tilda said, her needle flashing in the sunlight as she moved it through the chintz. "But you are less than half my age, Your Grace. There is a whole world outside these doors. Forgive my impertinence."

She didn't look repentant for said impertinence, though Joan wouldn't expect her to. Tilda had never been one to hold her tongue. When Joan first entered the household, Tilda had told her all she needed to know about surviving life with Stanmere.

"I can hardly afford to go outdoors, Tilda. What if someone recognizes me?"

"Why did I take the trouble to cut your hair if you won't even test out your disguise?"

Joan looked away. "It's risky."

"Shake the worry from your shoulders and enjoy being young." Tilda gazed out the window, her face soft and wistful. "Young folk like my Sarah don't remember to enjoy it as they ought. And you're hardly much older, Your Grace!"

"I've had more than enough excitement since the funeral, thank you. I don't need any more."

Tilda shook her head. "That wasn't excitement. You've been mourning your own life since your wedding day. You threw off mourning for Stanmere almost as soon as we arrived here. It's time to stop mourning yourself now too."

Joan stared at her. "I enjoyed many things about my life as a duchess."

"The balls and the dinners and the soft life. Yes, anyone would enjoy those. But you didn't enjoy the loneliness or the cruelty."

It had seemed selfish to be unhappy. How many girls would have loved to be in her position? How many would have done anything they could for the sake of the estates and the dresses and the connections? But then, how many would have stomached what Stanmere had done to Maurice? Or what happened to the housemaids who were sent away a few months into their employment? Joan had been too naive during her marriage to understand it. It was only during the parade of illegitimate children at the will reading that she had pieced the events of her own life together.

"Happiness was never listed among a duchess's duties," Joan said.

"And how could you have been happy with a man like him?"

Joan bit her lip. "I wasn't. You know I wasn't."

"His Grace was a right bastard—a thousand times more than the ones he sired. You don't even know the depths of his evil."

"From beyond the grave, he has denounced me as an adulterer and left me with nothing of note. I think I have some passing familiarity with his evil." She stared down at the scissors in her hand, and for half a second felt she could see a glimpse of his face in the cold steel. She shivered.

"Be grateful that it's all you know."

Tilda had been with the family for decades. She knew everything. But the look on her face prevented Joan from asking.

"You've been frozen scared like a rabbit for too long. It's time for you to thaw."

"I don't think I know how to do such a thing." There was a lump in Joan's throat the size of a boulder. She *had* been afraid, she realized. She had been afraid for years and years, for so long that she had forgotten it and had mistaken stability for happiness. "I don't know what would even count as excitement."

"Trust me, Your Grace. When you find real excitement, you'll know the difference."

In the end, Miss Balfour crossed her path when Joan was least expecting it, after she had come downstairs from talking with Tilda. Her head ached, filled with worries and fears. She was vexed with herself for not even realizing how much they had driven her life.

Miss Balfour was returning from out of doors, a bit of color in her cheeks, her curls beneath her bonnet mussed from the wind. She looked wonderful.

She *was* wonderful. She was unlike anyone Joan had ever known.

Some strange feeling leapt in Joan's breast and made her heart hammer like a bird sailing straight into a window. And yet she didn't think it was fear.

Was *this* excitement?

Joan swallowed hard. "Miss Balfour. Do you think you might like to take your daily constitutionals with me from now on?"

Miss Balfour's lovely lips fell open.

"We both need to walk, after all," Joan said, forcing herself to continue. "For our health, if nothing else."

Miss Balfour smiled at her, a sparkle in her eyes. "By all means, Mrs. Firth. For our health."

It was easier to breathe after that. It wasn't like a bird flying into a window after all. It was like being set free, the skies open and clear in front of her.

CHAPTER FOURTEEN

The next afternoon, Joan found it within herself to consider the manor and the surrounding land almost pretty. Birds flew overhead and bees buzzed in the garden and the sun was high in the sky, and the house didn't look quite so forbidding anymore.

She wasn't confident that it was the sunshine that had changed her perspective. A compelling argument could be made for the presence of Miss Balfour. Her face and form needed little adornment, lovely as they were, but adorn them she did, and with an eye for color and fabric and trim.

"Your frock is beautiful," Joan told her, deciding that there was nothing unexceptional in a compliment toward a woman she wished to befriend. "The braiding is a wonderful detail."

Miss Balfour gave a shallow curtsy. "Do you have your eye on it for when I inevitably sell it to Mr. Culpepper at the emporium?"

Joan froze. But when Miss Balfour laughed, Joan realized she was funning, and she joined her laughter. When had been the last time she had laughed? She hadn't found anything amusing in weeks.

Possibly years.

"It suits you," Joan said. "I would not dream of poaching it."

"I no longer ever look my best on a stroll these days, having sold my favorite walking dresses. But may I confide in you?" Miss Balfour leaned in, her rose scent tantalizing Joan. "I think my best looks rather better on you."

If this was Miss Balfour not looking her best, she was intrigued for the day when she would see her in full splendor.

"You are kind to say." Joan looked down at her sprigged lilac muslin. "I hope you have deep pockets to fill with my debt of gratitude. Leaving off mourning and wearing your wardrobe has been a tremendous help to me. I feel like a different woman."

"If you have left off mourning, then why have I never seen you out of doors except for the storm?" Miss Balfour asked idly, looking up at the cloudless sky.

The words stung. "Are we not out of doors at this very moment?"

"You stroll your own grounds, but you entertain no visitors. You do not stray beyond the garden's borders." She glanced at Joan from beneath her straw hat, her eyes well shadowed by the deep brim.

"You are impertinent."

"I thought that was the prerogative of friendship."

"Is that what we are?" She tried to match her voice to Miss Balfour's gentle teasing tone, but her heart was thumping as if it still had not decided how to feel in her presence.

"Do not forget that you have seen me in my night wrapper with my hair quite wild. Few can claim to have seen me in such deshabille. Any who do must consider themselves dear friends indeed." She patted her glossy black curls.

"This is true. And you have seen me in my shawl and night rail. And most shockingly, without any shoes."

"On several occasions, in fact." Miss Balfour laughed.

Joan tried not to wince at the memory of skulking around her own hallway in her stockinged feet when Miss Balfour had first visited her.

"It cannot be good for you to stay cooped up in this house. Grand as it is, it isn't healthy to stay inside when there is a stout sea air ready for one's lungs."

"Do you find it grand? I find it a touch frightening at times." She glanced at it over her shoulder. "It's imposing."

Miss Balfour raised a brow. "All the more reason to escape it in search of entertainment, is it not?"

Joan felt flustered. She had hidden herself away for weeks now, and the heap of calling cards in the salver had trickled to nothing. She had thought the dangers of socialization were long past now. "Eventually, I am sure to meet the owners of the other manor houses. Or I may attend the assembly rooms of an evening and encounter the visitors."

Joan had no plans for any of it to happen, but Miss Balfour didn't need to know that.

"Visitors!" Miss Balfour cried. "They are no different from the people you left in London. You *own* part of Inverley now. Your commitment to this county should run deeper than socializing with visitors."

The criticism struck her to the core. She had always taken her duty seriously, and Miss Balfour had a point. An inhabitant of a village should be part of its structure, whether social or financial or charitable. Was she letting her neighbors down?

"You seem to have strong opinions. Are you so attached to the social life here?"

Miss Balfour's smile was wistful. "When I lived with my mother before her remarriage, there was always something to do. On Mondays, we played whist at the assembly rooms while enjoying a dish of tea. Tuesdays were for strolling on the promenade. Wednesdays and Fridays we had our spa treatments. Thursdays were reserved for the library so that we could read all the latest society gossip. Preferably in the bay windows on the second floor overlooking the seaside. Inverley truly shows to advantage from those windows."

"It sounds like it was a nice life."

"It was nice." She raised her chin. "I haven't the money for public breakfasts and dancing and cards any longer. But what doesn't cost money is friendship, and so I am glad to lay claim to it wherever I may find it."

Joan smiled. "The benefits to friendship are rich indeed."

"You have the means to enjoy Inverley. I highly recommend you do so."

"I would not have the first clue where to go."

"I could show you." Miss Balfour's eyes were bright. "You are missing something special by staying on your own patch of land all summer. The promenade by the beach is heavenly."

"I don't like the ocean," Joan reminded her.

"You have hardly *seen* the ocean if all you have seen is your own cove. But you needn't see the shore to enjoy the town."

Joan's heart leapt. Again she questioned herself whether it was fear or excitement. She thought of the brooch Stanmere had left her and what Tilda had said about mourning her own life. She ought to seize the opportunity to live. She was feeling more hopeful now that the lawyers had filed the suit with the Court of Chancery.

And yet it felt a terrible risk. What if someone recognized her and announced to all and sundry that the duchess had been found?

Yet it might be best if Joan showed people herself that there was nothing at all interesting about the reclusive widow on the hill. She didn't know if Miss Balfour had spread any news of her at all, and it would be exceedingly strange to ask her to do so. The longer Joan knew her, the less she liked the idea of Miss Balfour gossiping about her.

"You could go to the lending library. Perhaps you might enjoy the theatre?" Miss Balfour looked away. "I do not have the money to do such things myself any longer, but I could show you where everything is. I would lead you to the very doors."

"If you were to do such a thing, then I would pay your entrance fees for your troubles," Joan said, shocked at how fast the offer tumbled from her lips.

Maybe Tilda had been right. Why not test the limits of her disguise?

The truth of it was that she *wanted* to go out into the world with Miss Balfour.

What could be the harm?

Besides the danger of wishing to confess every last detail of her life to her newfound friend, that is.

Miss Balfour could never discover the truth about her. How would she even react if she found out that she would be squiring about a duchess instead of a sea captain's widow?

And yet, as long as she were taking risks… "If we are truly to become friends, perhaps we should dispense with the formalities? Please do feel free to call me Joan."

"I would be honored if you would call me Maeve."

She took a deep breath. "I would love to see the sights of Inverley with you, Maeve."

Come what may.

❖

Maeve's thoughts were full of nothing but Joan the next day. Strolling with her around the perimeter of Fairview Manor was a fine thing. But offering to show her around Inverley was an impulse that she regretted. Having been granted the use of her Christian name, Maeve's curiosity about Joan increased tenfold. Spending more time with her was dangerous, for her time would never be rewarded in the manner of her wildest fantasies. How was she to control the overwarm feelings that flooded her in her presence?

It clouded her thinking.

Maeve was also embarrassed at what had motivated her to blurt out her offer. For although she did think it a shameful waste if Joan never found any enjoyment in Inverley, and she did believe that it wasn't healthful for Joan to remain in the manor day after day, her heart leapt at the thought of enjoying spa treatments and tea and cards again. Of being a woman of leisure. At least in pretense if not in fact.

How selfish of her.

She missed the indulgences of her previous life, sometimes so much that she ached. It was bliss to think of enjoying them again. But she was determined to spend her own money instead of Joan paying for her. Her pride insisted on it.

She simply needed to *earn* her own money first.

Mr. Culpepper sighed. "Do pay attention, Miss Balfour. I almost fleeced you out of five shillings."

Maeve was at the secondhand emporium to sell another dress. She blinked down at the coins in her hand. "Oh! You knave. I should have realized they felt lighter than usual."

"Where is your mind this morning? You're sharper than this."

"I cannot share all my confidences with you, Mr. Culpepper, as there are far too many to count. It would take up your whole day, and then how would you make any money from sales if you didn't attend to your clientele?"

He laughed. "There is no one here but us, is there? I wish nothing more than to help you. I esteem you, Miss Balfour."

For an instant she worried she had given him the wrong impression by coming so often to his shop. Surely an offer could not be forthcoming? But she detected no air of romance about him. "I esteem you too. You have been a fine friend to me, Mr. Culpepper."

"Now, what has you distracted? Is it an affair of the heart?"

Maeve paused. Could she trust him? It was a sensitive business, discussing her preferences. But his face was open and his eyes were kind, and she had a suspicion that he may have already guessed.

CHAPTER FIFTEEN

"First I need to make something clear," Maeve said to Mr. Culpepper. "I am not interested in attracting a suitor. For me, there is no greater felicity in the world than that of finding a very intimate female friend with whom to spend my time."

She was relieved when he did not look appalled.

"That sounds like a fine thing, Miss Balfour. I have several friends who live in London who are of the same persuasion, and pleased they are to have sorted such things out before any of them fell into an unhappy marriage."

"But not yourself?" she asked. "You are also unmarried, are you not?"

He shrugged. "If I may be perfectly honest, I do not possess any sort of romantic interest for any type of person. I tried a time or two to see if it would suit, but I cannot imagine experiencing some of the more intimate particulars, so I do not engage in any."

Maeve nodded. "It is always a relief to discover these things about oneself, is it not? I have only shared this with certain other people in my life, but it eases the burden of secrecy to talk about it where one may."

"I heartily agree. Now do tell if you are having any such experiences now? This is intriguing." He wiggled his brow at her.

"The affair that I am most involved with these days is with my purse, as you well know. I am in need of more than these five shillings." She plucked the remaining coins from his hand and put them all in her reticule.

"I can think of an establishment or two who may need a helping hand."

"Your first tip did not endear me to your recommendations, sir."

"The spa has need of a new attendant. One of theirs has up and married last week, leaving them short of staff."

"The spa?" Maeve sighed.

"What is your objection to the spa? Mr. Williams runs a fine establishment. It's clean and proper and serves a fine clientele. I had a nice dip last week and never felt better."

"I can have no objection to their services when I have enjoyed so many of them myself." Her stomach pitched. How could she encourage Joan to venture forth to her favorite places in Inverley when she may well be working in them soon? But Joan hadn't seemed to judge her for working. In fact, she had commended her when she had listened to Maeve talk about her experience with the general store. She straightened her back. "Well. If I must now work there, then so be it."

She was determined to go now while she still had her resolve.

The spa was located near the shoreline at the far edge of town. Maeve relaxed when she was greeted by her favorite attendant in the front room. "Miss Alice, it is ever so good to see you."

"Are you here for your seaweed treatment, Miss Balfour? It's been some time since we saw you here."

"Alas, no. I am here for a different purpose. To nourish my pocketbook instead of my skin." She managed a wry smile but was met with a blank expression.

"I beg your pardon?"

"I was wondering if I could speak to Mr. Williams about employment." He had always been most cordial to herself and Mama when they had frequented the establishment.

She told herself not to feel embarrassed, but her bruised ego didn't want to listen. She straightened the pink ribbon that she had tied around her waist. She could do this. She could belong here. She had to try.

The smile disappeared from Miss Alice's face, and her back was stiff as she ushered her to the office at the back of the building.

Maeve felt a flutter of discomfort at Miss Alice's behavior but managed to smile at the owner. "I do hope you are well, Mr. Williams."

"You are always welcome here, Miss Balfour." He rose to his feet and grabbed her hand, brushing a kiss against her knuckles. He was a jovial older gentleman with thick white sideburns. "I am most surprised to see you in my offices, but perhaps there is something particular you would like us to do for you? I am sure we could see to your needs, whatever they may be. We would like nothing better."

His warmth eased her, and she smiled as she sat down across from him. "I am delighted to hear you say so, sir. In fact, I do need something different. I am looking for employment."

He spluttered like a fish. "Employment? A woman of your stature?"

She swallowed the bitterness at his reminder. "My circumstances have changed with my mother's remarriage this summer."

"Why are you here instead of the assembly rooms?" he asked, slapping the desk as if he had come up with a brilliant solution to her troubles. "You must know that you are a great beauty. You could have your choice of husbands. Get to a dance floor posthaste and you have no further need to visit my office."

What business of it was his? Anger simmered in her chest. And yet she needed him, so she forced it down. "I am not interested in a husband, sir. Would you have a position available, or must I continue to seek employment elsewhere?"

"And how do I know you'll want to stay?"

"What on earth do you mean?"

"Why, you're Irish. Are you looking to return home?"

"I wouldn't have the funds to do so even if I wanted to. But no, I do not wish to leave."

"You've never even wintered here once and you think you want to stay?" He shook his head, his chin brushing against his high collar. "Inverley's a different place when the visitors leave."

"I suppose I shall learn that for myself."

"Then you can start today," Mr. Williams announced, startling her. "I could use another pair of hands, and it's all the better if they're a pretty pair. Customers like a fine-looking attendant. It's been a busy summer, you know. The owner of the Crown Hotel tells me this is the most we've welcomed to Inverley yet."

She felt a flutter in her belly. Start *today*? But it was out of her hands when he stood and ushered her to Miss Alice, who handed her a smock to cover her dress, and before Maeve knew it, she was smiling serenely at the entrance and welcoming women into the various treatment rooms.

The morning passed in a blur as Maeve rushed after Miss Alice. She learned where the tea service was kept and the time at which to offer it (precisely a quarter hour after any regimen, after the guests had freshened up their appearance and had time to settle into the parlor overlooking the beach). She prepared the towels that were part of the after-bathing ritual for the guests who chose to partake of it, after they were hauled out to sea in a horse-drawn contraption and dipped by attendants (soaking the towels first in sea water and drying them over hot rocks, the salt being highly prized to rub on the body after bathing). She pulverized seaweed into paste for her beloved seaweed treatment, wishing heartily she could apply it to her own face and relax instead of work.

Maeve had enjoyed dozens of appointments at the spa, and it humbled her to realize that there was four times as much work as she had thought to arrange even something so simple as preparing a glass of tonic.

It was exhausting.

Maeve walked slowly toward Fairview Manor at the end of the day. On the way, she passed Arabella and Caroline's cottage, and on a whim opened the door and called out a welcome.

"Oh, Maeve!" Arabella beamed at her when she popped her head into the parlor. "What a lovely surprise."

"I still have another quarter hour's walk before I am home," she said morosely, collapsing onto a chair. "I have been on my feet all day." Why, she was sore in parts of her legs that had never been taxed for more than a moment before. The spa had been much more strenuous than the general store had been.

Arabella was by herself, Caroline having taken her siblings to the shore where the younger ones wished to fly their kites. She brewed Maeve a cup of tea, and she had never felt more thankful for its restorative powers. Arabella was a most gratifying listener as Maeve recounted her day. Her emotions flitted across her face, and she gasped and laughed in all the right places, and by the time Maeve could see the tea leaves swirling at the bottom of her cup, she felt much better.

"You did it," Arabella cried. "I knew you could. You have found your place, Maeve. I'm so happy for you."

Arabella was always ready with a kind and cheerful word for her friends. It was an endearing quality. But though Maeve knew she should be happy at having found employment at last, part of her still yearned for more than waiting on customers. She missed having nothing more pressing on her mind than wine and cards and dancing and cozy sessions of gossip.

But that life wasn't available to her anymore.

Even if she showed Inverley's pleasures to Joan, she would be acting as a visitor to her own past. It wasn't the same as living it for herself.

She forced herself to smile. "Thank you, Arabella."

"I think there is more that you aren't telling me," she said, a crease between her brows. "If you do not wish to speak further, I understand. But I am here to listen."

Maeve sank into the chair and leaned her head back. "I am having a most difficult time in a most unexpected way."

Arabella poured her a fresh cup of tea. "Unexpected can be good."

"It's a matter of romance." She hadn't wanted to tell Mr. Culpepper all the details, but she was more than happy to confide in Arabella.

"Oh!" Arabella clutched her hand. "Oh, Maeve! How delightful."

"I have waited and waited for my turn." First Arabella and Caroline had fallen in love, and this past year, their friend Grace had tumbled into an infatuation with a bold and daring botanist. Maeve had wrestled with her jealousy, wishing it was her who had found a woman to flirt with.

But Joan was a complicated woman, and Maeve could not be certain that she would welcome her flirtation.

"I am intrigued by Mrs. Firth," she admitted.

Arabella's mouth fell open. "The widow? The one you are renting from? Oh."

"Exactly. *Oh.*"

"Has she given any signs that she might be interested in such a thing?"

"No. But there is something between us. I don't know what it is. Some connection, pulling us together. I feel drawn to her, but I cannot tell if she feels the same way."

"Do not hesitate to explore it, Maeve. If she does not share our preferences, then it is better to know than to wonder. Inaction brings nothing but the same daily routine. Without the unexpected, without the risk, you will never have romance."

She would have to risk her own confession. Time would only tell if they could be compatible, but the first step was one of discovery.

But without risk, Arabella was right. There could be no reward. More importantly, there could be no romance.

And romance was worth everything.

CHAPTER SIXTEEN

Joan agreed to a sedate visit to the circulating library for her first outing with Maeve. There was nothing so safe as a library, after all. People would be so focused on what there was to lend out that no one would notice two women in their midst, browsing the shelves.

But her legs trembled the moment they passed through the iron gate and stood on the cobblestone lane that bordered her property. She hadn't left it except for the single time that she had visited the secondhand emporium, under the protection of her widow's weeds. The lane stretched as far as she could see in either direction, lawns and hedgerows bisecting them on one side, and the patchy grass of the bluffs on the other.

Her nerve almost failed her.

Maeve was bright-eyed and enthusiastic, a vision in cream muslin with pink walking shoes. "Why are you hesitating?"

"I'm worried about what lies ahead." It felt good to express it, though she was a little embarrassed by her feelings.

"I've told you what lies ahead. Town." Maeve had a patient expression on her face, but there was a furrow in her brow. "Is that not where you wish to go today?"

Joan had tried to convince herself a thousand times last night that it was. "Perhaps I should call for the carriage."

"There's hardly any need to bother your driver unless you wish to leave the county itself. The library is a scant mile and a half from your front door."

"I should ask a footman to accompany us. Or Sarah. I think Sarah would like to see the library."

"We hardly need a chaperone."

The sly look Maeve gave her beneath the brim of her bonnet had Joan's belly tightening as taut as a drum, which made her even more nervous. What *were* these feelings that Maeve conjured in her as easily as anything?

But she couldn't tell her the truth—that as a duchess, she never went anywhere without someone following. It was terrifying to be venturing forth alone.

She wasn't alone, though. She was with Maeve, who stood there as steady as could be.

"Very well. Let us begin our journey."

It was a pleasant enough walk to the edge of town, where they encountered nobody except a farmer and his son who tipped their hats as they passed, but the streets of Inverley were bustling.

Thank goodness any of her acquaintances who fancied a trip to a resort were Brighton-bound in the summers, clamoring to be close to the Prince Regent and his circle. Inverley was not for the upper crust.

And yet her legs continued to shake and she could only listen with half an ear as Maeve pointed out the various landmarks and buildings of importance.

Joan paid for a subscription once they arrived at the library and was about to do so for Maeve as well, but Maeve slipped a stamped metal token onto the counter before she could.

"I decided to renew my subscription for the summer," she said, her head high as she showed the token to the attendant. "I was here yesterday tending to matters."

"I am happy to pay for you." She knew Maeve didn't have much to spare.

"I don't need your money," she said, her tone clipped, but then she grinned. "Do let us enjoy ourselves on our outing. The scandal sheets are at the back near the stairs and are always what I go to first." Joan stopped as Maeve sailed ahead. "I cannot wait to read the latest *on dits*," she called over her shoulder.

Joan followed her, heart pounding. "I hate the scandal sheets."

"Is that why you do not allow them in the house? I assumed it was so the servants wouldn't be distracted by them. Perhaps you could explore by yourself while I catch up on all the gossip I've missed." She sighed. "And how I have missed it! I haven't had any proper news in weeks."

Under no circumstances was Joan about to explore the library by herself when it had taken all her courage to enter the building. "You can hardly call it news when you don't even know those people."

Maeve laughed and picked one up. "Oh, no one here *knows* them. We have plenty of younger sons who rent lodgings for the summer, with a handful of minor lords and ladies scattered among them. And of course I've danced with plenty who have made a fortune in shipping or mining. But the ladies and gentlemen in these pages are a cut above the rest. That's what makes them so interesting."

Joan would have wagered a good deal of money that she could discern at a glance who the gossip was about, despite the thinly veiled attempts to hide their identities by publishing their initials instead of their names.

She was also quite sure that stories about *her* still circulated among the pages.

Maeve was an honest woman. What would she think of her deception?

"I thought we were here for the view from the second story," she said, and started for the curved staircase that hugged the far wall. Maybe Maeve would follow.

"You can't enjoy the view fully without something to read, and perhaps a cup of tea."

"We could look at fashion plates."

"Good idea, I'll add some." She picked up a few ladies' magazines and added them to the papers in her arms, then marched up the stairs in front of Joan.

If she had been in better spirits, Joan thought she would have enjoyed the fine wooden chairs and the graceful arched windows and parquet floors. Lost in her worries, she was so startled when an attendant brought them tea that she almost knocked the cup to the floor.

Maeve's face softened. "Is it the sight of the sea?"

"I find I don't mind it so much from a distance, compared to being at its mercy on the shore." Then she realized she should have lied, as it was the perfect explanation for her nerves. "But I do find that today I am somehow more affected than usual." She sipped the scalding hot brew, burning her tongue.

Maeve settled into her chair with one leg tucked under the other and her shoulders braced against the back. Joan almost said something, so shocked she was at the impropriety. They were in public, where anyone might see them! But then Maeve thrust a magazine at her without a word as if they had established some long-term routine, when this was the first time they had been here. Joan stared at the first page, the elegant drawing of the fashion plate blurred through a sudden veil of tears. It was a tiny exchange, already forgotten by Maeve who was now nose deep in her own magazine, but it felt disproportionately important to Joan.

It felt familiar, and warm. As if they somehow belonged together.

She had never been treated with such familiarity before, such lack of pomp and circumstance, such a casual expectation of reciprocal friendship.

This moment was valuable.

The library suddenly came into focus, the white paint gleaming and bright in the sunshine that poured in through the high windows. Warm wood was polished to a high shine on the banister and floors. It was a place of communion, people gathering—and she was part of it. She had been so long alone and so scared of people that she had forgotten what it felt like to be among a crowd. She hadn't remembered that there was peace in listening to the drone of conversation around her.

She felt more settled here, surrounded by strangers who thought her a nobody, than she had among the *ton* who valued only her title.

And it was because of the woman beside her, as comfortable here as she was in Joan's kitchen or the gardens or the cove. Maeve never looked out of place.

They whiled away a happy hour together speaking of fashion. It was most enjoyable to look through the drawings with Maeve, who insisted on peering at each one and always had a comment regarding fit or fabric, or a change she would make were she to order something similar from the dressmaker.

Best of all, no one paid any attention to the pair of them.

Joan had thought the gossip rags had been forgotten, but Maeve spied them at the end. Her heart sank as Maeve rattled off a few choice tidbits, and then finally came the moment she had dreaded.

"Oh, a new story about the duchess!"

"The duchess?" She failed to keep the quaver from her voice despite her best efforts.

Maeve gave her a look. "I know you know who she is, even if you never picked up a scandal sheet in your life. *Everyone* is talking about her. The one who ran away. What a spirit! I wish I could meet her."

Joan sat up a little straighter. "You do?"

Maeve's eyes were shining. "What a glorious adventure! Who doesn't think of running away sometimes and leaving everything behind? Mama and I did much the same when we left Ireland, though our circumstances were far less dramatic than the duchess's."

Joan blinked. Maybe Maeve would understand. Could she trust her with her secret?

Maeve continued to read. "It says here the family will continue the search *forever*. How very romantic. Can you imagine having a family who loves you so much that they would do anything to recover you? All this despite the number of love children she had from her wild affairs."

"We ought not make assumptions," Joan said. "The papers are unreliable."

"Most scandal is rooted in some truth."

"Even if it is, why should everyone be privy to it?"

"What if we found her?" Maeve's face was dreamy.

"*What*?"

"Well, it may be nothing but idle gossip here, but writing about it increases the odds that someone will recognize her and bring her home." She jabbed at the paper. "Look, they even have a new drawing! Is she not perfectly dashing?"

It was as vague a likeness as the previous versions had been, but Joan tucked an errant red curl beneath her bonnet as if its presence could give her whole identity away.

Joan could never tell Maeve the truth if she so whole-heartedly believed what was written in the papers. How would she ever understand Joan's side of the scandal?

❖

"To celebrate our newfound friendship, I begged a liberty of your Cook. I hope you do not mind." Maeve beamed at Joan as they walked past the holly bush with its bright red berries, which usually marked the end of their daily constitutional. Maurice sniffed at it and then bounded ahead in delight as he realized that they were continuing onward instead of looping back to the house.

"A liberty?" Joan sounded worried.

Maeve hesitated. Had she misjudged? "I asked Cook to prepare us a picnic. I thought our excursion to the library went well, and hoped to show you more of Inverley."

"However will we explore Inverley at luncheon? Must we go far?"

"You know I am no great walker beyond our usual two turns round the garden, and in fact would often prefer to sit than stroll. These days at the spa are taking their toll on my legs and I have no desire to walk further afield today."

"Then where are we going?"

"Just beyond your own stretch of land is a lovely treasure for the eyes. I thought we could explore the Roman ruins."

The ruins were a popular destination for visitors, and there were half a dozen people already strolling the overgrown road, still visible after centuries of disuse. The road continued on for a mile or two if one was wont to follow it, but the main attraction was a length of crumbled wall bordering a few sunken squares that were the old foundation to a fort, and the round base of a tower that Maeve imagined once looked out to sea. Maurice leapt into the foundation and chased his tail until he trotted back, satisfied with himself and ready for luncheon.

They could hear the ocean even at some distance, as it was audible from every corner of Inverley, but Maeve had wanted to take Joan somewhere that had no overt view of the seaside to avoid distressing her.

"Inverley has its own historical society," Maeve said. "They told Mama and I all about the ruins. There are ditches on each side of the road—see those grooves in the land there—though I must confess I don't recall their purpose. And you can see the pavestones peeking out from the grass. I think the society told me they were limestone. Anyway, it must have been magnificent when all this was built up." She gestured at the tower. "I suppose I am not a terribly knowledgeable guide. If all fails at the spa, I shall never seek employment at the historical society."

"I don't think we need to know the facts to appreciate its beauty. It is impressive to look at, whether we know that it's limestone or not. All of this was but a mile from my manor, and I never sallied forth to see it." Joan walked up to the wall and touched it with a gloved hand. There was a hint of sadness in her voice. "Now that I am a widow, I thought my duty was primarily toward myself. But I think I have been remiss. Perhaps I could become a benefactor to this society."

Maeve joined her and leaned against the wall. "You must have been accustomed to charitable work, then."

"I may not have been devoted to my late husband, but I was devoted to the land that he lived on and the people who lived there too. I was proud to do my share of hosting and visiting."

So Captain Firth had been landed gentry even before he had built the manor here. That made sense with Joan's elegance of manner. "Then why will you not entertain visitors at your manor? It sounds to me that you miss it."

"I do." A touch of wonder entered her voice. "I do miss it."

"I would be happy to introduce you to my friends. We could host a little party." She liked the idea of Caroline and Arabella meeting Maeve. Perhaps Mr. Culpepper could join them.

"Someday," Joan said, looking away.

"When—Yuletide?" Maeve asked with a smile.

"That might be acceptable."

Maeve had been funning, but Joan seemed in earnest.

The wind picked up and Maeve itched to reach out and touch one of Joan's ringlets as they escaped her bandeau. Joan tugged the cloth off from her head, her curls whipping around her face and neck, and Maeve realized with some surprise that her hair was actually quite red in the bright light instead of brown.

"Has your hair always been this color?" she asked, blinking at it.

Joan stilled, then resumed tying the bandeau. "Of course it has."

"I don't know why you wear it pinned and bound up when it's such a gorgeous shade."

"Do you think so?"

"I am sure anyone who sees your hair would have the same opinion. It's rich and vibrant with a beautiful russet tone. Truly, there are so many colors in your hair, it is a wonder that I never noticed before." Her hair was dark chocolate and amber, oakwood and ember red. She was beautiful with her hair pulled away from her face, but now Maeve wished more than ever to see it falling in luxurious waves around her shoulders.

Joan looked pleased, touching her hair with a shy smile.

One of the footmen from the manor approached with a wicker basket in tow.

"Our picnic arrives," Maeve announced. "Let us enjoy our repast."

The footman snapped a cloth over one of the flat rocks near the tower and poured them each a glass of wine before presenting them with sandwiches and cheeses and chocolates. Joan instructed him to return in an hour. Maurice, heartened by the sight of food, wagged his tail and looked up at them both with mournful eyes.

Maeve felt a pang of guilt. Perhaps Joan's refusal to entertain her friends was due to her social standing. Their acquaintanceship had been accidental, living as they did in the same house, but that didn't mean Joan wanted to be on familiar terms in general with people of her stature.

"I apologize if I have overstepped," she said as she stared down at the watercress sandwich balanced on a fine china plate.

It had indeed been a liberty to have asked Joan's cook to prepare all of this. Her money for room and board did not take hampers of foie gras and wine into consideration. Joan had offered to pay her entry to the sights of Inverley, but the ruins were free to visit. She hadn't thought of the expense to the household for the picnic.

"One must eat. What matters if we are to be seated amid the grass and stones or at the dining room table?"

"It matters that we ought not be sitting across from each other at either venue."

A shadow flitted across Joan's face. "I thought you said we were friends. Did you not mean it?"

Oh dear, she had put her foot in it now. "Of course I did. But I am not trying to take your hospitality for granted."

"Banish the thought from your mind, for it never crosses mine. I consider us to be equals."

But would Joan consider them as such when Maeve revealed her desires?

For that was the real reason for the picnic. She had wanted time away from the house for longer than the space of their daily constitutional, so that they might have a discussion without being overheard.

Talking with Arabella had made the gesture seem romantic, wonderful, inspiring—but in the light of day, it was terrifying.

"I am always keen to seek friendship where I can find it." Maeve adjusted her bonnet and lifted her chin. Now was the time for courage. "And even though I have never been married, I do not consider certain types of companionship to be unavailable to me."

Joan gasped. "You mean an *affair*!"

Perhaps the picnic had been a poor idea. "Surely such frank talk cannot shock a widow?"

"I am merely surprised." But she was shredding the corner of her sandwich.

"Do I not strike you as the sort to have indulged in intimacies before? I am eight and twenty after all, and never once considered myself a candidate for sainthood."

"I didn't think you the sort to hang after any man. You have always seemed to me to be opposed to the notion."

"You have the right of it. I am not interested at all in setting my cap at a man." She emphasized the last word. Her travels had brought her in contact with many worldly women who grasped her intentions after such a subtle mention.

Joan's blank gaze revealed that she was not that worldly a woman. Maeve wasn't one to take risks, preferring to take the troubles of each day as she found them without trying to add to the pile for the future. But if they were truly friends, then surely Joan would not toss her from the manor if she revealed her secret. Her desires might not be common, but they were not unheard of, and Joan had proved herself to be both sensible and thoughtful.

Maeve tried for plain English. "I would prefer to catch the eye of a lady than a gentleman."

Still Joan blinked at her.

She cleared her throat and wondered if her nerve would leave her. "I have not been chaste all these years, but I have only ever kissed the lips of the fairer sex."

"Oh!" Joan's mouth fell open. She looked away, color flooding her cheeks.

CHAPTER SEVENTEEN

Have you never heard of such a thing as a woman desiring another woman?" Maeve asked, struggling to keep her voice even. She lost all pleasure in the picnic. The foie gras could have been ash in her mouth, and she tipped the remainder of her luncheon to the grass for Maurice.

She had experienced this sort of reaction before. It never got easier to expose herself after facing rejection or revulsion. But she had hoped to trust Joan. In her loneliness, she had leapt too fast, hoping too much for intimacy.

For Maeve wished nothing more than to unravel all of her mysteries and reveal plain Joan before her. She wished to learn her secrets and her worries and to kiss the furrows from her brow. She wished to hear all the details of her life in London.

Most importantly, she wished to show her that widowhood could have its distractions.

If only she would allow them.

Joan was intriguing and pensive and hesitant, and yet there was genuine interest in her eyes for those around her. She listened, and she was kind.

She was marvelous.

Joan finally met her eyes again, her cheeks still pink. "The concept is not unfamiliar to me."

Maeve felt a glimmer of hope in her heart.

"But I confess I have not given it a second thought since my youth."

The hope died. "Pray do not give it one now if such a notion disturbs you."

A clamor erupted behind them, and for an instant Maeve thought the bowels of hell had broken loose at her confession. But it was merely the clatter of horseshoes striking the old Roman road, and a gentleman who grinned at them and shouted out a halloo as he sped past.

Joan grabbed her arm. "Was that man staring at us?"

"Why would it matter if he was? Do you think two ladies cannot have an innocent time together without someone thinking ill of it?" Maeve shrugged her arm from under Joan's hand.

"It's not that. It's—well. I worry that people may be talking about me."

"Whyever would they?"

She hesitated. "I know word must travel in a small town and I have not been terribly friendly to anyone."

"People think you are reclusive, but they are merely curious about you." Maeve gentled her tone, for Joan looked afraid.

She seemed to be struggling to say something. "What else do people say about me?" she asked, her voice hardly above a whisper.

"Many have asked me about you, knowing that I live in your house. Do not worry, I have not said much. I am no teller of tales! Not of the scandalous sort, at least. I may have mentioned a fact or two, but no *gossip*. The general consensus is that you must be very proud as you have not received a single caller, not even from the reverend. They respect that you have mourned so deeply for your captain, who they believe died a hero." She gazed at Joan. "Are you not more curious what I may say about you?"

The worry eased from Joan's face. "What would you say of me, then?"

"That your hair has more luster than a pearl. That your lips hold a perfect dip and curve, like a heart. That you have the loveliest voice I've ever heard. And obviously you have superior sartorial taste, given that you bought so many of my own garments to wear."

Joan laughed, her face bright.

As they packed up the remnants of the picnic luncheon, Maeve felt hopeful that she had found a true friend indeed.

And if she was lucky, maybe something more.

❖

As August came to an end, Joan learned more about Maeve. She discovered how Maeve liked her tea (scalding with the barest splash of milk) and that walnut was her preferred flavor for biscuits. She found that Maeve was apt to wander when she brought Joan around town, where Joan walked faster and preferred to have a set point to venture to.

When Maeve came home from the library one day with a handful of sheet music for four hands, Joan learned that she did in fact play the pianoforte. She played brightly with a tendency to rush, and they spent their evenings amid the sound of their own laughter as much as that of scales and harmonies.

What Joan didn't have the courage to learn about was Maeve's uncommon desires.

She had been shocked beyond measure when Maeve brought up affairs during their picnic, having been so recently accused of them herself. But nothing had prepared her for the confession of preferring the companionship of other women.

Joan hadn't heard of such a thing since she had been a girl in her first Season, when a bevy of debutantes had giggled over their schoolgirl exploits. They had told tales of sweet embraces and an intimacy that could not be matched in a husband.

She had never experienced such a thing for herself, but it had intrigued her.

Though she had not thought of such a thing in years, she was surprised that it intrigued her even now.

Most importantly, it gave a name to these things she had been feeling. Maeve's confession unlocked the words that she had not even thought of in such a long time.

Desire. Lust. Passion.

She craved, she longed, she wanted.

But what did she crave and how did she want it? That remained a mystery. Though Joan's skin tingled and her heart sped up when she sat next to Maeve on the piano bench or across from her at breakfast, she wasn't sure if it was from nerves or anticipation.

Her marital duties had not inspired her to think of experiencing such things again with men, but the notion of tupping a woman revealed significant gaps in her education. Did women even visit the bedchamber together? Her friends had not been at all specific when they spoke of it. Perhaps it was a matter of kissing and not much more.

Kissing Maeve sounded wonderful.

Tilda had advised her to find excitement where she may. Was this not the most exciting thing to have happened to her in months, if not years? Was this not a way to wake up from the doldrums of her previous life and to seize the present to enjoy it?

But before she could make any sort of decision, her previous life caught up with her in the form of a crisp white card presented by the butler one morning.

Lord Peter had arrived in Inverley and requested the presence of Her Grace at the Crown Hotel at three o'clock the following afternoon.

Asking her to wait upon him as a supplicant. As if she had not been his brother's bride. As if she were not still a duchess. As if she were of no more importance than a drop of water on his felted beaver hat.

At least it wasn't Chetleigh himself. A wealthy unmarried duke, arriving as the fashionable summer season in Inverley was still in full swing, would have been the talk of not only this town but of several towns over. Perhaps of the entire county.

A duke's uncle, long married and without any title or distinction of his own, would cause a lesser stir, but a stir nonetheless. No one of such rank came to Inverley.

Joan went to find the butler to give him her return correspondence. "Lord Peter shall have to come here if he has any hope of seeing me."

If she went to the hotel, her identity would be discerned within a quarter hour. There would be no hope of hiding the connection once curious minds realized that the reclusive widow on the hill had arrived the week the rumors had started about the missing duchess. It was better by far if he came to her home, where she could remain safely hidden.

The duchy might know where she was now, but she didn't need the denizens of Inverley thinking that a harlot lived in their midst. What would Maeve think about it if she knew the truth? Would she believe the rumors? Joan couldn't bear to think about it.

When Lord Peter was announced at Fairview Manor the next day, Joan was waiting for him in the Blue Parlor. She dressed in black for the first time in weeks, and her skin had crawled as Sarah buttoned her into the thin crepe.

She had never liked Lord Peter. Not since she had met him on the day of her wedding and he had told Stanmere mere minutes from the ceremony that he could have done a damned sight better.

"Thank you for joining me," Joan said, sitting down after the briefest curtsy that she could manage. "I had no desire to be seen visiting your hotel. To what do I owe the honor of a visit from the Astley family?" The black tar of anger, dormant since she had left London, bubbled inside her.

Lord Peter made a sound of amusement, then cleared his throat. "Perhaps I should have kept our rendezvous at the hotel. They have the manners to offer a guest refreshment there. Poor lamb, you are showing your true colours. You were never a true duchess, were you?"

She unclenched her jaw enough to speak. "How dare you question my manners in my own house?"

"And such a house it is." He took an unhurried look around the room. She watched him assess the curtains and the baseboards and the furnishings and the view out the window. She knew it wasn't fashionable like the mansions he was used to, but she had grown accustomed to her odd little house.

The most important thing was that it was hers.

Her own gaze was caught by the wrought iron poker beside the fireplace. Oh, if she only had the courage.

But she would never make a ghost by her own volition.

"I am but a messenger. You need to drop your suit, my dear duchess."

"I am not your dear anything." Joan surprised herself. She had never used to talk to anyone in the family with anything but deference. "How do you know about the suit?"

"London holds no secrets for those with power."

"Chancery is kind to widows cheated of their lot, and will rule in my favor. Public sympathy would be with me, not with the dukedom."

He shrugged. "I think not, with all those scandalous lovers in your past. Not to mention the children, Your Grace! How could you." He widened his eyes to a comical degree and made a little moue with his mouth.

"You know perfectly well those children are Stanmere's, and not mine!" Joan struggled to keep her composure. "They are cast in his image."

"Of course I know. It is not even entertaining how easily you believe anything you are told." He shook his head, then took a cigar from his coat pocket and gestured with it. "Do you mind? No?" He lit it with the tinderbox on the mantle and puffed out a cloud of smoke.

She did mind but knew it wouldn't matter to him. "I am not a fool."

"No, you aren't," he agreed. "But you are sadly ill informed. You know nothing of what you do."

"What do you mean?"

"Pursuing this in the courts will end in embarrassment for you, and Stanmere doesn't wish to displease the Queen so early in his rule with a petty family squabble. We will finish this now." He steepled his fingers. "Here is the God's honest truth for you at last. You will never receive funds from your dowry."

He truly must think her a goosecap if he wanted her to believe that. "Of course I will."

"The annuity that you receive is out of the goodness of Stanmere's heart."

This was even more ridiculous. "There was no goodness there."

He brushed her words away with a wave. "You should accept those two hundred pounds per annum and drop the suit."

"How would it embarrass me?"

"Because you are not entitled to a damn farthing if we prove that you have been adulterous."

"You were behind the rumors in the scandal sheets." She sat back.

"The scandal rags will print anything, and they do love to put their own salacious spin on things, don't they?"

"But rumors are not proof. I never was unfaithful to your brother. Neither in thought or in deed."

"I believe you," Lord Peter said, surprising her. "But it does not matter, because I can pay as many men as I can find to swear otherwise."

"That's unconscionable."

He shrugged. "It's nothing personal. Only business."

"It felt personal when Chetleigh stole my jewelry."

"Oh, that." Lord Peter grinned. "Maybe that was a little personal. But that wasn't the boy, that was Stanmere's doing. We Astleys like to keep our wealth, you see, and my brother didn't see why you should have any of the jewelry if you outlived him. You were a great disappointment because you bore no children. If your lawyers wish to look, I can show them where each piece has been catalogued in the ledger as part of the duchy's wealth, not as a gift to a wife. You are right that if they had been seen as a gift, you would have been entitled to them."

"You have so much, and you would deny me what is rightfully mine."

"What makes a rightful wife? An adulterous wife deserves nothing. It goes well with the story."

"Why are you telling me this?"

"So you will write to your lawyers and tell them to drop the suit." He leaned back in his chair and puffed out a smoke ring. "Do it now, Your Grace, while I wait."

She hesitated.

"Stanmere has given me something to encourage your cooperation." He called for his servants, and one of them brought a box with him.

"My jewelry box!" Joan exclaimed.

"We weeded out your own belongings from what my brother gave you. I believe there may be some sentimental folderol in there that may be of interest to you."

Joan opened the box and saw the jewels that had been passed down from her mother. It meant a great deal to be reunited with them. Not because of their worth, although they were valuable. Emotion threatened to choke her, and she trailed her fingers over the pearls and rubies and sapphires that she remembered her mother wearing when she had been a child.

"You see, Stanmere is willing to be reasonable, but you must do your part."

"I owe him nothing." Seeing her jewelry filled her with courage. "I am entitled to my belongings, and I am entitled to my dowry. We will prove that my land is providing income."

Lord Peter sighed. "Perhaps you are a goosecap," he said, though his voice was gentle. He leaned over and took her hand. She tried to snatch it back, but he held it firm, stroking his thumb over her palm and looking right into her eyes. "Listen to me carefully, my dear duchess. Your husband had three wives before you. The last one died young, six months before your own wedding night. Think about that for a moment."

Memento mori. That was why Stanmere had given her the brooch.

There was no escaping his reach. Not even in death.

Terror seeped through her marrow.

"Now write the letter."

With shaking hands, she wrote it, and he snatched it and looked at it. "Very good. I will deliver it myself."

"How did you find me?" Joan whispered, clutching her jewelry box.

"You cannot trust a lawyer, no matter how earnestly he lies on your behalf. The firm you hired may have been good enough to serve the likes of your father, but anyone who knows anything knows that they are not the best in town." He blew out a stream of smoke. "You should have seen what a low price they were tempted by to give you up. With the right persuasion, anything is possible." The tip of his cigar burned as red as the anger in her heart. "Then I had a gentleman come to town last week to confirm that you were here."

The man on the Roman road. Joan closed her eyes. She knew he had looked right at her. He had pierced through her disguise in no more than a moment.

"Why do you need my letter if my lawyers are already in your pocket?"

"We need it in your own hand so that no one will question it." He bowed. "I bid you good day."

Joan sat in the library, her head swimming, with no sense at all of the passage of time until Sarah came to find her before dinner.

Everyone had lied to her. Stanmere, her father. Her own lawyers. Over, and over, and over again.

"I heard Lord Peter was here, Your Grace." Sarah looked fretful. "I hope he wasn't too objectionable."

Objectionable. There were a thousand other words more apt to describe Lord Peter, none of which were suitable to say aloud.

"I am fine," she said, and rose to her feet on shaking legs.

It wasn't true, of course.

Nothing would feel normal ever again.

CHAPTER EIGHTEEN

Joan didn't attend dinner that night.

Maeve felt the loss keenly. She had grown accustomed to taking their meals together, and it was lonely to have her own thoughts as company when she so enjoyed the pleasure of Joan's conversation. Even worse was the realization that she ought not be sitting at the table in such circumstances at all.

There was nothing exceptional in accepting an invitation to dine from the mistress of the house. But to make the staff wait on her *alone* when she was a mere boarder! Why should Cook prepare milk-fed veal for a woman who only paid enough in rents for rabbit? Did the staff think her no better than she was, with airs and graces that she didn't deserve?

She hurried through the soup and took a bite of each course, hardly tasting anything, which was of real regret to her as Cook was excellent and she had never eaten so well in her life as she had at Fairview Manor. After dinner, Maeve sat by herself in the drawing room where she and Joan had the habit of retiring, though she did not dare ring for tea by herself after feeling so self-conscious during the meal. The room at least held the ghost of conversation, which made it more comfortable than her bedchamber. She curled up on the Chesterfield sofa and watched the sun set, her thoughts scattered.

Was Joan ill? Would it be considered impolite of her to inquire?

Maybe Joan had finally decided that Maeve was unnatural. Someone that she could no longer associate with. Maeve had flirted with other women who were fickle about such things. Desires could run hot while judgment and prejudice ran cold.

She knew what desire looked like.

And she could see plain as daylight that Joan did desire her. Maeve had caught her looking when Joan had reason to believe Maeve to be preoccupied. She had felt the graze of their hands as they strolled the gardens together. It couldn't always have been accidental. Two women needn't stand so close together when acres of land surrounded them, after all.

How could Maeve think of seducing a woman who she paid monthly? As a spinster with no immediate family in England, she would be forever subject to the vagaries of the household. She had already seen it with Caroline and Arabella, whose family had needs more pressing than her own. Joan could remove her from the household with nothing more than a word to her staff, and Maeve would have nowhere to go.

But she didn't think their friendship was so inequal as that. Joan was trustworthy, and kind. Although she *could* end their arrangement at any time, Maeve severely doubted that she ever *would*. And there was a world of difference between the two sentiments.

The truth was that Maeve wanted to stay.

Oh, how she *wanted*.

Though she had spent all evening longing for Joan's presence, Maeve was caught by surprise when Joan did enter the drawing room, Maurice padding along beside her. She wore a white silk evening dress with a small train in the back and a square neckline cut low on the bodice. Maeve had donned it once to an assembly the previous summer, and she was glad that Joan had purchased it because it suited her far better than it had Maeve. Her hair was pulled back under a white lace bandeau decorated with satin rosettes.

Joan's eyes were wild and glittering, and the lines around her mouth were tight. An air of determination squared her shoulders beneath one of her thick sumptuous shawls.

She looked like a lady on a mission.

"I hope you enjoyed your dinner," Joan said.

She took a seat next to Maeve on the Chesterfield. Even her voice sounded different. Lower. Tense. Purposeful. Her posture had always been a credit to any governess, but tonight Joan crossed her legs at the knee and leaned against the back of the sofa. Her foot, shod in an elegant cream satin slipper, was kicking her petticoat with fervor.

"The artichoke soup was superlative." It wasn't what Maeve wanted to say. *I missed you. I wanted to tell you about my day.* But her true thoughts might not be what Joan wanted to hear from her.

"And yet it did not inspire you to ring for further refreshment? I see no teacup beside you. I must provide proper hospitality." There was something sharp and brittle in her manner.

Maeve covered Joan's hand with her own, wishing neither of them wore gloves. Wishing her touch could soothe. "You are always generous in your hospitality. I do not need refreshment."

Joan snatched her hand away. "There is sherry in the sideboard." Though Maeve demurred, Joan poured two glasses and clinked hers against Maeve's after she passed it to her. "To friendship."

"To friendship." Maeve took a sip while Joan gulped hers. "Forgive me, but are you well? You do not seem like yourself tonight."

"I have never felt better in my life."

Maeve frowned. "Is this your first drink of the evening? You have had no dinner."

"Am I to account to you for every glass of wine I enjoy in my own house?"

"Of course not. I never meant to suggest such a thing." She rose, trying to keep the hurt from her face. "Perhaps you would enjoy the room to yourself."

Joan looked up at her, her eyes wide. "Don't go," she said, her voice quiet. "Please."

Maeve sat again. "Are you certain?"

Her shoulders slumped, and she pulled her shawl around her like a blanket. "Everything is fine," she said, sounding anything but. "But I confess I am in need of company tonight."

"That is no trouble. We have always entertained ourselves."

"What manner of entertainment?"

Maeve knew what kind of entertainment she wished for, but instead said, "Cards would do nicely." That should be a safe enough activity. She didn't think she could sit next to Joan on the piano bench, their thighs pressed together as they played a duet. Taking a turn about the room together would naturally invite them to link arms, and she knew from experience that it was all too easy to steal looks at Joan's bosom while they walked.

But cards could be played quite well with an entire table between them.

"I imagine we could find cards here somewhere." Joan rummaged through a few drawers, and Maeve was about to suggest ringing for a maid to help when Joan held up a pack in triumph. "There is even a set of fish for wagering."

She tossed the deck and a handful of fish onto the table, the carved ivory tokens clattering against the glossy lacquered wood. Maeve fanned out the cards in front of her. They were finely drawn, paper knaves and queens winking at her with cherry painted lips and knowing looks.

Why had she thought cards safe? They invited gambling. Risk. Chaos.

If only the idea weren't so appealing.

"Are those emeralds?" Maeve studied a fish in the candlelight. It was the length of her little finger, scales and fins etched into the ivory, with a tiny jewel sparkling from its eye.

"Did you never have a bejeweled set?"

"You move in circles beyond mine, I'm afraid."

Joan's smile wavered on her lips. "Perhaps I shall bring the fish to market and see what price they can fetch me."

"I suggested the cards, so you should choose the game."

Joan frowned. "My preference has always been for vingt-et-un or whist, but I suppose those cannot be played with two."

"Then let us play patience together."

"*Patience*? This is a paltry suggestion. Patience is for one person."

Maeve started to shuffle. "Any game that can be played by one can be better enjoyed by two."

"Black cards on red, red cards on black, all proceeding in a dull manner from highest to lowest. Do let us find another pastime."

"If you aren't interested, you may watch me play alone."

"We shan't need counters then if we're playing a game with no winning."

Maeve grinned. "I always win at patience."

In the end, they sat as close together as they would have at the piano bench, for to see the game properly Joan brought her chair so close to Maeve's that their knees touched. Maeve hoped Joan's presence wouldn't distract her overmuch, for she did have every intention of winning. Would Joan be open to returning her desires? She intended to find out by the end of the game.

Maeve dealt seven cards onto the table, the first facing up with the following six facing down. She placed six cards atop the ones facing down, with the first card again facing up, and continued for four more rows in the same manner until almost half the pack was dealt. The rest were placed in a stack face down.

"Look, there's an ace of spades. We're doing well already." Maeve moved the ace from the third column and placed it above all the rows and turned the card that had been beneath it over. "Luck is on our side again! A black nine to put on that red ten at the last column."

"You cannot mean to move anything there!" Joan protested. "I dislike having such a long column—the cards are then so difficult to move. Here, we can put six over seven instead." Joan snatched up the black club and moved it atop the red diamond in the second column.

"It's *my* game, is it not?" Maeve protested. "I saw that play."

"It was you who said patience could be played by two. If you saw it and didn't move it, then it counts as *my* move."

"We aren't playing that way!" Maeve cried, indignant.

Joan plunked a fish in the center of the table. "We shall keep track of who moves the most cards."

And after that, play was fast and filled with laughter as they uncovered cards and tossed fish and downed half the bottle of sherry between them. Maeve had played hundreds of hands of cards over the years, at private dinners and public assemblies and at home by herself. But never with so much at stake, though there had been no wager at all.

Finally, Maeve slapped the final card on top of the last column, with Joan's hand covering it a moment too late to claim it. "Ace of diamonds," she said, breathless.

Joan stared at their hands, and Maeve didn't dare move. She felt Joan's heat next to her, her sweet violet perfume layered with the sherry and the beeswax candles.

The pile of emerald-eyed fish twinkled at them from the table.

"The game is over." Joan sounded disappointed.

Maeve drew in a breath. Now was the time for risk.

If only she dared.

❖

Joan was entranced. It had been a common enough evening, two women playing a simple card game, and yet the possibilities spilled before her like a treasure chest, worth far more than the emeralds on the fish. Those were but a token. The woman before her was the prize.

She had spent the afternoon in her bedchamber, pacing and fretting after Lord Peter's visit. Nothing had calmed her. Not wine, not Maurice. Not until she realized where she could seek safe harbor.

With Maeve.

Her presence, her laughter, her very self was a delight. She could turn Joan's mood from sour to sweet, from horror to peace.

She was a rare woman.

Joan's hand still rested on Maeve's. Her index finger brushed against Maeve's wrist, where she felt her pulse beating fast.

Just like her own.

"Have you ever read your fortune from a game of patience?" Maeve asked, her voice low.

"I have never even heard of such a thing."

"There are two ways to divine your fate from the game. The first is if you asked a question before you started. If you win the hand, then the answer to your question is positive. If you lost, then the answer would be negative."

Joan thought back to the beginning of patience. When she had sat down, she had asked herself if this had been wise.

If that didn't prove that fortune telling was ridiculous, she didn't know what would. There was nothing wise about how she felt right now.

"And the other way?" she asked. Surely it would be some commonplace superstition that would encourage her to finally move her hand away and end this evening without betraying her desires. She could acknowledge to herself what she felt, but she wasn't ready to voice it aloud. Not yet.

But then she looked into Maeve's eyes. When would she be ready? Was Maeve even still interested?

Lord Peter's visit had stripped the fear from her and replaced it not only with rage, but a raw wanting for more. More than what she had. Maybe more than what she deserved.

Maybe it was time to find out exactly what more *meant*.

"The other way is to look at the last card played, as each ace holds a meaning for what shall come for you. Hearts for love. Spades for single blessings, which I always thought particularly apt for spinsters such as myself. Clubs for marriage."

Joan took an unsteady breath and gazed down at the last card. The ace of diamonds was still half-hidden by their hands. "And diamonds?"

"Diamonds are for courtship."

Courtship.

Joan moved her hand away and shifted on her chair, her silks rustling in the sudden silence. "Have you ever been courted, Maeve?"

She was shocked at her daring, her ears ringing with her own words.

Why had she blurted out such a thing? Had it been the sherry? The excitement from the cards?

She swallowed. She knew why. Deep down, she knew.

She asked, because she wanted to *know*.

Maeve's smile was a reward in itself. Her lips were full and a most becoming shade of pink. Joan had spent the last few weeks admiring them. "Some have tried. Few have succeeded. I am selective in my favors." She took a sip of sherry, her eyes gleaming over the rim of the glass. "What was your experience?"

If only she hadn't been married to an unscrupulous duke with coffers where his heart should have been. Thinking of Stanmere dimmed her pleasure in the evening. And yet, if she wished to know any of Maeve's history, she must share at least some of her own. She felt helpless in this web of desire, this uncommon thread that seemed to bind them. The difference was that Maeve was sincere. Unlike herself.

Joan set her sherry aside. "Well, I was married, wasn't I? Things ran their usual course."

"But did your husband *court* you? Did he woo you, with words or gifts or actions?"

Joan had been presented to His Grace at a meeting with her father, and then given to him at St. George's four weeks later. She had seen the groom twice in her life before their wedding.

Their betrothal had nothing to do with her.

And her marriage had nothing to do with the unexplained feelings that Maeve arose in her, the heat that tingled her skin and the tension between them. "No," she said quietly, unable to lie. "I have never been courted."

"Would you like to be?"

CHAPTER NINETEEN

Maeve held her breath. Sitting here, with the cards still splayed on the table, that damned ace of diamonds seared into her mind, with Joan a scant handspan away from her—time seemed to stand still.

Had she truly asked to court Joan?

What had she been *thinking*?

Once spoken, the question became part of the magic of the moment, lingering in the air like the warmth from the flickering candle or the sound of the sea in the distance. She could almost see Joan puzzling it over in her head, her brow furrowed, her lower lip caught between her teeth.

It was foolish to put one's trust in a game of patience.

But her own patience had worn thin.

"I'm not sure what you mean."

"By courtship in general?" Maeve forced her voice to be light. "Or courtship by one such as *me*?"

"By you?" Joan stared, but she didn't seem horrified. She looked... intrigued.

If the words could not be withdrawn, then by God she would stand by them. If Joan wasn't interested, then it wouldn't be for want of effort. The cards had spoken, after all. She had won the game. Now it was time to put a new one into play.

Maeve moved closer to her. "You deserve sweet words by candlelight and flowers for your hair. You deserve to be told that the emerald on that fish pales in comparison to the sparkle in your eyes when you smile. You deserve to know that the tone of your voice is so warm that were you to speak to me in winter, I would have no need of blankets." Maeve took a deep breath. "I could tell you those things. If you want them from me."

Joan's hand rested at her throat and her eyes were dreamy. "I rather like hearing them." She hesitated. "Particularly because they were from your lips." She swallowed. "I like your lips, Maeve."

"Would you like them on yours?"

"Oh. *Oh*. Please."

Maeve's patience was well rewarded, for Joan's lips were as soft as a dream. It had been so long since she had held someone, so long since her lips had touched another's, and it was even better than she remembered. She slid her hands under Joan's shawl, reveling in the warmth of her bare arms beneath the scrap of fabric that passed for sleeves on her dress. Her lips were sweet with sherry, as soft as the silk that she wore, and they parted at the merest brush of her tongue. Every movement Joan made beneath Maeve's touch was so delicate and so slow and so subtle, her elegance unmarred in passion.

It made her wonder what it would take for that composure to dissipate, for her to move with abandon, seeking her release. She ached with desire for far more than kissing, and she pulled away.

"What comes next?" Joan was breathless. There were a thousand questions in those wide eyes.

Maeve slid one of her fish across the table to Joan. "I would happily wager to kiss you again."

She cupped Joan's face in her hands and met her eager lips with her own, a rush of delight filling her lungs along with her violet perfume, almost dizzied from the pleasure that she had not known for sure if they would ever share. Her kisses became hurried, small presses of joy against the corners of Joan's lips and across her jaw and at the base of her throat.

Joan's breathing was unsteady. "I think I am in dire need of a distraction tonight."

Maeve frowned. She didn't wish to be a distraction. What she dreamed of at night, her pillow clutched in her arms, was a grand romance. She wished for love, for an honest relationship with a woman who would value her above diamonds and who would ride to hell and back for her.

And she wanted to love a woman who would inspire her to do the same.

Being a distraction wasn't an auspicious beginning to such an end. But what were the odds that the woman sitting across from her was to be her grand passion in life? Maeve had found occasions in the past for a night or two of pleasure. It had never amounted to much more than that. But she had taken the opportunity anyway, because she had found there were precious few enough moments in life to snatch even a fraction of such happiness for those such as herself.

If this were but another moment for such an occasion, why should she not take what was offered?

Maeve smiled. "I would be happy to be such a distraction for you. But are you sure of what you are asking?"

"I think we both know what we want," Joan said softly. "Ever since I met you, I have admired the curiosity that you have for the world. You are always looking around and talking to people and asking questions and wanting to know more. I find myself growing curious too. I also wish to know more. To learn." She swallowed, and her voice dropped to a whisper. "To take."

Maeve saw the color wash back into Joan's face and noticed the tiny pulse at the base of her throat start to throb. Her eyes were glassy, and she saw her own need reflected back at her.

She wanted this woman, more than she had wanted any other.

She wanted to show her exactly how much desire a woman could have for another.

"But I have something to tell you first," Joan said. Her face was pale, and her bottom lip quivered.

Maeve's curiosity roared to life. She had plenty of questions about Joan, though she thought she could well guess what she was about to say. "I gather you did not have satisfactory relations with your husband?" She took Joan's hand in hers, trying to warm her clammy hands. "I understand. It doesn't have to be that way between us. Truly. I promise you." She gazed into her eyes.

"Oh. Well. Yes, that is something I wanted to say." Joan averted her eyes. "This is difficult for me."

"I don't mean to be indelicate, but exactly how much experience do you have in such matters?"

"Admittedly not much." She swallowed. "But I do know I would like you to be a good deal less than delicate with me."

"That could be arranged."

❖

Joan couldn't quite believe that she was leading Maeve down the hallway to her bedchamber by the light of a single candle, her skirts fluttering in the draught like ghosts. There were altogether too many spirits in her mind tonight. Ghosts of Stanmere's nocturnal visits with his rough hands and passionless embrace. Ghosts of her previous life, when she used to float along the surface and never bothered to check what riches lay beneath the glamor. Ghosts of insincere smiles, of friends and family, crowding her mind with unpleasant memories.

She was indeed in need of distraction, and there was none better than to take her pleasure with than Maeve, sweet in her sincerity.

Joan had almost spilled her secret to her tonight.

But now that she had indulged in the pleasure of her kiss, she wanted to forget about being a duchess. She wanted to forget that she was living in a house of lies, that Lord Peter was in Inverley, that at any minute her world could fall apart.

Those worries could wait for tomorrow.

The cards had decreed that tonight, she could have a taste of paradise.

As soon as Joan led Maeve into her bedchamber and closed the door, she pressed her lips to hers again, sliding her arms around her neck. Her lips were full and lush and as beautiful to the touch as they were to look at. Joan felt clumsy in Maeve's arms, wanting so much but unsure what else to do than move her lips and stroke her tongue against hers.

Such a simple thing, kissing was, but it was so much more than she had ever imagined it could be. It was powerful, and wonderful, and sweet.

The only kiss she had ever received was a dry brush of Stanmere's lips at the altar. They certainly had never touched hers again, so perfunctory were his nocturnal visits.

It was with great relief that kissing Maeve banished all thought of her late husband. She had not known the peace of it in months.

"Are you sure you know what you are asking for?" Maeve asked her, her lips brushing against her ear.

"No," she admitted, touched that Maeve had asked her. "I'm not at all sure that I understand what two women can do together. But I find myself eager for tutelage."

It was a relief to confess it. She didn't want to pretend to be worldly, to be other than she was. Perhaps being a duchess had been a pretense all along, and this was who she was meant to be. Plain Joan, an ordinary woman with extraordinary desires that felt sweet and pure and loving.

There was nothing that transpired between them that could be called uncommon.

Maeve smiled. "What can happen between women is not so different as what can happen between a woman and a man, or in fact a man and another man. Lovemaking can be as simple or as complex as we choose to make it. It is a matter of exploration, of learning what pleases you, whether it is with my fingers or my mouth or anything else that you might think of."

Oh. She blinked. Maeve's mouth. *There*. That had not been anything she had ever thought of before.

"The truth is that I don't even know the words for these things. For…myself." It was difficult to even allude to what she meant, and she gestured vaguely beneath her waist.

"What do you call it?"

"My private area."

"There are other words," Maeve said. "Technical words, and lover's words, and naughty words."

"Naughty words." She liked the sound of it.

Maeve kissed her again, this time moving her hand and cupping her breast. "I assume you are well aware about breasts and nipples, though I am not yet as acquainted with yours as I would like."

Her hand felt glorious against her breast, her thumb brushing over her nipple, which puckered beneath the silk.

"Yes, I am familiar enough about them."

Maeve skimmed her hands down her waist and settled them on her hips. "It is more this area."

She swallowed. "Yes."

"We shall get there, in all due time."

Maeve undid the laces at the back of her dress and tugged the silk to the floor, then did the same with her stays and her shift until Joan stood before her unclothed. She pulled the bandeau loose from her head and let her hair fall to her shoulders.

Joan thought she would feel shy, but she didn't. There was such joy in Maeve's movements, such reverence in her eyes. It was impossible to feel anything other than perfect.

They lay on the bed together, and Joan was delighted that there was more kissing, but also touching. She learned the shape of Maeve's breasts, full and plump, by her hand and then by her mouth when she dared to kiss her ruched nipple, as pert as Maeve could be. She loved hearing Maeve's breathing speed up as she settled her body against hers, her skin smooth and warm under her touch.

"I think I am ready for more knowledge," Joan said, feeling a restless ache that she knew could not be satisfied until she had learned all she could manage tonight. "I mean, I know what I *have*, though I am unfamiliar with the words."

"Lover's words include garden," Maeve told her, the back of her hand brushing against her curls. "The sensitive spot at the top is your crown, and you have a pair of lovely nether lips."

Garden. She liked the sound of that.

"A physician would tell you that the proper words are vagina and clitoris and labia."

Joan swallowed. "And the naughty words?"

Maeve kissed her, and this time her hand slipped between her legs and Joan gasped as she stroked her. "There are many, but the one I like the best is the ace of spades." She traced her gently with one finger. "See how your body complements the name with its lovely shape?"

Joan sighed with pleasure. "You did say that spades were singularly suitable for spinsters, so I do hope that mine suits you well."

Maeve laughed. "You are a delight. Every inch of you."

She slid her fingers deep between her legs and moved them slowly until Joan began to arch her hips, the pressure inside mounting as Maeve eased a finger inside of her. Then she was lost as if swallowed up by the sea fog, emotion and sensation blurring together as her lips sought Maeve's and she grasped her shoulders for dear life, until she was shipwrecked against the pressure of Maeve's hand against her body.

When she regained enough strength, Joan nudged Maeve onto her back and began a slow exploration, kissing each rib and the hollow of her waist and the sweet curve of her hip. She thought she would feel inept when she moved her hand between her thighs, but although she lacked experience, she felt confident and powerful and deeply satisfied when she found Maeve slick with need and panting beneath her. It didn't take long for Maeve to cry out with pleasure, her hips working against Joan's at a frenzied pace.

Afterward, Joan felt as if she had walked the length and breadth of all of Inverley with how much her legs trembled.

"Is it like this every time?" she asked, stretching her neck. "I wonder how anyone can move after such activity."

"No, not every time." Maeve kissed her shoulder. "Sometimes it's sweet, and sometimes it's slow. But sometimes a powerful need overtakes you and it's fast and heated. I think it's lovely that we seem to be particularly compatible in this area."

She was so tired that she didn't even have the energy to pull up the coverlet, and instead snuggled against Maeve for warmth. "I always thought sexual activity was something that was done *to* someone," she said, closing her eyes.

"Sometimes it is, but I think it is much better when the doing is *together*."

Joan felt Maeve settle the blanket over her and drifted to sleep in her arms.

CHAPTER TWENTY

When Maeve sauntered into the breakfast parlor the next morning, Joan couldn't even attempt conversation. She fumbled her teacup as she lifted it to her lips and didn't know if it was the steam that heated her cheeks, or if it was a blush.

Intimacies in the dark had turned out to be wonderful. She had no regrets whatsoever about last night. But in the daylight, she was shocked all over again that she had indulged at all. How adventurous it felt!

And what an education she had earned.

Joan dropped the butter knife into the jam dish and then tipped the sugar over as she tried to set everything to rights, prompting a footman to rescue her from further gastronomical disaster by removing the offending dishes to the sideboard.

Maeve buttered her muffin and sliced her herring as neat as you please, as if nothing unexceptional whatsoever had happened between them the previous night. She looked well rested and content, her face dreamy as she bit into her muffin.

"I must be away to the spa now," Maeve said. "Otherwise, I think a perfect day would be spent here with you. In the library with a good novel, perhaps. Or…in other environs of the house. Doing other things."

Maeve winked and left the room in a swirl of rose perfume.

Joan stared into her teacup.

Anyone might have watched Lord Peter enter her estate yesterday afternoon. Anyone might wonder why he was visiting the widow on the hill and start to wonder if there was more to the story of the missing duchess.

Anyone might mention it to Maeve.

She had been so close to saying something last night, but fear had stopped her confession. How could she tell her now? And yet what if she found out from someone else?

Why could she not simply be *Joan*?

She took a deep breath. Maybe she could be. Maybe this was her opportunity to start her life anew.

Lord Peter would have left for London with her letter at first light, so it was entirely possible that his stay had been so short that it had gone unremarked. And the duchess was missing no more. Once the papers announced that she was found, they would move on to another story. This one was sensational enough that the specific location of where she had been found was likely of little interest.

Her name might be ruined in London, where people knew her. But no one in Inverley need ever discover the truth.

As awful as Lord Peter had been, his visit had finished the matter. The duchy had already stripped her of everything. She had dropped her suit, albeit under duress. It was a fact that would haunt her the rest of her life, but it meant that she no longer needed to worry. The worst had come to pass.

At least she still had Inverley.

She set her teacup on the saucer with a clink. There was only one more detail that she needed to know for sure.

Tilda brightened when Joan entered the parlor where they often did their sewing together. "My fingers can't abide the scissors today. Be a dear and cut a few pieces for me, Your Grace?"

Joan sat down with the scissors and dutifully snipped out a series of squares, which Tilda methodically took and wrapped with fabric and sewed together, her movements slow but steady as she passed her needle through the cambric.

"Do you like it here in Inverley?" Joan asked her.

"Why, I like it as well as anywhere. It's a very pretty spot."

"Is there anything I can arrange to make it more comfortable for you?" She watched Tilda make a fist and release her fingers a few times before she threaded her needle again, as if loosening the joints. "There are plenty of doctors in town. Miss Balfour tells me that the spa in town has many health treatments."

Tilda deserved to be treated well. She deserved to be happy.

Anyone who had lived through Stanmere's rule at Astley Park did. "I'm well enough." Tilda sewed another neat line. "I suppose I never saw myself as retiring anywhere but Shropshire."

"I am sorry that your dreams have been dashed." If Stanmere had seen fit to take away everything from her, she couldn't imagine there being a scrap of generosity for her elderly maid.

"There is nothing for me there anyhow. I was meant to grow old together with my Thomas, but he died long before you married into the family. He was the stable master, you know, and had worked decades for the family. He saw a lot of nasty work go on in those stables." She bent down and ruffled Maurice's ears. "Poor Maurice wasn't the worst of it. Not by far."

"I've never heard you speak of Thomas. What was he like?"

"Wonderful. Good man. Strong. The quiet type, the kind that gets under your skin when you're not paying attention and then they are as much a part of you as they are themselves." Her needle flew faster and faster, her shoulders hunched over as she worked. "Not many out there like my Thomas. But the good die young, and he was among the very best."

"Was it an accident?"

But Tilda wouldn't say. "Enough of the past, Your Grace. I don't like to return there much. Better to think of what lies ahead than what came before, that's what I've always thought."

"Sometimes the past catches up with us," Joan said quietly. "Lord Peter paid me a visit yesterday."

Tilda's fingers stilled. "Sarah didn't say anything to me."

"Perhaps Sarah didn't know." It was a falsehood, but Joan hoped it was small enough that she wouldn't be caught out.

The look Tilda gave her was searing. "Your Grace, there is no secret that the household cannot uncover. I suppose she meant to do me a kindness." She jabbed at the square. The hurt was clear in her voice.

"She does you credit. It was well done of her."

"I beg to differ. I'm not useless, Your Grace. You cannot spare me from any greater pain than I have already endured."

Tilda's elbow bumped the basket of fabric scraps, and they scattered across the floor, bright patchwork squares everywhere. Joan bent down and picked them up and was startled by the look on Tilda's face when she gave them back to her.

It was fear.

"It wasn't a pleasant visit." Joan looked at the unfinished quilt in Tilda's hands. It was sturdy, the paper still basted to each square and triangle and hexagon to maintain the crisp and orderly lines of the pattern. It should have been soothing to look at, but the colors were not harmonious. Burnt orange and crimson red looked like flames across a background of saltwater gray and forest green. It filled her with dread. "Lord Peter forced me to give up my petition to the Court of Chancery. I shall never have more than I do now, which I suppose means that I must learn to economize."

"Who is he to tell you to stop? You can do as you like, Your Grace." Tilda huffed as she continued her sewing.

Joan hesitated. "It sounded to me like a threat." She remembered his grip on her hand, and the deadly serious look in his eyes. *Memento mori*. "He asked me to think about Stanmere's previous wife."

Tilda's mouth trembled and her shoulders sank, and she looked ten years older in the blink of an eye. "Emily. Katherine. Louisa. Dear girls, all of the wives were. I think of them often."

"What happened to the last one?" Joan whispered.

"Louisa—oh, foolish, headstrong Louisa." She shook her head.

"Did he murder Louisa?" Her lips were numb. Was she in danger? Were they all in danger?

"Oh, don't be foolish, Your Grace."

Joan sighed in relief and put down the fabrics.

"Without a doubt, he murdered all three."

CHAPTER TWENTY-ONE

Maeve folded the salted and dried towels and put them back on the shelf for tomorrow's round of customers looking to be rubbed down after being dipped. She had learned to love her routine here, but the work continued to take its toll. Her legs were sore after hours of standing. Her back ached from the two hours that she had spent applying seaweed treatments.

Though last night's acrobatics played a role there as well.

"I will see you tomorrow, Miss Alice," she said, slipping off her smock and hanging it on the peg in the storage room where they kept their ointments and salves and tonics. She couldn't wait to return to Fairview Manor and see Joan again. Last night had been one of the best experiences of her entire life.

Miss Alice's head jerked down in a quick nod.

Maeve hesitated, her fingers still on the cotton smock. "Is anything the matter?"

"Why wouldn't it be?" Her tone was short.

"I always considered us friendly, but I feel as though things have changed of late." Miss Alice gave her the more difficult clients and never seemed inclined to talk while they scrubbed down the treatment rooms at the end of each day.

"Do you expect everyone who you consider to be your inferior to wish to be your friend?"

Maeve was shocked. "I never thought such a thing. You are by no means inferior! I thought we were much the same."

"We will *never* be the same. I have lived here forever, and my family too. We are from these shores, and this is our way of life. I don't need to be friends with someone who still thinks they are too good for it."

"I never meant to give that impression." Maeve felt shaken. "I am so sorry."

"The reason you have this position is because Mr. Williams thinks you're pretty."

That hurt. He had mentioned it when he hired her, but she knew she did a good enough job now to have earned her place here. "He also says I am good with the clients." She *knew* it was true. She loved nothing more than chatting with people during their treatments and had learned an enormous amount about absolutely everyone who came through the doors.

Miss Alice looked away. "I need this job, Miss Balfour. I need the income and my family needs it too. I can't afford for it to be taken away by a visitor in her fine silks and fancy shoes, playacting at my livelihood."

"My station in life has changed," Maeve said quietly. "I need money too these days."

"Then why don't you marry?" Miss Alice cried. "A dozen well-to-do men would make an offer with but a glance from you! You are being picky when the reality is that you are spoiled for choice."

How unfair that marriage was the sole answer anyone ever tossed her way, as if it were the simplest thing in the world. "I shall never marry."

Miss Alice shoved beside her and flung her smock across the peg. "Your choice limits the choices of others who might need this job. Married ladies whose families cannot make do. Single women waiting for a suitor and still living at home."

Maeve had never thought about other people who might have needed the position. She was silent.

Miss Alice sighed, exhaustion plain on her face. "You don't even understand anything about Inverley outside of the fashionable season. It's September. The visitors will be gone next month. Business has already tapered off and will continue to do so. Mr. Williams only ever keeps one employee through the winter months."

Maeve frowned. "I am sure he will be fair. We are both good at what we do."

"Of course he won't be fair. And you won't be either. You will take what you think is already yours." Miss Alice pushed her way out the door.

Maeve dragged her feet on the walk back to Fairview Manor, and not because her shoes pinched. Many people had reiterated to her the reasons she ought to marry, but she had never considered that her choice might affect anyone other than herself.

But how was she to earn her place in the world when there would always be others in more need?

It was a thorny question that pricked her conscience any way she looked at it.

She stopped at Arabella and Caroline's cottage, her habitual refuge. She was beset by their cats, Byron and Shelley, and their purrs comforted her.

"What if I am selfish for wanting to keep my employment at the spa?" she asked them after she told them what Miss Alice said.

"You aren't," Arabella said. "We know you. You have always been an open book to us."

Maeve cleared her throat. "If that is the case, then I have something new to read to you from my pages."

"Do tell!"

"The widow and I have become intimates." Open book she may be, but she was only willing to say so much. Joan deserved discretion.

"Oh, Maeve! A conquest!"

"It could not be further from a conquest. It truly felt like a meeting of equals." Maeve sighed. "She is different from anyone I have ever known."

Caroline grinned. "This sounds like great fun."

"It is not strictly physical desire, like most of my previous experiences. I want to hold her, and kiss her—but I also want to know her. There is something fragile about her, but also spirited. I want to *protect* her." She shook her head. "Why, I have never in my life protected anyone more than to offer them my parasol on a particularly sunny walk!"

"She sounds lovely," Arabella said.

"These developments are all very new. It may come to nothing."
God, she hoped not. She wanted it to be something wonderful between
them. Something permanent.

"You look sad at the prospect."

"Do I? I suppose I know how these things have ended for me
before. Nothing has lasted longer than a few passionate weeks. Desires
fade. People become less interesting. And less interested."

"Not always." Arabella gazed at Caroline. "Sometimes it can last
forever."

"That's what I want," Maeve said. "But we shall see what the
future holds in store for me."

The ace of diamonds that had been revealed during the game of
patience, after all, had promised courtship. Nothing more.

❖

Joan wasn't sure what would happen when she and Tilda sat down
together the next morning. Tilda had refused to speak any further after
her shocking revelation the previous day, and Joan wondered if she
would be more forthcoming today.

She didn't know if she wanted to hear more details or not.

It was a strange thing, this explosion of her former life. Her
marriage had been far from happy, but she had at least thought she
understood the basic structure of it. After all, she had *been* there. She
had lived through it. It was vastly confusing to learn that she had it all
wrong from the start.

But Tilda seemed determined to speak only of the increased price
of cambric, and of Sarah's dismal efforts to help with the piecework.
Her face lit up when Maeve entered the parlor, a cloth bag in tow.

"Is this where fine ladies of leisure do their needlework?" Maeve
asked, winking at Tilda.

"It certainly is, Miss Balfour! You are more than welcome to join
us."

Joan blinked. "I thought you were at the spa this morning?"

"I quit," Maeve announced, sitting down with a flounce and pulling
fabric from her bag. "As I have a sudden increase in my available time,
I decided to enjoy more genteel pursuits today."

"You *quit*?" Joan asked.

"Never mind Mrs. Firth," Tilda said. "She is of a mind to be nosy these days."

Joan spluttered. "Concern for my friends is not in the same category as nosiness!"

"It's quite all right, I have no secrets among my friends. I thought about it all night and decided it was the right thing to do for Miss Alice to keep her position. I had not realized that the spa would keep but one employee when business slowed."

Maeve's voice was light, but Joan's heart ached for her. Being employed had meant a great deal to her, and Joan knew it could not have been a decision that she made easily.

"The decision should have been the owner's," Tilda said. "You're a good girl. What if you were the better choice?"

"I'm not," Maeve said firmly. "Miss Alice is truly excellent at her work and has been there for years. When I tried to quit, the owner did try to talk me out of it. He wanted to keep me instead. But I told him he didn't appreciate what he had if he couldn't see Miss Alice's value, and I left."

"Very noble of you," Tilda said.

Maeve ducked her head, but Joan saw her blush. Maeve never blushed. She reached out and touched Maeve's knee. "Tilda is right. That was a kind and generous thing you did."

She shrugged. "Well, as a result I have no employment of my own now. It was the right choice, but perhaps not the wisest."

"I hope you aren't worried about room and board," Joan said, struck with shame. "You must consider yourself a guest." She should have made the offer far earlier.

Maeve bristled. "I can pay my own way."

"Circumstances have changed," Joan said softly. "Haven't they? You are my friend. Not simply a boarder."

Maeve smiled. "They have changed, haven't they?"

"Now do tell us what it is that you are working on, my dear?" Tilda asked, interest in her voice.

Maeve brightened at the question, her lap now filled with trims and swatches, a pincushion balanced on her knee. "I asked Mr. Culpepper if I could take some odds and ends that were in such poor condition that he could not sell them."

"Whatever for?"

"I have not bought a new frock in months, nor even a single ornament for my hair. I patched my stockings last week because I didn't think I should purchase a new pair when I could still wear these around the house." She stuck out her foot and the heel of her blue satin shoe slid down, revealing the clumsy darning in the silk around her ankle. "I have discovered that if I want something, I need to work to get it."

Joan nodded slowly. "And to that end, you purchased…rags?"

"I'll have you know that Mr. Culpepper gave them to me for free. They would have gone to the rag man otherwise." She studied the bag. "Some might yet go to him when I'm done, though I can also use them for my hair to curl overnight."

"But what is it that you are doing with them now?" Tilda asked.

Maeve held up a plain straw hat with a wide brim. "I cannot afford the fancy ribbons and rosettes at Mr. Jackson's general store, so I thought to retrim one of my old hats with scraps."

"That is a fine idea," Tilda declared. "You have such an eye for fashion, Miss Balfour! You are always so elegantly turned out."

"It is kind of you to say, ma'am."

They worked for a half hour together in comfort. Joan stole as many looks at Maeve as she could, her head down and the tip of her tongue peeking out most adorably as she braided strips of velvet. Maeve had slid into her life so seamlessly that it was as if she had always been here, like they had known each other for years.

Tilda admitted that she could not work any longer due to the strain on her eyes and bid them good day. "You must come back again, Miss Balfour," she said to Maeve before she left. "I will want to see that hat when it's finished."

Maeve leaned back in her chair after Tilda left. "This is a pleasant way to spend the morning."

Joan set down her embroidery. "Yes, I have been enjoying it greatly. I agree with Tilda—I am most intrigued how your hat will turn out."

Maeve twisted the velvet braid into a rosette and stuck a pin through it to hold it steady as she sewed the edges together. "I admit to being intrigued by more than our crafts."

"Oh?"

"I am intrigued by *you*."

"I have enjoyed the time we have been spending together." Joan meant so much more, but her tongue couldn't move to push the words from her mouth.

After the horror of what Lord Peter had threatened and what Tilda had revealed, this morning's routine was a balm to her soul. It was an hour that was precious in its normalcy, and she wanted to clasp the feeling to her bosom and never let it go.

She had enough of excitement. She wanted something deeper than that. Lingering looks across the breakfast table as they spoke of their plans. Kisses good night amid conversation of whether it would rain the next day. A shared life of peace and comfort, to erase her past.

It was almost absurd. They were seated a chaste distance from one another in an ordinary parlor, ordinary cups of tea steaming in front of them. And yet, an extraordinary feeling ached inside of Joan, and she knew that it ached inside of Maeve too.

It hadn't been satisfied by only one night together.

"I want to know more about you." Maeve's eyes were bright with emotion. "We live in this house together, but still I feel as if I only know pieces of you. I want more than the mystery."

"I am not mysterious." Joan stared down at her skeins of embroidery floss, and though it had always felt true, recent events were proving otherwise.

Maeve laughed. "Of course you are. You almost never speak of yourself! That is the essence of mystery. Why, I don't even know how old you are, or how long you were married, or any of the important things."

"Are they important? I thought knowing someone was more than that." Joan gazed at her. "I know you like scandal sheets and short walks and prefer quail to pigeon."

"All very true, but that doesn't make up the fullness of my life."

Joan smiled. "I know you are warm and honest and are not afraid of anything. I know you work hard and value friendship. You are beautiful, but you are more than that. You are curious and kind and you make me laugh. But I don't know the name of the town you grew up in, or what education you have, or how long ago you left Ireland. Do those things define you?"

Maeve pursed her lips. "I suppose you are right that the specifics do not matter so much as their essence. I could tell you all about myself. I hide nothing."

"I am five and twenty. I married five years ago and have been a widow for four blessed months. He was the worst thing that ever happened to me, so do forgive me for believing that neither he nor my marriage defines my life."

It didn't matter if Stanmere had been a duke or a pauper. There was truth in the words, and it lanced a wound she didn't even know could be healed.

Maeve's hands stilled, the rags twisted in her fingers. "I am sorry to hear it. I shouldn't have asked."

"You were right," Joan said softly. "He does not bear speaking of, but my experiences do."

Maeve nodded slowly. "Who we are in front of each other is more important than who we were before. I confess that my life has changed a great deal in recent months, and I suppose it must have changed me too." Her eyes shone. "I want you to know me *now*, Joan. I am my best self at this moment in time. And I want to know you too. As you are. Not as you were."

It touched her that Maeve wanted to know. No one had wanted to listen to her before, to really know her. Not her father, or her husband, or the people she thought had been her friends. They had only ever wanted to take from her. She had been a duchess to them, but not a person.

But she mattered to Maeve.

And Maeve mattered to her. More than she could have guessed she ever could when Maeve had asked her if she had a room to let.

Tears threatened her vision.

Maeve fixed a scrap of lace to the hat above the velvet and silk rosettes and wrapped a thin length of scalloped leather trim around the base. "There," she said, holding it up. "All done."

"It's lovely, Maeve! You have a real talent for this." Joan was impressed.

Maeve placed the hat on her head and went to admire it in the mirror above the mantel. "I'm pleased with it."

"You should be. You know, people would pay good money for such a hat."

Maeve looked at her reflection again. "Truly?"

"I would have bought it if it had been in the bag you sold to Mr. Culpepper."

"I have dressed all of my straw bonnets myself. I draw the limit at plaiting the straw itself, of course. My fingers could not bear the cuts from such harsh work."

"Perhaps you should consider showing Mr. Culpepper. Vast as your wardrobe has proved, you cannot sell every stitch of it. Why not make something to sell instead of selling what you already own?"

Maeve made a little hmmm, sounding pleased. "I think such a fine idea deserves a reward."

"A reward?"

"Yes, involving rather less clothing from both of us."

CHAPTER TWENTY-TWO

As Maeve led Joan to her bedchamber, she couldn't believe that she had been so lucky to have started an affair with someone so wonderful. She had been intimate with a handful of women in her past, and the encounters had been enjoyable enough that she continued to seek them where she could.

This was the first time that anyone made her feel so seen.

Joan appreciated her face and form—Maeve had caught her looking at her enough times—but she also appreciated who she *was*. She laughed at Maeve's witticisms, she encouraged her to pursue employment if she wanted to, and she praised her hat-trimming talents.

Talent.

She hadn't believed she had possessed much of it. What use was it to anyone except herself if she could restitch lace from one dress to another, or spend a morning trimming a hat? Most women could say the same of themselves, with varying degrees of success.

But the admiration in Joan's eyes when she had looked at Maeve's hat had been something lovely.

Something special.

It made her believe she could sell a thousand hats at a moment's notice, one to every inhabitant of Inverley.

And it certainly made her wish to fling every stitch of Joan's clothing to the far corners of her bedchamber and to have her way with her between the sheets.

Joan was a soft woman, sweet and perhaps a touch naive. But she wasn't weak. She was resilient, and hopeful, and kind.

And it made Maeve all the more upset whenever she thought of the injustices done to her. To not even be given the proper knowledge of her own body! Too much had been denied this woman.

Maeve didn't want to deny her anything.

Her fascination with Joan had begun the day they met in the secondhand clothing emporium, where a dress had brought them together in ways she never could have imagined.

Now she tugged that same dress off of her, the blue and white stripes falling to the floor atop the flounced petticoat and followed by her shoes and her silk stockings. Her own frock followed, and they sank into the bed together amidst kisses and caresses and murmured words that meant nothing and yet everything at the same time.

Maeve moved with leisure, determined to give Joan sensual pleasures instead of merely sexual. She skimmed her hands all over Joan's body, traced kisses across her spine and bottom, pressed herself slowly and deliberately against her sweetness as she tongued her breast. They fit together as if they had always meant to be here in this moment, giving each other delights untold.

Joan had proved herself a quick learner in the study of love. Maeve trembled at Joan's barest touch, her nipples tightening at just one look of desire from her. She had never experienced satisfaction like this, such complete abandon in another woman's arms.

But what satisfied her more than anything, even more than finding her release, was the expression on Joan's face as they made love. Her dark blue eyes were filled with joy and wonder, her soft lips a constant moue of surprise or pleasure, as if every single moment needed to be grasped to her bosom and enjoyed to its fullest.

Maeve had known desire plenty of times in her life.

But this was more than desire. It felt like they were building something with bricks as fragile as glass, each discovery about one another adding to the walls, and each new routine they established were windows and doors leading toward something glorious.

It was as unfinished as the Roman ruins, and she didn't know what it would look like when it was finished. She could only hope that nothing would happen to shatter the bricks.

Because with time, she knew that it could become a castle.

❖

Every day that passed increased Joan's fears until she thought she could take no more. She found solace at nights in Maeve's arms, distracted from the past as she indulged in the present, but worries chained her to memories and she wanted to banish them once and for all.

She needed the full history from Tilda, and she told her so when they next sat down with their sewing.

Tilda sighed. "Those old sins. He's accounted for them, Your Grace. Stanmere is dead and buried. It can all be forgotten now."

"Everyone has hidden so much from me, but you can help shed some light so that I may understand." Joan put her hand on Tilda's knee. "These things have shaped my life until I cannot make sense of it anymore."

"I was with the family for almost fifty years. There's a lot that happened."

"Anything you could tell me would be appreciated." Joan poured her a cup of tea. "Please, take your time."

Tilda settled into her chair and gazed out the window for a long while before she spoke. "I was born on the estate and started work as a housemaid at fourteen. Pleased as punch I was when Stanmere married and I became the first duchess's lady's maid, ten years after I started working for the family. My family was proud, and my future seemed bright."

"What happened?"

"Stanmere took his duty to the duchy seriously and married as soon as he came of age, hoping to fill the nursery at once and start his legacy. But Emily never conceived in the twelve years they were wed, and he grew impatient. I never had proof, of course, but I didn't like the look in his eye when he came home that day to find the west wing burning. It wasn't normal, Your Grace." She shook her head. "My Thomas tried to save her but lost his own life in the effort."

Joan felt sick. "I had no idea the depths of his evil."

"Then along came Katherine, and she had a sunny disposition. I stayed by her side the first few years as if we were sewn together. Tried never to let her out of my sight. She bore Edward—the Marquess of Chetleigh he was, from his birth—and then two daughters. Stanmere was delighted to have an heir, disappointed as he was that there were no more sons. For years, all seemed well. I struggled to adjust to life without my husband, and I didn't work the long hours I had done before." Her voice trembled. "I let my guard down and let *her* down. My attention was divided trying to raise my children in Thomas's memory."

"You are not to blame," Joan said, grasping her hand. "You did not cause any of this to happen."

"No, but I bore witness. I saw him push Katherine from the horse. I was too far away, but my screams alerted the staff. We got to her right away. Even still, it was too late." She swallowed. "He knew I saw. I never said a word about it to anybody, and yet he took his revenge."

Joan's lips were dry. "No, Tilda."

"Not me. It would have been better if it was. But he bided his time, and when my Gabby joined the household, he seduced her." She dabbed at her eyes with the cambric. "She bore him one of those illegitimate sons you saw at the estate. The eldest. Alexander. And then the second one, not long after the first. James."

"Oh, Tilda. Your own grandsons!"

"They were raised with us for a time, but Stanmere didn't want much gossip to stir, so he sent them off to London to a boy's school. I haven't seen either Alex or Jamie in years." She sounded wistful. "I would like to think them innocent. I doubt Stanmere had much to do with them, despite being obsessed with the notion of lineage, and proud of any son that he sired. Maybe my grandsons are still good lads, like they were when they were young."

"I'm sure they are." Joan's heart felt close to breaking.

"After that, I think Stanmere was greedy and careless. He always wanted more, and he set his sights next Season on a debutante with a large parcel of land. Louisa." Tilda shook her head. "Louisa was a firebrand. I miss her dearly."

Joan shuddered. "He was after her land, the way he was after mine."

"I think she found out about the children. She certainly knew about the affairs. She must have confronted him, for the marriage didn't last long. Under six months. We found her at the base of the grand staircase at Astley Park. Her family petitioned for her dowry to be returned, there being no children, of course, and they were successful."

Joan sucked in a breath. "And then I was his next attempt at the same thing."

She wished for her shawl to wrap around herself. It was cold comfort to finally know the details when they were so horrifying.

"Do you think we are in danger?" Terror seized her throat. "Is the *household* in danger? Sarah, Luke—Miss Balfour?"

"Lord Peter had the opportunity already if the duchy had wanted to take it," Tilda said. "They know where you are now. Edward isn't his father. We can't judge him on his father's sins."

But she didn't look convinced.

"What should we do?"

"There is nothing we can do. Justice cannot be served against a dead man."

"Their families should know," Joan said quietly. "Everyone should know." Her heart ached for Emily, Katherine, and Louisa. She felt a kinship to them, despite having never met them. It almost didn't seem fair that she alone had survived. "I am grateful to have escaped with my life. The jewels and furs are no matter. Chetleigh can keep them. All I want is to stay safe and protect what we have here together."

It wasn't much, her household on the hill. But by God, it was hers, and she had never been more grateful for it.

❖

Maeve entered the emporium with her newly trimmed hat in her cloth bag. She had only ever sold professionally made items to Mr. Culpepper. Fabrics that she knew were fine quality with trims that had stretched her budget. Garments that had garnered her compliments aplenty when she had worn them.

This was the first time she would try to sell something from her own handiwork, and she worried it wouldn't measure up.

"Are you in the doldrums, Miss Balfour?" Mr. Culpepper peered at her.

"A lady of fashion might cultivate an air of ennui on occasion, but I would never admit to a fit of the doldrums." She sniffed.

"Call it what you may, but I detect at least one doldrum." He leaned close. "I see it as plain as the weave of your dress."

Mr. Culpepper was rather dear to her now. She liked to watch him with customers, whom he treated with the same respect and attention as if they were in a fancy London establishment. They were all worth his time, and if a customer was dressed particularly shabbily, she noticed that he charged them far less than the usual rate.

Old ladies tottered in looking for a petticoat or a shift, taking their time perusing all the wares for the best deals. "Help me find one that needs a bit of mending," one woman announced. "Gives me something to do in the evenings as my girl is off with her man and I don't see the grandchildren until tomorrow."

Young women rushed in after working in the taverns and eating establishments that served the gentry, harried and looking for a new apron as theirs smoldered yesterday while fixing their husband's dinner on the hearth.

Fishermen came in with a briny scent clinging to their beards and clothes, fellows who had no sweethearts to mend their shirts so they dropped them off here for Mr. Culpepper's sister. She took on tailoring and mending work from her home, and Mr. Culpepper brought bundles of clothes to her each day after the shop closed.

It was a different sort of clientele compared to the general store and the spa, but Maeve liked to be part of the crowd wherever she was and couldn't help but talk with them alongside Mr. Culpepper and to help find clothing and tally up the mending until the last customer left.

"You have such a talent with people," Maeve said to him. "You have made a real meeting place here, haven't you? It isn't the clothing. You like helping *people*."

"Ah, like recognizes like. You have the gift of it yourself, don't you?" He smiled at her.

"I certainly like to talk, but I wouldn't presume to know these people the way you do, living here all your life."

"I might sell them an outer shell, but it covers up the same flesh as we all have. We're all just trying to get by, are we not? If we listen to one another and are kind to one another, then we rub along together fine."

She frowned. "I suppose. I don't much know these days where I am trying to get to." Since talking with Miss Alice, she had given the matter a lot of thought but hadn't come to much of a conclusion.

"You were born to belong somewhere altogether different, but you're not so far removed from these people."

"Am I not?"

"When your fancy threads have all been sold, and you continue to age into a spinster with no husband or family, will you not be coming here to purchase your dresses instead of selling them?"

Mr. Culpepper's smile was gentle, but she felt the truth of it like a pinch. Sliding into poverty was what she feared most since Mama had remarried, and she needed to remember that she still had to find a way to earn her coin.

"As it happens, I have something to show you." Maeve drew the hat from her bag and pushed it across the desk. "I retrimmed one of my hats, and I wanted to know if you thought you could sell them if I made more of them."

"You did this?" Surprise was clear on his face as he studied it.

"Yes, from the scraps that you gave me the other day."

He squinted at it. "I would never have guessed. Miss Balfour, I commend you. That is an ingenious way to use up clothing. I would indeed be interested in repurposing what we cannot sell and finding another way to generate income from it."

"I could trim a few a week, if you think you could sell that many. Or I could make other things. I am quick at netting reticules."

He hesitated. "In fact, I have been mulling something over, Miss Balfour. My business pursuits are growing as of late. The emporium provides a steady enough income, but my sister's mending business has seen a sharp increase this year. Enough that she has hired a woman to help her with it."

"I have little talent for mending," Maeve warned.

"No, no. There's no need for that. But it got me thinking about other services we could provide for the clients that we already have. I have been planning to open a laundering business in the vacant building next door. If people want to bring their mending here because they have no one to help with it at home, then it might be convenient for them to bring their laundry here also instead of hiring a washerwoman. I have talked to a few women who I would wish to hire, and they liked the idea well enough of being employed here while I arrange the contracts with the clients."

Maeve raised a finger. "I would like to mention that I am as poor at laundering as I am at mending."

He laughed. "What I mean to get at is that I would need someone to help me with the emporium, as I will be hard-pressed to manage the shop and to start with the new endeavor. I want to work with someone I trust, who I know would be good with the people here. Would you be interested?"

A rush of happiness had her skin shivering from her nape to her toes. "Perhaps I had been beset by doldrums, for I find this news has chased the very last of them away. I would like nothing better than to work with you, Mr. Culpepper."

Maeve looked around the emporium. She had been humbled to lose what little standing in society that she had enjoyed before Mama remarried. It had taken all this time to realize that what she had now was far richer than what she had given up. She had once only seen the dust and clutter in places like this and mourned the loss of luxuries.

But her priorities had changed. It wasn't so much the fine living that she missed, but instead it was the company and the crowds that she had enjoyed when she was part of society. Now she had the opportunity to have it every day.

Different people, but Mr. Culpepper was right—not so different in the end.

Maeve was brimming with ideas to improve the shop alongside Mr. Culpepper, but already one thing was certain. This was somewhere she could see herself belonging.

She couldn't wait to tell Joan.

Chapter Twenty-three

Joan was delighted when Maeve gave her the news about Mr. Culpepper as they strolled the garden on their daily walk. She stopped and swept Maeve into a wild hug, holding her tight.

Maeve buried her nose in her hair and then kissed her cheek. "You've never held me outside before." Her voice held a trace of wonder.

"And now I regret every missed opportunity, because you feel every bit as wonderful here as you do indoors." She rested her head on her shoulder. "Oh, Maeve. I am so proud of you. This is perfect for you."

They resumed their walk, linking arms. Now that the air had a brisk chill to it in the afternoons, Joan appreciated how closely they walked together. Maeve had pushed a thick wool walking dress at her before they had left, telling her that she might as well give it to her directly. "It's too cold these days for silk," Maeve had scolded her. "You'll catch your death."

Joan hadn't liked the phrasing, but she did appreciate the warmth of Maeve's dress against her skin.

Maeve squeezed her arm as they walked past the holly bush. "These past few months have been lucky for me. I am grateful to have found employment." She hesitated. "And even more grateful that I have found you."

Her words warmed Joan more than the wool. "Then we are in perfect accord. I love the routines we have established, and our evenings at home have been some of the happiest of my life." Time was precious, and it was important to seize happiness where one could find it. "You deserve this opportunity. And we deserve to enjoy these moments together."

Maeve's eyes were watery. "I am not the sort to cry," she said. "But I suppose there are always exceptions in one's life." She slid her arms around Joan again. "So much has changed in my life. They are good changes. Necessary ones. But I fear they have quite overwhelmed me."

Joan drew a handkerchief from her pocket and offered it to her.

Maeve wiped at her eyes. "Your handkerchief carries the scent of your perfume," she said. "It is all the cheering up I need."

Joan laughed. "I shall have to remember it the next time you are in need of comfort. I could carry a vial with me wherever I go."

Maeve's smile was brilliant though her eyes were still reddened. "I should like nothing more than to know that you will be there for me next time, too."

Joan wondered if emotions were as easy to catch as a cold, for she found her own eyes welling up. She wanted to be there for Maeve. She wanted to be the one to hold her.

Always.

In the space of the time it took for them to complete their two turns around the garden, everything had fallen into place, clear and simple.

"We need to celebrate your good fortune," Joan announced.

"I do like to celebrate," Maeve said. "Those are cheering words."

"We shall host a dinner party. I would be delighted if you invite Miss Seton and Miss Reeve. And Mr. Culpepper and his family, too."

Maeve's face shone. "I would like nothing better."

"The numbers will be off and we ladies shall greatly outnumber the men, so it won't be as formal as I might like."

"If you plan it, then I am sure it will all be quite perfect."

Joan had entertained no one for months, and she knew that Maeve must realize that this was a significant choice for her. There was not much that she still believed in from her years as a duchess, but the importance of dining with one's associates was a practice that she thought held merit no matter one's social standing. Business deals were best sealed through such invitations.

She was determined to give the Culpeppers a good dinner and good entertainment, as best as she could manage. For Maeve's sake.

She would do anything for her.

But what she really wanted was to tell Maeve the truth.

There would be time enough to explain everything after the dinner party. After all, Maeve deserved to celebrate her new opportunity and bask in the attention of her friends without being distracted by the horrors in Joan's history.

Until now, Joan hadn't planned on telling anyone in Inverley that she was the missing Duchess of Stanmere, hoping to start a fresh life now that her past was truly behind her. Her relationship with Maeve was a beautiful thing that had emerged from a time of upheaval in both of their lives. She would never forget that they had learned to embrace each other for who they were now, and not who they had once been.

But Maeve deserved someone who could share her whole life with her. Not only her present and her future, but her past.

If she wanted any kind of future with Maeve, she needed to have honesty between them.

Because if she were being fully honest with herself, she was falling in love.

❖

Maeve dressed with care the evening of the dinner party. Her gown was pink satin with a sheer white gauze overskirt, and her bodice and sleeves were edged with a deep white lace flounce. She had sold most of her evening dresses, having fewer occasions for which to wear them, and it was a pleasure to dress her finest.

It touched her that Joan had gone to such trouble to arrange the party. Cook had even shown her the marzipan for dessert that had been shaped into a replica of Fairview Manor itself. It was a remarkable effort.

How wonderful it was to feel so cared for! She felt Joan's affection in the way she looked at her, and the way she held her, and the way she loved her through the nights. But tonight felt different. Although they walked arm in arm outside and sat perilously close together in the parlor of an evening, this party felt like a more public display of affection.

It changed things.

No one would recognize the evening as momentous except for themselves, and that made it all the more special. A secret affection between them was all that Maeve could hope for, after all, and she well understood the importance of keeping their affair discreet.

"Welcome to Fairview Manor." When the grandfather clock struck six o'clock and their guests began to arrive, Joan was at the top of the steps with a halo of light shining down on her from the candles in the chandeliers. She was resplendent in a black velvet gown that showed an appreciable amount of decolletage, sapphires dangling from her ears, her hair swept up in an array of pinned curls. She wore a thin black ribbon around her throat, with the tiniest picot lace edging in white. Even if all she owned was mourning, she had told Maeve earlier that evening, she wanted to wear her own clothing tonight, with her mother's earrings.

Joan had blossomed in the past few days since announcing her intention to host a dinner party. She spoke with more confidence and brimmed with excitement. It was understandable if she wanted to lay claim to her own clothes the way she seemed to be embracing a new life with this party. It was exactly how Maeve would have felt herself.

Arabella and Caroline arrived first, in muslin gowns that had seen better days and which Maeve had seen them wear to countless engagements over the past two years of friendship. It warmed her heart to see them arrive hand in hand, opinion be damned. Above all, it was nice to finally welcome them to the place where she lived.

The place where she considered home.

The person she shared that home with.

She swept them into a quick hug, then stepped back. "Mrs. Firth, may I present to you Miss Arabella Seton and Miss Caroline Reeve?"

"Otherwise known to me as your dearest friends in Inverley," Joan said with a warm smile at them. "I am so pleased to make your acquaintanceship."

"You have a lovely home," Arabella said, gazing at the furnishings with great interest. "I appreciate the opportunity to see it from the inside. I am a watercolor artist and have painted your house dozens of times from the bluffs on the opposite side of town."

"Have you!" Joan sounded delighted. "You simply must paint one for me to hang here in the hall."

Mr. Culpepper arrived soon after with his father, Culpepper Sr., and his youngest sister, Miss Diane.

Culpepper Sr. was an older gentleman with brilliantly white hair and a face wizened with wrinkles, and who walked with a wooden cane.

He beamed at them. "It was well worth the long hike my rapscallion son insisted on to come here. A quartet of charming young ladies to greet us? Fortune smiles on us."

"I shall arrange for my carriage to bring you home, sir," Joan said. "I would not have you tired out on our account for anything."

"Oh no, it's good exercise and I have strong legs." He tapped his cane on the ground. "Just need a bit of help for balance. Plenty of life in me yet."

Maeve wondered if he might be a good match for Tilda, who had the same attitude. She caught Joan's eye and saw a knowing look there that told her they had understood the same thing.

This harmony with another person was heaven.

Joan ushered them into the drawing room and a footman poured wine while the ladies plied their fans.

"It is such a pleasure to be invited out," Miss Diane said. She had dark blond hair and shared the same brown eyes as her brother.

"It is a delight to be among new friends," Maeve said.

Culpepper Sr. nudged his son. "There is nothing like friendship turning into courtship."

Mr. Culpepper laughed. "You know I am a devoted bachelor, Father. Miss Balfour has graciously agreed to become my business partner, not my wife."

"Please pay him no heed," Miss Diane said to Maeve. "Matrimony is a subject dear to his heart, and Frederick and I are sore disappointments to him by remaining unwed."

Culpepper Sr. twinkled at her as he sat down. "If my son shall not do his part, then may I pay court to you fair ladies myself?"

Maeve sat across from him in an armchair. "I am as devoted a spinster as Mr. Culpepper is a bachelor, I am afraid."

"We are enjoying our spinsterhood as well," Caroline said to Mr. Culpepper. "Leading apes into hell with a sprightly step, if I may say so myself."

"She does have an energetic turn during a quadrille," Arabella agreed.

"Ah! Young people have no fear of the future." Culpepper Sr. shook his head. "When you've got knees that ache with the tides and a back sore from working your whole life, you may yet change your minds. It's no bad thing to have a helpmeet."

Maeve stilled. A helpmeet. Was it possible for her and Joan? Could happiness be theirs to hold for more than a season? She tried to imagine twenty or thirty years into the future. Would they still be here strolling the garden in their fifties? Would Joan still think her fashionable when her hair had grayed and her step was slower than ever?

Maeve watched her move among their guests, as gracious as any fine lady in her attentions to their comfort. She knew she would find Joan as fascinating at fifty as she did tonight.

Dinner was a feast. Cook had gone to a great deal of trouble to prepare course after course of fish, beef, meat pasties, and buttery vegetables. Maeve took a bite of mackerel with mint and sipped her wine and could almost imagine herself transported to the finest establishments of London.

She could lose herself in memories of years past, when she had enjoyed such dinners without much thought. Or she could focus her attention on the present company and enjoy each moment of friendship and partnership and companionship, amid people she loved.

Love.

Oh, God.

Her throat felt tight, and she gulped her wine.

"Come, we are boring Miss Balfour with our talk of politics," Culpepper Sr. cried.

"I am hardly bored," Maeve insisted, hoping no one had noticed her mind wander. "My mother taught me that boredom cannot exist with a curious mind, and mine is curious indeed."

"What are you most curious about?" Miss Diane asked.

"The future," she said quietly, and looked over at Joan.

Joan raised her wineglass. "To the future! Tonight we celebrate Miss Balfour and Mr. Culpepper's joining together in business. May you both be prosperous."

There was a general hubbub of congratulations, and Maeve let the moment wash over her, lost in a bubble of joy.

There was a commotion from the entryway, raised voices audible from down the length of the hallway.

"Are you expecting more guests?" Caroline asked.

"I am not." Joan's voice shook, and the color faded from her cheeks at an alarming rate.

Maeve got to her feet and murmured to the footman to fetch Sarah and the smelling salts. She stood beside Joan and squeezed her shoulder, not daring to do more in front of their guests, but needing to touch her. To comfort her. To reassure her, even if it was only through a look, that she was here for her. She would help Joan handle whatever she was afraid of.

The sound of heavy boots and the clack of heeled shoes echoed down the hallway, getting louder and louder.

"Are we too late for dinner?"

A man and woman appeared in the doorway.

The man was in his early twenties, his hair fashionably tousled and his starched collar almost reaching his ears.

"How rude to start without us!" the woman cried. She was in her forties and clad in a beautiful black crepe dress.

Maeve stilled. Mourning attire. Like Joan's.

"What are you doing here, Chetleigh?" Joan asked, her voice low. She remained sitting, glaring up at them both.

He sighed. "Chetleigh? Do not forget that I am the Duke of Stanmere."

The collective gasp was sharp as gunshot.

He raised a brow at them. "Did she not tell you?"

Joan rose, her shoulders back and her chin up. "It is true," she said. "And I am the missing duchess."

CHAPTER TWENTY-FOUR

A duchess.

Maeve couldn't breathe.

Her Joan was a sea captain's widow. She could not possibly be the Duchess of Stanmere.

And yet, she looked positively regal in her black velvet, and the look on her face could have belonged to a queen.

Caroline and Arabella were whispering to each other. The Culpeppers looked mystified. Her stomach churned. This was not how the evening was supposed to end.

"I asked you what is your business here," Joan said, her voice cold and unfamiliar.

He shrugged. "Any duke worth his salt ought to inspect his holdings." He prodded the back of one of the chairs, tilting it on one leg as he examined it, then let it drop back down with a thud. "Do finish your dinner. Or would you prefer to withdraw to the drawing room to catch up over a snifter?"

Mr. Culpepper rose. "It appears you have some pressing family business to take care of, Your Grace," he said to Joan. "I am much obliged to you for your hospitality, but it might be best if we took our leave."

"I understand." Her eyes were glassy as she looked around the room. "Thank you all for coming to Fairview Manor. It was a pleasure to have you with us tonight."

Even under duress, she spoke calmly.

Just as Maeve imagined a duchess should. She felt a little glow of pride in her heart. She was reeling in shock and could make neither head nor tails of the situation, but one thing was clear. Joan was a rare woman to retain her dignity and composure in such a moment.

Caroline and Arabella hesitated, looking at Maeve. She nodded at them. Joan was right, it was best if the party disbanded for the night. She would stay and get to the bottom of the mystery at last.

"You must leave with them, Miss Balfour." The hardness in Joan's voice returned.

"I don't understand your meaning."

"Leave." Her eyes were cruel as she looked at Maeve from the crown of her head to her pink evening shoes without a hint of familiarity. "You might deign to dine with a duchess for an evening, but I would never stoop to have such commoners stay a moment longer than necessary."

"Finally, it is good to hear some common sense from you!" The fashionable lady waved them away. "Farewell, all."

Maeve struggled to breathe through the pain. "I am not common," she managed to say.

"You are mistaken to think you are anything but."

Then Joan turned away from her and poured wine for the two new guests.

She had thought Joan afraid of these two. But clearly all she had feared had been the threat of discovery from those she had dallied with below her rank.

She felt sick. Had she truly thought herself in love with this woman? Who *was* she?

Arabella grabbed her arm. "Let us be gone from this place," she whispered, and though Maeve would have never even considered abandoning Mrs. Joan Firth to the company of strangers, she had no qualms about leaving the icy Duchess of Stanmere.

She stumbled her way after Arabella and Caroline and found it easier to breathe in the crisp October air where the Culpeppers waited for them outside.

"Those are strange goings on," Mr. Culpepper said to her with a frown. "There's something deuced odd about that house."

Maeve shivered. "It wasn't always like that."

Joan's face had been terrible to behold. Maeve was accustomed to seeing affection and warmth in her eyes, and kindness in her smile. To see her stripped of all emotion was shocking.

Did the Joan that she fell in love with exist at all?

Miss Diane grasped her hand. "You shall stay with us for as long as you need to," she declared. "We have plenty of room and would be happy to have you."

"It is generous of you, and I am grateful. Thank you." She knew Arabella and Caroline would have made the same offer in an instant despite the fullness of their cottage, and the warmth of their friendship seeped into her bones.

At least she could rely on them. Good honest people, who had helped her adjust to her new life after her mother's remarriage without a sneer for her lowered social standing. She had thought the same of Joan, and yet had watched her turn her back the instant that a duke came calling.

Her allegiance to rank must be of greater importance than anything.

Why had the duchess been missing in the first place if she was so quick to return to the family's fold? What did these past few months mean to Joan? Now Maeve would never understand the mystery surrounding her. The difference now was that she no longer cared.

The shock and hurt of tonight's revelations crowded every inch of space inside herself, leaving little room for anything else.

She lagged behind her friends in the dark, with but a single lantern between them as it was all they had time to beg of the butler before they had departed. They walked Arabella and Caroline to their cottage, and then Maeve and the Culpeppers continued to the center of town where most of the professionals of Inverley lived.

Their townhouse was nothing as grand as the manor, but Maeve was glad enough of a bedchamber of her own and a grate to fill with hot coals to stave off the worst of the night's chill. She stripped to her shift before climbing beneath the covers, wishing for nothing more than her worn flannel night wrapper to bundle herself in as she cried herself to sleep.

❖

Joan led Chetleigh and Lady Mary into the library for the sole reason that it was a room she had not spent much time in. She didn't want their presence to taint the spaces in this house that she had learned to love, that held such precious memories of Tilda and Sarah and Maeve.

Oh, Maeve.

Joan's heart had cracked at the agony on Maeve's face when she had told her to leave. It had taken all of her resources to steel herself into cruelty toward the woman she loved, but there had been no choice. It had been the only way she could make sure that Maeve was away from here tonight.

Out of danger.

Because after Lord Peter's visit and Tilda's confessions, Joan didn't know what Chetleigh was capable of. If there was any chance that the duke could stoop to murder, she had to keep Maeve clear of it. Even if it meant that Joan was still in danger.

Chetleigh sat behind the oak desk as if he were lord and master of the manor. Lady Mary perched on the edge of a leather armchair, her full skirts artfully arranged in a cascade. She snapped open her lace fan and plied it, but it didn't hide the malice in her smile.

Joan stood by the window, uncaring that the draught was strong enough to move the drapes. It was nothing to compare to the chill in her heart. "I did what Lord Peter demanded. I dropped my petition to the Court of Chancery to sue for my rightful dowry. So why are you here? Fairview Manor cannot be so interesting as to merit a social call from London."

"No?" Chetleigh cocked his head. "I would have thought the wine cellar, added onto the house ten years ago and carved into the sandstone, would be of some interest. Or the widow's walk, twice as long as standard. Inverley may well become the next craze in resort towns. How fortuitous it would be to have a manor here."

Joan saw pinpricks of light for a moment. She forced herself to steady her breathing, gripping the windowsill to help compose herself. How did Chetleigh know these details? She herself had not known the provenance of the wine cellar. "I do not recall giving Lord Peter a tour when he was here."

"Oh, there are other ways to get information. On the pretense of wishing a house to be built, Uncle Peter found the architect and visited his offices in London. He was happy to show him blueprints of his work, including this one."

The notion that the duchy knew the layout of her house and the location of every room deepened her unease. "I meant that my house cannot be of much interest to you, specifically."

"That is where you would be wrong on both accounts. The first is that the house is not yours. And the second is the matter of my interests. Seven bedchambers and four parlors may not be grand, but it has enough stature to be worth my time."

"And the location!" Lady Mary sighed. "What an ideal part of the country for a charming house party. I cannot wait until next summer."

"This house is not part of the dukedom." She forced the words out past numb lips. "I purchased it. The manor is mine."

Chetleigh's smile was as patronizing as it had been when the will had been read, as if he were a tutor with all the patience in the world for a particularly inattentive student. "And with what money did you purchase it, Your Grace?"

"My father gifted me with the money."

"And once you were given that money, you bought this property?"

"Yes."

"Then it could not be clearer. Any money or property that came to you during your marriage automatically belonged to your husband. You were two halves of the same coin, with that coin quite naturally falling into his own coffer."

"But the deed has my name on it, and Stanmere didn't even know about the house."

"It does not matter. Anything you owned was his. So this house then became part of the estate upon my father's death. And as he left all of his holdings to me, it is now mine." He glanced around the room. "It needs a refresh, but it's fine enough land."

"A gift is given free and clear!" she cried, no longer able to keep in her emotion. "Fairview Manor is not yours. You will have noticed that there was no mention of it in the will, and I assure you that you shall not find any transaction detailing its purchase in any documents that Stanmere kept."

"Any unlisted property was mentioned in the all and sundry terminology. But I suppose you didn't learn much about legal matters from your governess, did you?"

She felt sick. He was determined to ruin her life for his gains, when he already had a princely fortune and a king's ransom in land.

"This is not right. This is my house." Without it, she truly had nothing left.

"I do wonder where it was that you left the deed?" Chetleigh tapped his chin.

She whirled around and with trembling hands pried open the safe hidden in the globe near the desk.

But the safe was empty.

From his smirk, Chetleigh had already known it.

Lord Peter. He had been with her the whole time during his visit, but he had brought three footmen with him. She had thought the reason merely his sense of self-importance, but his servants must have taken the deed while he had distracted her with threats.

"You have stolen it."

"It is not theft when it rightfully belongs to the duchy. Uncle Peter took back what was already ours."

Lady Mary laughed. "How very entertaining! I am glad I accompanied you to Inverley instead of staying in London."

"I thought we were friends." Joan looked her in the eye. "I held you in the greatest esteem."

Lady Mary sniffed. "My brother had the most pedestrian of tastes in women. You are as insipid as the other wives were. Do not disguise shopping and theatre for friendship when they are merely pastimes."

"I imagined you to have more integrity."

"You never had an opinion of your own that we didn't feed to you. Why, I used to remark to my husband all the time that it seemed you never had a moment's original thought in your life."

Joan had opinions now. Plenty of them. "That is better than having nothing in my head but vitriol, Lady Mary."

"The sea air has changed you." She tilted her head, considering her. "You are feistier than you once were. A small improvement, but improvement nonetheless."

"I am not concerned about her personality," Chetleigh said to Lady Mary. "This has never been personal. It's a matter of business."

"If this is some perverse business deal, then why do I not have a chance to bargain?"

"Because it is men's business," Chetleigh said. "Because it is a simple matter of the law. The fact that it negatively impacts you is unfortunate for you, but has nothing to do with me being the beneficiary. If you wish to be provided for, find a husband and his money can sustain you instead of mine."

"It has been an awfully long trip," Lady Mary said, yawning behind her fan. "I would appreciate if we could end this tedious conversation and retire for the evening."

"There are plenty of rooms at the Crown." Joan glared at her.

"Where is your sense of family, Your Grace?"

"I could ask the same of you, Lady Mary."

Chetleigh stood. "We shall not be leaving. Your butler assured me that rooms were being readied for us."

Joan watched them leave the library, Lady Mary's lily perfume lingering in the air.

Fairview Manor had intimidated her when she moved in. But over time, it had become home. It was where she wanted to build a future with Maeve, if Maeve could only forgive her.

Joan slept poorly that night. It was difficult to rest when her bedchamber and sitting room were full of guests, the doors barricaded with furniture. Maurice snored by the fireplace, Tilda and Sarah were sleeping on the sofas in the sitting room, and Luke was sprawled in an armchair.

She had insisted that they gather together tonight, terrified to leave any of them out of her sight after the tales Tilda had told her.

Joan hated that there were enemies in her house. She hated that she even had enemies. She had never asked for any of this.

One way or another, she would find a way to keep this house. She would make sure that she had a future. She would survive.

Duchy be damned.

CHAPTER TWENTY-FIVE

Your Mrs. Firth is a duchess." Caroline shook her head. "This is all rather unbelievable. It is as if you have stepped right into the pages of the scandal rags yourself."

Arabella sighed. "Imagine falling in love with a duchess!"

"I am not in love," Maeve snapped. "Not anymore. And there is nothing so wonderful about the rank when it is the ruin of everything I have wanted."

They were on the beach, bundled in warm sweaters and thick socks. Maeve had borrowed mittens from Arabella and was consequently upset because she couldn't grasp her glass. The wine bottle that Caroline had insisted that they bring with them was stuck firm in the sand, and a fire crackled and snapped in front of them.

Despite the fire, it was cold, and the breeze from the ocean whipped at their hair. The waves were loud as the tide came in, lapping at the shore. Dusk was falling, the sky darkening fast in the late afternoon. Within the glow of the fire and the circle of her friends, Maeve felt safe enough to fall apart.

"What if I don't even know her name?" Maeve whispered.

Arabella unstoppered the bottle and handed it to her. "Here, this is easier than holding the glass. Drink up, and cheer up. This is cause for celebration."

She drank, the wine soothing her throat. "How?"

"Because nothing fundamental has changed. When Caroline inherited a fortune, she was the same as she always was. We fell in love when I was poor and she was rich, and it didn't matter one whit."

"Forgive me, but Caroline's fortune paled in comparison to that of a dukedom's. You know the gossip about the Duchess of Stanmere as well as I do. Her family has come to take her away with them to London, I am sure of it. The papers said over and over again how much the family loves her and misses her." She drank from the bottle again. "And yet why has she never spoken of them? Why did she leave them in the first place?"

It was one thing to learn that Joan was a duchess, and it was yet more shocking that she was *this* duchess. The *missing* duchess. If the stories were to believed, she was a scandalous adulterer with multiple children.

Maeve frowned. That part didn't hold water. Joan had understood so little of lovemaking. It couldn't have been an act. And she couldn't have made up what she had said about her husband. The duke must have been an absolute brute for her to flee.

But what parts were true, and what were lies? How was Maeve to know?

"It is mysterious," Caroline said. "But running won't help you understand anything more clearly."

"What other option do I have? Joan clearly wished to keep things secret. She sent me away and called me common." The word stuck in her throat. "Even if not everything in the papers is true, it's clear that she resumed her life as a duchess the instant that she saw the duke, like she was an actress on Drury Lane. You all are witnesses to the change in her. She was not the same person at the end of last night as she had been at the beginning. These past months must have paled in comparison to her real life."

All of their strolls, the laughter on the piano bench, the flash of needles as they sewed, the game of patience. Lovemaking until dawn. Images tumbled through her mind like the patchwork pieces of Tilda's quilt, sharp and stiff with their paper backing—though once the sting had eased with the passage of time, the memories would one day be soft enough to hold around oneself for comfort.

Like her night wrapper.

But if all she had were remnants, it meant that she had been left alone again, the same as when Mama had left her behind to start a new life.

Maeve moved closer to the fire, seeking anything to warm her.

"I know you are suffering," Arabella said, her hand on her shoulder. Warmth of a different kind, and much appreciated. "I am so angry that she hurt you. But I don't think she meant to."

Maeve laughed. "Not meant to! I should hate to see her try to do so, if that was the result of inadvertent success. Besides, you cannot possibly fathom to understand her motives. We do not know this woman. At least, I never did." The flames blurred in front of her eyes, and she wiped away tears with her mittens.

All of their talk about knowing each other in the present had been idle chatter. Maybe Joan had convinced herself that she fancied a commoner's life for a summer, but the truth was out. What they had was too fragile to withstand Joan's return to the nobility.

"I think you need to talk to her again," Arabella said softly.

Maeve sighed. "Of all of us, you have always had the kindest heart. I know it is hard for you to assign sinister motives to anyone. But some people do not deserve the benefit of the doubt."

"But aren't you still curious about the mystery?"

"That is a low blow, Caroline." She glared at her. "You know that I will ache with curiosity until my dying day."

"Then maybe Arabella is right and you need to find out more." Caroline held up a hand when Maeve started to splutter. "I am not saying that you must rekindle your love for her and throw yourself at her feet. But you must return to the house for your belongings, right? Perhaps you can talk with her then."

Maeve took another drink of wine. "Mr. Culpepper can help me with clothing."

"You will never mend a broken heart by hiding in the shop."

"Maybe she's already on her way to London, and I cannot return to the manor anyway."

But the idea made her want to howl with rage. Joan belonged here, to Inverley.

To her.

She wiped her tears away again. "Tomorrow," she promised with a sigh. "I will go to the manor tomorrow to see her. To find out why."

"Or you could find out now."

Maeve turned and saw Joan, her hair wild and tangled beneath her bonnet, her cheeks red and her lips parted. Her chest rose and fell as if she had been running. Maurice barked with joy when he saw Maeve.

"I will answer anything you want to know."

Maeve's heart soared. "You're here."

Her foolish heart didn't want to remember that Joan was a duchess, that she hadn't been honest. All she wanted was to rush into her arms, to kiss her until they both lost all sense of time.

"I'm here." Joan stood outside of the ring of light and warmth from the fire, her eyes anxious.

Caroline tugged Arabella to her feet. "We are decidedly de trop, Your Grace." She dropped a curtsy nowhere near low enough for a duchess, and one of the cracks in Maeve's heart mended when she realized that Caroline meant it as a show of support. No matter what events transpired with Joan, her friends would be there waiting for her. She *belonged*.

"Do excuse us," Arabella said, and took Caroline's hand as they walked toward their cottage.

Maeve didn't know what to say once they were alone. A hundred questions warred for priority in her mind, a thousand emotions raced through her heart. The sound of the waves almost drowned out her thoughts. "We're near the ocean," she blurted out. "You are afraid of the ocean." It was the least of her concerns, but she was so shocked that it came tumbling out of her.

"I don't think I ever really will like it. I am a creature who craves safety and security, and there is none of that on the shore." Joan took a step toward her, the firelight dancing on the folds of her skirts.

Maeve's skirts, once upon a time. It was the wool gown she had insisted Joan wear now that the weather had turned cooler. Joan had thrown off her mourning once more, it seemed.

Was it a sign?

Maeve didn't want to guess at anything anymore. She wanted answers, not more questions between them. Maybe a dress was sometimes simply a dress.

It grew darker and colder as the fire started to burn down to embers, but Maeve didn't want to move. They had nowhere to go. No house to return to anymore. No life to resume together. If all they had was this evening on the beach, as the faintest stars began to glow in the heavens, then she would try and stay out here forever.

"I know where safety and security are for me—with you." Joan's hands twisted in her skirts. "I am so sorry for what I said last night. Those were hateful words."

"I certainly didn't like hearing them."

"I was afraid of the duke and what he might do." Her brow creased. "My husband conspired to take everything from me and has cheated me out of my dowry. His son is continuing the family tradition by taking over Fairview Manor. They made up those lies about adultery so that if I challenged them, the law would be prejudiced against me and the court would be justified in ruling against my petition. Then they forced me to drop my suit against them." She paused. "I know this might sound unbelievable, but Tilda also thinks my husband murdered his three previous wives."

Maeve gasped. "Murder!"

In all her wildest imaginings, she had not realized that Joan had been in grave danger.

"I had to make sure you and your friends left immediately. I still do not know how much Chetleigh takes after his father."

"You wanted to protect me." Maeve touched her hand to her throat. "That is the most romantic thing I have ever heard."

"Because I love you," Joan said with dignity, her chin in the air. "I love you, Maeve Balfour, and I would do anything to save you from harm. I am a bad bargain. I have powerful enemies. Right now, I have no house and very little fortune."

"But I love you anyway." Maeve flung her arms around her. "Even if the world has turned upside down, I will love you."

"Will you?" Joan pulled back, concern on her face. "Are you certain? This is no trivial matter."

"Yes. Because I love you the way you are, for who you are, and for what we have become together."

Her feelings could not be expressed properly by more words, so she took Joan's face in her mittened hands and kissed her, the scent of violets mixing with woodsmoke and the salt in the air. This moment was everything. It was fire and ice, it was desire and tenderness, it was calm and adventure. It was all that they had built together, her castle of dreams completed at last.

Tonight she had pulled the ace of hearts. Whatever came ahead, she had already won. She had the heart of the one that she loved best.

"I want a future together," Maeve said after they broke apart. "I know it might look unusual to outsiders, but I want to live with you and take care of you and love you for the rest of my days."

"That's what I want too." Joan reached up and kissed her again until she was breathless. "No matter where we are, I want it to be together."

"I take back what I said earlier," Maeve said. "About you trying to save my life being the most romantic thing."

"Oh?" Joan's mouth went small. "I'm not sure how much further one can go for another person."

"It was indeed romantic," Maeve assured her, "and I would be greatly appreciative if you did the same again in a similar situation. But I would love you even if you only spared me the pain of a spider bite. Our real romance has been our everyday moments. Those are what I ache to return to. Watching you add sugar to your tea. Admiring the play of light on your hair. Sitting beside you and laughing as we play the chords incorrectly for Mozart. There is no greater romance that I can imagine than a life shared in perfectly ordinary moments with you and you alone."

"I never meant to be dishonest." Joan gazed into her eyes. "Anything I kept from you was out of ignorance of my own situation, or fear of what might come. I don't want to feel that way anymore." She pressed Maeve's hand to her breast. "I want to feel more of this. The peace. The bliss. The safety that has been here all along, between us. All of those moments we spent together were real and meant the world to me. There has always been honesty in my affections."

"I know," Maeve said. "I know now that you were as honest at every turn as you could be. I would have done the same thing in your situation, to keep my loved ones safe from harm."

Joan blinked, looking up at the sky. "Is it beginning to snow?"

Small white snowflakes were falling on the beach, glittering in the dying firelight, and Maeve smiled. "You see? Even a simple thing like a snowflake is beauty beyond measure when I am with you. How pretty they are, dancing from the sky! I see the whole wide world in your eyes when you look at them."

"No, sweetheart. That's when I look at *you*."

Joan kissed her again as snow fell on their eyelashes and noses, melting on Maeve's spencer and Joan's shawl, whirling around their hair in the wind. Maurice barked in excitement, trying to catch the flakes, and they broke apart in laughter.

"Lovely though they are, I suppose that is a sign that our evening is over."

Joan smiled. "It can always begin anew somewhere else."

"Surely it is not safe to return to Fairview Manor?"

"Oh no. I am no longer living there. Chetleigh forced us out after breakfast. He stood there like a warden in my bedchamber, making sure I didn't take more than a carpet bag with a few clothes in it. He insists that everything else is his property."

"He sounds perfectly dreadful."

"Any negative thing you could possibly think of him is a vast understatement." She dug into the pocket of her dress. "Which reminds me that I meant to get rid of this at the first opportunity." She held up a large carved brooch, and Maeve could see there was a lock of hair in it. "I mean to rid myself forever of ghosts, and this is primary among them. A bequest from the duke."

"What do you plan to do with it?"

"The ocean can have it." Joan whirled away from the fire, striding out of the light and toward the shore with Maurice on her heels.

"Do be careful! The tides are high, and you will freeze if seawater gets into your boots." Maeve scrambled after her.

It was dark, but Joan nimbly climbed up a rock and looked out to sea. "It's as dreadful from this vantage point as any other. What horrors do you think lie beneath the waves?" But instead of fear, she sounded fascinated.

"Be careful of your footing. It's slippery." Maeve stood on the sand beside the rock, and raised her arm up so that Joan might reach out and steady herself. "I imagine there are countless ships and sea beasts down there."

"I shall add one more beast to the briny depths." She threw the brooch as far as she could, launching it into the ocean, then hopped down from the rocks. "I feel a great deal better. Let us leave now, and perhaps I shall be brave enough one day to face the sea in the daylight."

Maeve shoveled sand onto the fire like Caroline had taught her to prevent any chance of the fire from spreading. With the shovel in one hand, she picked up the bottle of wine with her other one. "Where are you staying if not in the manor?"

"The King's Anchor. It's not as nice as the Crown, but it suits us well enough."

"Us?"

"Sarah and Tilda and Luke. And Maurice, of course. I have to pay extra to keep a dog in the room, but I cannot leave him and refuse to let him stay in the stables where he might be ill-treated. He means the world to me."

They started to walk back to the cottage.

"How are you able to afford it if you left under such duress?"

"Your five guineas a month," Joan said with pride. "I kept them in the drawer with my shifts and scooped everything into my carpet bag with no one the wiser. The hotel is twelve shillings a night for all of us, even with breakfast. We have plenty for the month if we need it."

Maeve was delighted. "I am so glad that it has been useful."

Maeve returned the shovel and the bottle of wine to Caroline and told them that she would be off to the King's Anchor tonight.

She and Joan had much to catch up on.

CHAPTER TWENTY-SIX

Once they entered the rented room at the King's Anchor, Maurice curled up in front of the fire with a contented sigh and settled into sleep. Joan frowned down at him and nudged him gently. "Come on, Maurice." She snapped her fingers, and he followed her into the hall, where she knocked on Sarah's door and asked if she would take Maurice for the night.

Joan wanted all of her attention on Maeve tonight.

"The room is not much to offer you." It was clean and tidy, with just enough space for an iron-framed bed, one armchair, a dresser, and the fireplace. "It's not quite the seven bedchambers and four parlors that I previously entertained you in."

"To call a spade a spade, you only entertained me in several of those rooms," Maeve said with a laugh. "And when entertaining with a certain spade, we limited ourselves to but two of the bedchambers."

"Maeve!"

"We are in private here, and can speak as we wish, can we not? Anyway, I am not fussy about my lodgings. I am only fussy about my women." Maeve kissed Joan. "This woman in particular."

Joan felt boneless, her head tipping back as Maeve kissed her throat. She unwrapped her from her shawl and ran her hands over Joan's hips.

"My lover has turned out to be a duchess. Should I humble myself on my knees?"

Joan shook her head. "Of course not."

"I wouldn't mind," she said softly, her eyes gleaming in the firelight. Her tongue touched her bottom lip and Joan felt a jolt of awareness between her thighs. "Your Grace."

It was as if every illicit thought that she had ever had burned through her mind like wildfire. Joan didn't know what came over her, but the way Maeve looked at her made her feel like a queen. Her eyes were uncharacteristically serious, burning into hers with an intensity that lit her body afire.

"I do not like the title. Not between us."

"I could call you anything you like." Maeve's voice was quiet, hardly above a whisper.

"Call me darling, or sweetheart, or anything you please—for what pleases you must surely please me too." She smiled. "As long as I am always your Joan."

"My sweet Joan."

An alarming thrill raced through her as Maeve sank to her knees on the carpet. She slid Joan's shoe from her foot and cupped her hand around her stockinged arch. The warmth felt wonderful. She pressed her thumb into the arch of her foot and Joan bit back a sigh of pleasure.

Maeve nudged her to sit on the bed and she settled between her open knees. She slid her skirt and petticoat up to gather around her waist and ran her hands up Joan's calves and brushed the sensitive part behind her knee.

"You're so beautiful," she murmured, her breath teasing Joan's skin. "Rosy in the firelight." She kissed her inner thigh. "I am so glad that you are mine."

Maeve moved her hand up her leg and over her hip before slipping it between her thighs. Joan bit back a moan. She was more than ready for her pleasure, shifting on the bed to allow easier access as Maeve touched her gently, easing her finger inside.

Then Maeve pressed her lips to Joan's center and gave her the most intimate kiss she could imagine.

Joan had known what she was about to do, and yet in no way did it prepare her for the sensation that rocked through her. It was lightning and thunder all in one, soft and yet fierce, with a blazing heat.

"Maeve," she gasped.

Maeve drew back and looked up at her. Oh, but she was a vision, her own face flushed with pleasure, her green eyes expressive with her desire, her lips damp with the moisture from Joan's own body. She felt something deep inside clench.

"Are you overcome?" Maeve asked gently, her hands on Joan's trembling thighs, soothing her. "If it's too much for you, we can always try something else. It's not everyone's preference."

"I liked it," she managed to say. "I was merely surprised."

A slow smile spread across her face. "I like surprising you."

She kissed her again, and Joan ached inside as Maeve's lips moved across her most sensitive parts. She was so careful with her, handling her like she was precious. Delicate. Loved.

When Maeve's tongue tasted her, Joan writhed and twisted her hands in Maeve's dark curls, her breathing coming in short gasps as every inch of her felt the fire spreading in waves, until she came apart under her mouth. Her body shuddered, and then she collapsed, falling backward with her arms above her head.

Maeve pulled down her skirts and curled up beside her. "I enjoyed that greatly." She kissed the top of Joan's head.

"You are wonderful," Joan said after she regained her senses. "I never thought we could do such a thing with our clothing on."

"There is so much to explore with regards to such activities. I confess to looking forward to each journey we take together."

"When each trip ends in such paradise, you shall find me always to be a much appreciative traveler." She trailed her hand over Maeve's hip. "And I will never leave you behind."

Joan kissed Maeve, a little shocked to discover her own scent on Maeve's mouth, and she reached beneath Maeve's beribboned cotton petticoat to find her ready. She moved on top of Maeve, their skirts swirling together around them as she straddled her hips, both of them bared to the waist. "I once heard a naughty joke that I did not fully understand," she said softly, adjusting herself so that her hand had easier access to Maeve's center. "It was about a gentleman riding a lady, and it was quite coarse so I won't repeat it in its entirety."

Maeve caught her lip with her teeth. "You are welcome to tell me any naughty jokes you may have heard. Though I am surprised that you know any, with how few words you possessed for such things."

"Well, I did not know it was naughty until this very minute when I have pieced it all together. I am better equipped to understand such things now." She stroked a finger inside of Maeve as she pressed her body forward, and Maeve's hips bucked beneath her. "This is rather like riding, isn't it?"

She thrust again, settling into a rhythm. The palm of her hand brushed against Maeve's clitoris, and she felt Maeve twisting underneath her, urging her on, her face wild with need, until she arched her back and cried out and grew limp in her arms.

"It was exactly what one would mean by riding," Maeve said drowsily, "though there are several ways to do it."

Joan settled beside her. "Oh?"

Maeve curled against her, resting her arm on her hip. "One can do such a thing from behind, for example."

"Oh!" That sounded naughty indeed.

"There are also items one can purchase that can facilitate the process, if you would like to think about it. I've never tried such a thing myself, but I have met women who have enjoyed it exceedingly."

Joan cocked her head. "Items?"

"I am not so knowledgeable about them, but there are apparatuses that one can use instead of a finger. Leather, I believe."

She wasn't sure she wanted to try such a thing, but the idea was fascinating. "Where on earth would one procure such a thing?"

Maeve shrugged. "I think they could be found easily enough in London. Perhaps we shall save the idea for our next trip to the capital, whenever that may be."

Joan felt a little flutter in her belly. Next time. She would never get tired of hearing such words from Maeve. The idea that there would be today, and then tomorrow, and then every day after that.

❖

The breakfast served at the hotel was surprisingly serviceable, though Joan had to hand over an extra shilling to pay for Maeve's share. Crowded together around a small table, they all agreed that the weather was lovely for October, and they were glad that the snow had not lasted more than a half hour the previous evening, and wasn't there something ever so comforting about eggs and toast and nice strong tea when one was in an unfamiliar setting?

"Now that we are done with pleasantries," Joan said, pushing away her plate, "we must speak of plans."

"Are we going back to Astley Park?" Sarah asked, looking worried.

"No, pet, we shall never return," Tilda said.

"But however will we survive? We don't know anyone here."

That had been her own fault. Joan had never thought of the wider repercussions of hiding away the entire household, but her fears had limited all of their opportunities. She stared into her teacup. How had she been so short-sighted?

"I know people," Maeve said. "The winter will be quiet, but there will be choices when the visitors return in the summer. I can introduce you wherever you wish to work. And if you are looking to stay in service, I know plenty of people who frequented the spa who I could ask."

"I'd like to work with horses," Luke declared. "Nothing better!"

"There are not so many people with horses and carriages in Inverley," Maeve admitted. "But the horses that pull the dipping machines out into the water must be driven and cared for. And there are men who walk donkeys up and down the beach, hiring them out for riding."

"I could make do with that." He snagged a crumb of Cheshire cheese. "I think I will like staying in Inverley."

"What about you?" Maeve asked Joan. "What are your thoughts for what you want?"

I want you, she thought, and by the way Maeve smiled, she knew that she had understood the look in her eyes. "I want Fairview Manor."

"Of course you do. We all do. But it's done." Tilda shook her head. "You have to move on."

"I most certainly do not."

Maeve stared at her. "Whatever do you mean?"

"I am going to take back what's mine." Her jaw was firm. "My jewels. The deed. Anything I can get."

Maeve clasped her hand. "Although I am in favor of you getting anything you want, let's talk this through somewhere a little less public so that no one calls the magistrate."

They left the King's Anchor for the Culpeppers' townhouse, where they found a warm welcome and another pot of tea at the ready. Leaving behind her anonymity was a difficult thing for Joan to become accustomed to, but she was heartened that the Culpeppers treated her no differently except to call her Your Grace on occasion instead of Mrs. Firth.

"Chetleigh won't anticipate me going to London. He will assume me stuck here with no way out, with very little funds." She sat up straight. "Even if he thought I had enough coin, he would doubt I have enough spine."

"But you do," Maeve said. "You have plenty of courage in you." Her reassurance was all Joan needed to believe it.

"If you don't have enough money, I would be happy to give it to you," said Mr. Culpepper.

Joan was touched. "That is a kind offer for an acquaintanceship that has lasted the length of a single dinner without even being served dessert."

"The entertainment of the evening was more incendiary than I thought it would be," he said. "But until then, it was a most enjoyable night."

Tilda frowned. "I don't like the idea of you going to London, Your Grace. It isn't safe."

"Chetleigh and Lady Mary are here, and Lord Peter and Lord Paul have their own estates to tend to. Stanmere's daughters are never in London at this time of year. Besides, I won't go alone," Joan promised. "Miss Balfour will be with me."

"I'll drive the carriage," Luke said. "Always wanted to do that."

"I can arrange to borrow a carriage and horses from a neighbor," Mr. Culpepper said. "He will be glad enough for someone else to exercise the horses for a few days."

Tilda huffed. "Well, if this plan is going ahead, then I will have you know that I am not too old to be of service. Don't forget that I know the Hanover Square townhouse backward and forward. I know all the staff. I can get us in without anyone being the wiser."

"I'm not too old yet either! I can be a lookout," Culpepper Sr. piped up.

"Father, think of your back," Miss Diane said as she poured him a fresh cup of tea.

"We're not lifting anything heavier than the deed to the house," Culpepper Sr. said, holding his hands up. "A paltry piece of paper is all we need." He grinned at her. "I won't even lift that, as I'll be too busy knocking any rapscallions down." He lunged forward into a credible parry as if he held a fencing spear instead of a wooden cane.

"Hanover Square!" Maeve leaned back in her chair, shaking her head. "I never thought I would see the day that I would ever take breath in such rarified air."

"This is no casual task," Joan said quietly. "I would be remiss if I did not warn you all of the real danger we will be facing. The Astley family is well connected. The Stanmere dukedom is one of the richest and most powerful in the kingdom. My late husband likely murdered people for his own gain, and his son has shown every sign of being as capable. I want the deed back to show the Astleys that I will not back down anymore, but none of you need to take this grave risk with me."

"I will stand with you," Maeve said.

Tilda and Luke agreed.

"To prevent harm from befalling another is well worth the risk," Culpepper Sr. said. "We shall stop for the night before London, then we nip into the city to fetch the deed and be back in a blink. I used to do the same all the time, except I was fetching yarns and fabrics back to Inverley in my days as a weaver. I never did any thieving." He grinned. "Even in a life as long as mine, there is always something new to look forward to."

"You may take any clothes you need from the emporium if you wish for a disguise," Mr. Culpepper offered.

Someday Joan would wear her own clothes again. Not from her duchess days, or from her brief mourning period. Not anything of Maeve's, and not secondhand dresses. Other people always had an opinion on what she should wear. Her mother had chosen all of her debutante fashions, and Lady Mary had steered her toward colors and patterns and styles that she declared suited Joan.

She had followed where others had led.

At this point her life had changed so much that she didn't even know what fashions she might prefer when she had the luxury of choosing such things for herself, but it was lovely to think about having something made for her from her own decision and according to her own preference. Something fresh to begin her new life with.

Joan looked at Maeve, laughing with Culpepper Sr. and Miss Diane. Perhaps clothing didn't matter so much after all. As long as Maeve was beside her, she could be happy wearing a flour sack.

Joan smiled to herself. Of course, Maeve would have an opinion on *that* as a sartorial choice. But as long as the sack came off each night, Joan didn't think she would complain all that much.

It was wondrous that amidst the turmoil of Chetleigh's deception, she could still find a thread of hope and a yard of happiness. Maeve had helped steady her in the worst of times.

After all this was over, Joan wanted nothing more than to spend the rest of her life trying to be good to her woman.

Maeve was worth every effort.

CHAPTER TWENTY-SEVEN

If the sense of urgency hadn't been so great, Maeve thought she might have enjoyed the trip to London. Culpepper Sr. was a delightful traveling companion and filled the time with interesting tales of Inverley through the decades. From the way Tilda looked at him, it appeared she thought so as well. It warmed Maeve's heart that Tilda might find love after decades of mourning her Thomas.

They stopped for the night in Swanley, a few hours from London, and paid for two nights of accommodations. It would be an easy drive into the capital the next morning, and they should be done with their mission and back by the next evening.

If all went well.

Joan had been quiet during the trip, though Maeve couldn't blame her. Tomorrow would be frightening even with the best of outcomes. After all, they were preparing to break the law and defy a dukedom.

She would wager that none of them had ever dreamt of doing anything half so illicit in their life.

Maeve had never considered herself vengeful, but she had never encountered a situation like this before. It would all be worth it for Joan to have what was rightfully hers.

It still angered her to think of the things that had been denied Joan in her life. She had lived a life of untold luxury in so many ways, and yet at what cost? She had never been taught the words for her own body, had never been told to think for herself, and had been taken advantage of at each turn. The men in her life had seen her as a pawn to use as a means to further their own gains. How many other women were likewise being raised in ignorance and obedience?

They made love that night in a bed that creaked and groaned, under coverlets that smelled less than fresh, and atop pillows with more lumps in them than not. But what mattered was not what was around them, but what was between them.

Love. Patience. Comfort. Security. Maeve tried to convey it with every touch and every stroke, every sigh and murmur. She was slow, and thorough, wrenching cry after cry from Joan until they both lay panting and sated.

But hours later, before the dawn, Maeve woke up and discovered her duchess was missing once more. Her heart pounded in her chest, and she shot out of bed, hands trembling as she dressed faster than she ever had in her life. Taking stock of the room, she could see everything was accounted for—their carpet bags still on the table—their hairbrushes on the dresser—then saw Joan's reticule was gone, and so was the dress she had thrown over the chair yesterday.

Had Chetleigh found them?

Had the duke somehow persuaded Joan to leave?

Maeve grabbed a brass candlestick holder and wrenched the door open, stumbling her way down the stairs. She would find them, by God. No one would take Joan from her. No one would harm one hair on her head. No one—

But no one was with Joan when Maeve found her.

She was sitting by herself in the corner of the darkened front parlor of the inn, her chin propped on her hand. She was fully dressed, including her bonnet, with her reticule on her lap.

"You scared me half to death!" Maeve exclaimed, setting the candlestick holder down.

Joan looked at it, her brow creased. "You took a candle but did not light it?"

"It wasn't for lighting the way, my sweet Joan. It was for smashing Chetleigh's head in if he had dared appear here."

"Good Lord! He isn't here, is he?"

"No, but when I discovered you missing, I didn't know what to think."

She sighed. "I came down to talk to the night porter and find out when the mail coach passes through Swanley to London. It should be here in a quarter hour, before the clock strikes five."

"Ah." Maeve was quiet for a moment. "You thought to go alone, then."

"I want this so much. But it's my battle to fight, and my life to win or lose."

Joan's hands trembled as she clutched her reticule. There were dark shadows under her eyes from her poor sleep, and a crease across her brow. Maeve's heart ached for her. She had endured so much, and still wanted to think of others to prevent any harm to them.

"I want to be in this with you. I love you, Joan. Being together with you makes me feel whole. It would be sad to think that you wanted to shoulder this burden alone when you are surrounded by people who would help carry it."

"But it isn't their burden in the first place. I should never have brought anyone else into this. Tilda, Culpepper. You." Her voice broke, and she covered her face with her hands. "This was a terrible plan, because I have never planned anything properly in my life! It always goes awry."

Maeve drew her into her arms. "You planned to go to Inverley. You planned to protect yourself and your household from harm by masquerading as a captain's widow. You planned to protect me when the duke came to Inverley. I think your plans have had a high success rate."

"They felt terrifying when I was executing them."

"And so does this. That's good news, is it not? Your terror did not conjure the things you feared to pass."

"But they happened anyway," Joan pointed out. "Otherwise we would not be in Swanley and you would not have come down here before the sunrise, brandishing a candlestick holder."

"But nothing has come to pass because of your plans or lack of them, or because of your fears of the outcomes. All of this is happening because you are dealing with a horrible person who deserves to have a bit of sauce for the gander when we take back the deed."

"You are too casual about this!" Joan cried. "I do not think you comprehend the danger. What if we fail? What if I have placed the lives of those I love in jeopardy?"

Maeve held her tighter. "I do not mean to make light of the situation. Of course you are scared, and you have good reason to be. What I cannot comprehend is how you survived being married to such a terrible man for five long years. But I think our odds today are good. There is risk, but it should be minimal with Chetleigh still in Inverley."

The mail coach rumbled up to the inn, the wheels crunching on the gravel.

"Do you still want to go?" Maeve asked. "Because if you do, I will follow. I will stay with you today wherever you venture, until your fears have all been laid to rest."

Joan gazed out the window. From the light of the lantern hanging outside, they could see the driver ushering people into the coach, cheerful and loud.

"No," Joan said. "I will wait for our friends. I wish I could think of a way to resolve this without involving them, but our chances of success are best if we are together."

"No one forced us to go to London. We all volunteered. This is what friends do, Joan."

"None of the friends from my past ever did anything like this for me."

"With all due respect, I don't think anyone in your past life was a friend to you at all."

"That may well be the truth." Joan rested her head against her shoulder. "Why do you make so much sense before dawn? It is a specialty of yours."

"I like to think I make sense at all hours of the day, but there is something special about this hour that inspires naked honesty, isn't there? Come, let us lie in bed for another hour before we must leave. We will need all the rest we can get."

Joan followed her back up the stairs and Maeve tucked them both into bed.

Today was going to be an important one.

Despite her reassurances to Joan, Maeve hoped they were not headed straight into disaster.

❖

London was as cold and dreary as Joan's memories of it had become. Once they had been vibrant, for she had spent years enjoying what the city had to offer a young wealthy person of excellent breeding and high social standing. Whether she was attending court or the theatre or a private ball, the evenings had been pleasant and the company amiable. She had felt among friends everywhere she turned.

The city had seemed gilded, filled with people shimmering their way through life in pursuit of pleasure. Her memories now turned her friends into an indistinct crowd, unfamiliar to her though she hadn't been away for long. The years blurred together, for though they had been lovely when she wasn't with her husband, they had also been insignificant.

Even the Thames, twining its way through the city, orderly and stately, had lost its dignity. She was so far removed from her past that after the warmth of familiarity had faded, she saw the dirt and grime of the city streets, and the debris that floated in the river.

When they arrived at Hanover Square, Tilda led them to the servant's entry. She wandered off to talk to the housekeeper, as they had planned. She would distract the household with her return, knowing that her welcome would include copious amounts of tea and cake and all the news from the housemaids about who had a beau and who had a child and all the goings on that she had missed over the months. Everyone in the household loved Tilda and would be delighted to see her again.

Culpepper Sr. remained outside to stand guard, declaring himself to be as inconspicuous as could be. An older gentleman strolling up and down the street on his daily walk would garner little interest or attention.

Joan and Maeve slipped through the empty hallway to the study. In the end, Joan hadn't bothered with a disguise. There was no use denying who she was to the staff, who would recognize her in an instant no matter what her dress looked like. Joan could only hope that Tilda could hold their attention as long as possible.

It was strange to invade a building that she had once called home. Joan had walked this hallway countless times over the years, without a single thought to any detail in it. Now she was aware of the click her shoes made on the white marble tiles, and the ornate framed mirrors along the wall that reflected her and Maeve, beaconing out their presence to anyone who glanced their way.

The study was a small room at the end of the house, with windows along the south wall and bookshelves lining the north. A desk took up a significant part of the room, and the rest was filled with a pair of leather armchairs and a curiosity cabinet that Joan had already warned Maeve not to look at, recalling several unpleasant items that Stanmere had kept on display.

"I heartily dislike being back here." The memory of her husband was strong enough that he could have been in the room beside her, for Chetleigh had changed nothing. She stood motionless until Maeve tugged at her hand.

"Remember our mission," she urged her. "We haven't much time."

"Yes, of course." But it was harder than she thought it would be to concentrate. "There is a safe in the master bedchamber where the deed might be. But although I think I know which painting the safe is behind, I would not know the first thing about cracking it."

"We shall look here first and come up with another plan if we don't find the deed in this room," Maeve said. "But I have confidence in you. You have sound judgment. You decided to look here for a reason."

It filled her with resounding joy that Maeve believed in her. She took a deep breath. "What we need are the ledgers. The Bow Street Runner said there was no proof of anything regarding my dowry, but he would not have had access to the duke's ledgers. I want to see for myself if there is anything that could prove that my lands are profitable. Then I intend to pursue my suit again. Chetleigh cannot continue to cow everyone in his path. It isn't right."

Maeve perused the shelves, then selected a thick book. "This section seems to have what we're looking for," she said after she flipped through a few pages. She sat at the desk so she could start combing through them for the right year. "While I look through the books, you look for the deed." She licked her finger and started flipping pages.

Joan turned her attention to the desk, searching through the papers stacked inside the drawers. "I think Papa must have felt guilty about what he did to me. The Bow Street Runner had told me that Papa was paid for his complicity in what happened with my dowry, and that was the year that he gave me the money that I used to buy the manor. I think he was trying to give me something of my own, knowing I would have nothing in the end."

Joan had been heartbroken when she had thought that Papa had betrayed her and conspired to leave her with nothing. He had treated her like a child her whole life, even when she was a woman grown and married, but he had been indulgent and affectionate and there had never been a cross word between them.

She had loved him. And she found that she loved him still, despite the pain that he had caused.

All of them had their choices to make. Whether or not he had been coerced into signing the papers that had led to the land's enclosure, in addition to receiving the money, she would never know. But his gift had not been insignificant, and he could have used that money in any way he pleased.

He had chosen to give it to her.

"Nothing is enough to repay what was stolen from you. But at least his gift has returned dividends, in that Fairview Manor will be enough for you to live in comfort," Maeve said quietly. "It was a far greater kindness than your husband ever showed you."

"That's the best way of looking at things," she said. "The past is the past. But I can embrace what Papa gave me, for Inverley has given me everything that I love."

She could be content there for the rest of her days.

But first they must find the deed.

There was no clock in the room, but as Joan worked her way through all the drawers and Maeve started flipping through the second book, she realized more than a half hour must have passed already. Sweat gathered on her brow.

"We aren't going to find it," she said, slumping into one of the armchairs. "It's over, Maeve."

Maeve kept turning pages. "We can't give up now!"

She had gathered her friends here to face danger for nothing. Joan rose and shook Maeve's shoulder. "Come, we must be away. We cannot count on Tilda to distract the staff for much longer."

Maeve sighed and closed the book. "I'm so sorry, sweetheart. I wanted so much to find it for you."

Joan took the book to replace it on the shelf, and a slip of paper fell out as she moved it.

Neither of them moved.

"That's it," Joan said in a hushed voice. "That's—that's the deed."

Maeve scooped it up and flattened it on the desk to study it further. "You're right. You found it!" She flung her arms around Joan, squeezing her. "You did it. I knew you would."

"I didn't do anything," she said in a daze. "It appeared as if out of the air."

"Stuff and nonsense. It shook loose as you moved it. I saw it clear as day. You found it."

Even without the proof in the ledger, it was important to Joan that she take possession of the deed. She had never looked at it before and was relieved that her name was plainly written there on the paper. Her land agent had bought the house on behalf of Joan, Duchess of Stanmere. There was no mention of the duke, or her father.

Fairview Manor was hers.

"Thank God," she breathed. "Now let us leave this place behind us."

But as they turned to go, Joan saw that the door was already open. And standing there was Chetleigh.

CHAPTER TWENTY-EIGHT

W hat are you doing in my house?" Chetleigh asked. He stood square in the doorway, blocking any possible exit.

Maeve wondered if it would be possible to heave a book through the window and escape that way. She thought they could run fast enough to where the carriage waited for them. Or perhaps with the two of them, they could tackle him and scramble out of the main doors.

Joan brandished the deed. "I am taking back what is rightfully mine. I am here to claim my dowry and to fight for my house."

Maeve thought a better idea might have been to try to tuck the deed down her bodice, but Joan's eyes were full of fire.

If only she had that candlestick holder from the inn. But if needs must, she could always heave a book at him instead of the window.

"You agreed to drop the suit for the dowry, and I can always simply take the deed back again. Really, Your Grace, you are not very good at subterfuge."

"She doesn't have to be." Tilda stood behind him, her arms folded across her chest. "Subterfuge is the Astley way of working." She nodded at Joan. "Culpepper raised the alarm."

Chetleigh sighed. "Even if you keep the deed, the lawyers will set things to rights. A wife's property belongs to her husband, and thus reverts to me as the heir."

"But if the funds came from my father, and my husband did not even know about the house, I think there is a case here. I intend to pursue it."

"This is for the lawyers to argue over, but I think you will lose."

"Why are you doing this, Edward?" Tilda asked. Her gentle tone surprised Maeve. "You don't have to be the man your father was."

Anger flashed in his eyes. "I want to be every inch the man he was."

Maeve moved closer to Joan. She radiated fury, her nostrils flaring and her hands clenched around the deed. She put a hand on her back, and her touch seemed to calm her. They were in this together, come what may.

Tilda sat in one of the armchairs. She was so calm that Maeve wouldn't have been surprised if she had pulled out her sewing basket and started quilting then and there. "I know the Astleys always put pressure on their children. But you were a good boy. Remember the jam tarts you used to make with Cook, and how you and the other children on the estate would run around the garden maze? You remember my Gabby, don't you? You used to play together as children."

"Of course I remember Gabby." Chetleigh was a little flushed, as if embarrassed at having his dignity reduced by admitting that he had once been a child.

"Your father took advantage of housemaids like my Gabby," she said flatly. "That is the kind of man he was."

His face twisted. "Housemaids are disposable. They are a dime a dozen."

"That is my daughter you are talking about. Your childhood friend. She was not disposable. She was my family. You can make better choices than your father did."

Chetleigh collapsed into the chair beside Tilda. "I want something magnificent to pass on to my own sons, once I have them. And the dukedom is only magnificent if it's intact, the way it has been passed down for generations. It's my duty to continue it. The money from that dowry helps keep the fortunes of the rest of the duchy intact."

"This obsession with perfecting the family legacy is poisoning your family. The sins of the father don't have to multiply in the son."

"Father always said it was business first."

"If it's business, then the deal died with your father. You never struck any such deal with Joan's father. You can honor your father and still let this go, because this has become vengeance. Let Joan live her life, Your Grace. It is nothing to you. I know there's a good man inside of you. I remember the boy that you were." Tilda rose and nodded at

Maeve and Joan. "You don't even have to do anything, except let us leave."

He glared up at her. "And if I don't?"

"You will," Tilda said, and her whole body drooped. "For I have not yet told you the worst of it. You know how your father conspired with Joan's regarding her dowry. You know about his illegitimate sons. But I do not think he ever told you anything about his wives."

"Why would he?" His brows raised.

"There is no easy way to say this. But you remember your mother, Katherine, don't you? The way she sang you to sleep and helped you count each star in the sky so you would fall asleep? I was her lady's maid. I was there for everything. I saw the love you had for her."

"She was my mother. Of course I loved her." He looked puzzled.

"Stanmere murdered her."

"Murder?" He recoiled. "You are sorely mistaken."

"I saw it," Tilda said, as gently as she could. "I was there for *everything*. The bad with the good. That's how it is with service, and I prided myself on providing my best."

Chetleigh sank deeper into the armchair. He pulled at his starched collar, freeing his neck from the constraints of his cravat. "I cannot believe it. I do not believe it."

But from the pallor of his face, he did believe it.

"We will take our leave now, Your Grace," Tilda said. "Let this be over now."

He waved them off. "This is more trouble than it's worth," he said, his voice raspy and exhausted. "Sue the dukedom. Take the deed. I do not care anymore." He closed his eyes.

They did not wait for him to repeat himself and fled down the hallway.

❖

In the tap room at Swanley, Culpepper Sr. insisted on ordering champagne and oysters for all of them. "I knew we could do it!" he crowed. "That was a fine adventure."

Joan pulled him into a tight embrace and kissed his cheek. "You were wonderful, Culpepper. You warned Tilda at the right moment."

He popped the cork and passed round champagne flutes.

Adventure hadn't been the word that Joan would have used. Nightmare would have been her choice.

For nightmares ended with the morning, and she could think of no brighter dawn than the one on the lawns of Fairview Manor. Hers at last, for good.

The champagne fizzed on her tongue. Joan patted her pocket to reassure her that she still carried the deed, satisfied when she heard it rustle. She may not have been able to take any of the jewels that Stanmere had given her, but the manor was the crown among them. Besides, she didn't want any more memories of Stanmere in her home. She was content to leave them behind her in London, for a future Duchess of Stanmere to flaunt.

She wanted a simpler life.

A peaceful life.

And against all odds, she was going to get it.

Maeve grinned. "You were all magnificent."

"You truly were," Joan said. "And I cannot thank you all enough for what you have done. You are true friends. I will never be able to make it up to you, but I will spend my life trying." Her heart felt as if it would burst from gratitude.

"Should we return to London tomorrow and find you a new lawyer?" Maeve asked. "I know you won't want to return to your previous firm, as they were the ones who told Chetleigh where you were."

"I don't think I need a lawyer after all," she said thoughtfully. She took an oyster and sucked it neatly out of its shell.

"You cannot mean to petition the Court of Chancery yourself?"

"I mean I don't think I'm going to sue anyone. All I really need is Fairview Manor, and I have the deed. Chetleigh won't argue for it again. He doesn't have the heart."

"But you cannot mean to let him win and keep the dowry, after all that!" Tilda was aghast. "If the Bow Street Runner saw with his own eyes that your land is being used for profit, then we can use that to our advantage at court. You can win, Your Grace!"

"Not pursuing the suit does not mean that I am letting him win." Joan sipped her champagne. "Chetleigh looked to be a tortured man, torn between love and duty, wanting nothing more than to fulfill the legacy that he was raised to idolize. When I think of continuing to chase for my jewels and for my property, I feel like I was consumed by greed to have wanted them so badly."

"It isn't greed to want what is fair," Culpepper Sr. said.

"But what is fair?" She had done a considerable amount of thinking in the carriage ride from London, trying to make sense of her past and her present so that she might make the right choices for her future.

"Your father paid the dowry, and your husband stole the profits. It seems a simple matter in this situation to determine who was right, and who was wrong."

"I thought so too," she said. "But right and wrong have turned out to be more complicated than I realized."

Maeve put her hand on her shoulder. "What are you thinking?"

"I cannot stop thinking about Stanmere's sons." Joan thought back to the will reading, and the Chesterfield crowded with unruly boys. "His illegitimate sons. Two of them are your own grandchildren, Tilda."

Tilda drew herself up. "They are indeed. Alex and Jamie. And the duke was not their only parent. My Gabby mothered them, for as long as she could before they were taken away from her. She loved those boys." Her voice broke, and Culpepper Sr. patted her hand. "I could not believe my eyes when I saw them from a distance on the estate. They were little lads when last I saw them."

"Stanmere may have been obsessed with his lineage, but they have their mother's blood in them, and yours too, Tilda. I don't know who the mother of the other boys is, but I saw housemaid after housemaid leave Astley Park after mere months of service. Those children must have nothing to their name other than what Stanmere settled on them."

"I would assume so."

"My feelings are clear on the matter. I have all that I have ever wanted in Fairview Manor, and it is greedy of me to wish for more, all because I had expected to have it. What makes me more deserving than they are? If all of the money from the enclosed land of my dowry is going to the upkeep of those boys, then I shall not challenge it. They did not ask to be brought into this world, after all. What is fair to them in all of this? If I take up my suit up again to the Court of Chancery and win, then they are the losers, not the Astleys. The duchy is worth a fortune, but they will not see a pittance of any of the wealth that the family has hoarded for the legitimate generations."

"That is a wonderful idea," Maeve said, and her smile warmed Joan's heart.

Joan turned to Tilda. "You deserve far, far more than you ever got from the Astleys. Your grandchildren deserve to be well taken care of, and if I cannot give you a cottage to retire in, then I am proud to give what I can in honor of your lineage and your legacy. If there is any grace in this world, then they will take after you instead of the Astleys."

Tilda took a gulp of wine and wiped her eyes. "I would like to think that Alex and Jamie are fine lads and will do well with the opportunities that have been given to them. Imagine, my grandsons with an Oxford education!" She sounded awed.

Culpepper Sr. bowed to Joan. "Very commendable, Your Grace." He kissed Tilda's hand. "You were magnificent as well. A credit to your years of ducal service."

"Ah, but I never served the duchy," Tilda said. "I only ever served the wives."

"You served us well," Joan said softly. "All four of us. I know Emily, Katherine, and Louisa must have been as grateful for your help and support as I have been."

"I will always have regrets." Tilda stared out the window. "There were times I failed them, and it will never rest easy with me."

"From what I can tell, you did your best," Culpepper Sr. said. "One's best isn't always what's needed in the moment, and sometimes we stumble. But stumbling doesn't mean we didn't try."

"That is a kind sentiment," Tilda told him. "You are a kind man."

Joan nodded. "You never failed me, Tilda."

"It is true, my dear. I didn't fail with *you*. Not when it mattered." She patted Joan's hand. "My nerves didn't fail me either."

"I know, and I appreciate you being here today. It was terrifying to confront Chetleigh like that. You were wonderful. I don't think he ever would have listened to me, but you stayed calm and you helped him to understand the truth of the situation. Thank you, from the bottom of my heart."

"Oh, today." Tilda blinked. "No, I didn't fail today either."

Joan stared at her. Did she mean....?

But Tilda merely smiled and looked serene.

CHAPTER TWENTY-NINE

"I have always been curious about the widow's walk," Maeve said at breakfast.

They had been back in Inverley for a week and settled back into their routines. Maeve had never been happier in her life as she and Mr. Culpepper began planning for the future of the emporium, and as she and Joan spent each evening together. Simply being together was satisfying beyond measure. Maeve didn't think she needed anything else to keep her happy.

Joan set her teacup down. "That is an easy enough curiosity to satisfy. I have never been past the third floor, let alone the fourth."

The housekeeper had the key to the roof, and they went up to explore after luncheon.

The November sun was not warm, but it was bright. It was windy atop the roof, and their hair was lifted and tousled in the breeze. The walkway was narrow, hardly wide enough for the two of them, and it went the length of the roof. A sturdy wrought iron railing ran along all four sides of the walk, decorated with swirled balusters that mimicked the undulating waves.

Maeve peeked over the side. The widow's walk was at the tallest point of the manor, and she could see the spindles and spires and trelliswork that decorated the rest of the roof.

"We are very high up," Joan said, looking up. "I think I could almost touch the sky."

Maeve rested her hands on the railing, glad that it was there so she could steady herself in the wind. "I can see why it is named Fairview."

The vantage point, four stories high, offered a spectacular prospect of all of Inverley. The ocean glittered in the sunlight, and the town spread before them in a series of twisting lanes and avenues, the bright white townhouses rented out to visitors contrasting with the old brick of the business sector where the emporium was. The bluffs across town, where Arabella had done her watercolors of the manor, were tall and craggy, the grass brown and patchy now that it was approaching winter.

"It is beautiful."

"It doesn't distress you?"

Joan smiled. "I think I have come to terms with the ocean. I can see that it is behaving itself admirably today and I can pay it no mind. When it throws a tantrum in poor weather like an unruly child, I shall wait inside while it composes itself again. Everything in nature has its rhythm, after all, and if I am to live here, then I must accept the ocean's vagaries." She looked out to sea, pushing her hair from her face. "Next summer, if we choose an exceedingly nice day, I shall accept to visit the promenade with you."

"I should like that."

The red in Joan's hair shone, a brilliant hint of ruby red within strands of brown, chestnut and coffee and cinnamon and darkest amber.

But Joan was worth more than rubies.

Maeve withdrew a card from her pocket and slipped it to Joan. "The ace of clubs."

The paper card was crumpled from where she had kept it close during the past week since their return from London, as she had been waiting for the right moment. Then she had realized that there was no reason to wait, because each moment beside Joan was right in its own way.

"Marriage," Joan whispered.

"You remembered," Maeve said, pleased. "It's the last of the aces, you know."

"The last of them?"

"We have collected each one, have we not? We played the ace of diamonds for courtship during our game of patience. Then I found your pretty ace of spades when we made love for the first time—for spinsters, I hope you remember." Joan blushed, and Maeve grinned at the memory. "The ace of hearts was won on the beach, when you told me you loved me. And now we have before us the ace of clubs." She flicked the card.

"But we cannot marry."

"Not in the strictest sense, no. But having been married before, I thought you did not recommend it?"

Joan thought. "It's true, I don't."

"Then what we have shall be better than marriage. A union of equals. We do not own each other, nor do we supersede each other. Therefore, we serve ourselves as well as each other." She gazed into her eyes. "I never want to take from you what so many others have, Joan. I want you to be independent and free, to make every choice you want to make. But I want to be the one beside you, cheering for you and encouraging you and loving you through each one."

"Some of my choices may well be mistakes."

"Some of mine will be too." She looked down at the ace of clubs. "But some of them will be like this. Moments of glory set in a lovely life, shinier than any jewel."

Joan smiled, her eyes bright. "That is exactly the kind of life I want with you."

Maeve kissed her, deep and thorough on the rooftop. "Then let's begin ours together."

EPILOGUE

When Joan turned five and fifty, she was convinced that there could be no greater happiness than what she already had.

She had employment that satisfied her, for she had become the primary benefactor to the boarding school that Arabella and Caroline had founded thirty years prior, and she served on its board of directors.

She had love beyond measure, as she woke up every morning and went to sleep each night beside Maeve.

And she had a family so large that Fairview Manor fairly burst at the seams each summer.

The year after Joan and Maeve had started to make their home together, they had started to invite Alexander and James Astley to Inverley for the summer season.

The first few summers had proven to be difficult, as their father still had some influence over them. At first, Alexander had refused to come at all, and James would stay but a week without his brother before declaring the town the dullest he had ever seen, without a lick of spirit or fun to be had in any corner of its environs. He claimed he was better entertained in London with his friends from school.

But over time, they grew more and more like Tilda and their mother Gabrielle, who also came to stay for the summers, and by this point, they each had a large brood of their own who loved nothing more than spending time at the seaside.

"Aunt Joan, we have found the skeleton of a fearsome sea beast!" Alexander's youngest son cried out to her, waving a fish bone.

"Careful, mind that the skeleton is kept away from the dogs. Sea beast bones can cause fearsome choking."

He pouted and wandered off back to the cove to search for more treasures.

Maeve found her in the Blue Parlor before dinner and drew her to her feet for a quick kiss. "As happy as I am to see the Astleys each summer, is it wrong that I am already looking forward to October and a quiet winter together?"

"I look forward to it too," she said, gazing into her eyes. Maeve was nearing sixty, her hair white as snow and a myriad of fine lines creasing her eyes and brow. She only grew more dear with age, and Joan was grateful every day that they had found each other.

Maeve grinned. "Good, because I see plenty of games of patience in our future."

Joan laughed. "You have always been right that a game played by one is better fun when played with two. I am always happy to wager with you."

"As long as you don't bet against me."

"I never would." Joan leaned against Maeve, safe and secure in her embrace. "It's remarkable, but I think I have everything I have dreamed of having in life. Is that not marvelous?"

"Do you know what I reckon that means?"

"I have no idea."

Maeve kissed her forehead. "It's time to think up dreams to last us the next thirty years. Is this not all great fun?"

And it was, just like every day had been before, and every day there was to come.

About the Author

Jane Walsh is a queer historical romance novelist who loves everything Regency. She is delighted to have the opportunity to put her studies in history and costume design to good use by writing love stories. She owes a great debt of gratitude to the local coffee shop for fueling her novel writing endeavors. Jane's happily ever after is centered on her wife and their cat and their cozy home together in Canada.